I0683321

Lands Edge

From the Series

THE SPIRIT CHILDREN
By Jan Hawkins

This is a Companion Book
Book 1
Rating YA & G

It has a friend that is a view
through other eyes.

A companion book is a given set of circumstance in which there are
two accounts from very different outlooks.
Both books are whole stories within their own right.
This story is told through the eyes of teenage Jeremy.
You can also find the tale as told through the adult eyes of Tom in

Through Other Eyes
Book 2

Dedication

To the Story Tellers and the Songmen of this Land Australia.
Particularly to those who tell the story of
Cadigal People of Sydney Town

ABOUT THE AUTHOR - Jan Hawkins

Australian Author, Jan Hawkins, was raised in the Australian bush on the outskirts of Sydney on the Georges River. Now residing in Queensland, she spent 20 years in education at secondary level in the IT field. Her love of computers pales in comparison to her love of the Australian bush and Jan now has quite a portfolio of photographs, which serve to inspire her stories.

Jan is passionate about the history of her country and a strong desire to discover and experience new places fuels her desire to travel extensively throughout the land. Along the way she relishes being able to listen to people and to share and enjoy the adventure she calls life.

Books in

The Dreaming Series

Book 1 - **Shadow Dreaming**
Taipan & Aine

Book 2 - **Sky Song**
Sean & Jenna

Book 3 - **Spirits of the Rock**
Andrew & Ngaire

Book 4 - **Caverns of The Dreamtime**
Tom

Lands Edge

The Beginning

Jeremy:

You could still taste the sweet chill of the night in the air but it was cosy laying here close to the earth. The light was growing slowly as I lay back to watch the day arrive and gather my wits. The dark shadows were drawing back across the ground, fingers of light lacing through the forest canopy leaving those small dappled touches in the first light of dawn. It was peaceful, quiet, but the morning song was beginning to break into the silence of the night hours.

The heat of summer had been cooling a little lately; it seemed that to me, and I was looking forward to the first of the winter chill promised in the damp air.

The earth against my bareback had a good feel about it. I wondered for a minute if I should still be asleep or even if it would make any difference. I wanted to enjoy the feeling of peace knowing that I was not quite fully awake yet.

I knew I had to wake-up properly soon though and it was then that I decided that the Oruncha men hadn't been around, or if they had, it wasn't apparent. I didn't know how to gauge these things, none of us did but we all hoped that we would be chosen. Those amongst us who wanted to be shaman that is.

It was near time to re-join the others. They'd be preparing for the day and the morning campfire would be roaring soon. The mothers would be stirring-up the embers from last night and no doubt they would be coming together now at dawn with the youngest of the kids. They would be talking companionably as they did around the campfire, discussing the day ahead and perhaps the ceremony that was theirs.

The kids would be done with quiet night hours and would be looking for trouble to get into while their mums were busy with the youngest of them. I knew they would expect a hand from all and anyone about as the camp stirred.

The girls would help the mothers but with the younger men it was expected that we would give an eye to the older boys for a time. Everyone had a job around the camp and it was expected that we would do any job that was needed doing, either that or leave. We all had responsibilities to the Community.

That was unless we had escaped already, or hadn't yet returned from our own ceremony and at that thought I smiled. I had escaped for the time and it was accepted that I mightn't return this morning. I had been in ceremony last night with the others at the corroboree for the men. But even amongst these young men, we would mostly be re-joining the camp and it seemed now that I would be amongst the initiates this morning that hadn't been chosen.

Most of us would be there, the Oruncha spirit men only chose a few and it had been a long time since they had chosen anyone that I had heard about. The day was to be like so many others and everyone would be moving back towards the camp. I knew I should make a move soon too and join the others. Breakfast would be ready as well, I was reminded as I felt the pangs of hunger stir.

Mostly the ceremony was over for me anyway. It was all part of taking on the responsibilities of a man and all that stuff. Another year and I would be finished with school and as a young man there was still a great deal to work out. Now though it seemed I was not ready yet to join the ranks of the shaman. There was a disappointment in that for me but I had to accept it anyway.

I had always wanted to be a shaman but so far this choice of mine hadn't done much to choose me and deep down I knew my worth to the community was in dance. It was something I loved, even storytelling and I knew I could spin a tale, especially in dance but maybe I was meant to be no more than this to my family. There was no shame in that, what was important was that I had a place already.

Thinking back over how the dance had chosen me I smiled, they had been good times. I remembered when Taipan had pointed me out to the community, to my family. How he had put the marks of the dancer on me, placing his hands on my shoulder blades leaving the tell tale clay imprint of his hands to push me forward into a world I loved. I had led the dance that night when I was only a kid and I had led it well.

That was when the dance had claimed me. I liked the high step of the men pounding the earth, talking to the country and the caricature of the dance. It felt good to make the kids laugh, help them to enjoy the dance as well as when it was time for a more serious step or story.

Taipan had been a mentor for many of us and he had been a force in my life even then, when I had been just a kid. It seemed like years since he had been in the community and it was an age since he had moved down to Sydney with his woman, Aine.

It wasn't the same with his brother Sean who had taken on the roll of mentor for so many of the young men. I respected and admired him a great deal and I understood how it was; they also had their women now and young families. Even Andrew, who no longer had his wife, had his kids to deal with but it was good that he somehow found time for us even though his new woman was due to have their baby any day now.

Thinking of Andrew I eased myself up and tried to figure out how far off the full glare of daylight was. Reminding myself again that I should get back. The path that led back to the camp was not a well-worn track and I would have to think about finding my way soon.

The creek below me twisted restlessly into the bank beyond it. The force of the water had gouged away the earth from the small rock and earthen cliff leaving a steep bank on the other side. It wasn't deep here now, the rainy season had all but passed and I thought about taking an early swim before getting back to the others. That thought however was silenced at the sound of footsteps, of someone coming through the bush near the track.

It couldn't be the men; I knew that they never came to get you after the ceremony of the night before. I hadn't been the only young man in ceremony and I understood I was not the only initiate to be left near the caves. The Spirit Men, the Oruncha, would emerge from their sacred caves and would choose only one, perhaps two of those amongst the initiates. They would choose you if you were lucky, or more likely they would choose none of us. Then for a moment I wondered what it would be like to be chosen in such a way.

We all hoped though that in the spirit hour, in the breath before dawn, we would be chosen and drawn into the caverns to be initiated into the secret ways of the shaman. But it hadn't happened for me and it would be this way for most of us. There were other ways to become a shaman within the community and I knew all of us would likely be making our way back into camp in time. We each had our own path to walk.

Quietly, with a slow lazy smile I watched the forest wake about me, these were sounds that I knew and loved. I listened contented and then again I heard the sound in the tread of a foot, the rustle of others moving along the bush track close by as they approached the creek and the unexpected sound of their hushed voices.

I was very quiet; I didn't want whoever it was coming down the track to know I was here. It had to be women, this was their land and their place and I was here only because I'd been in ceremony and had the permission of the women. I had leave of the Spirit to be here but whoever it was might not know this and I didn't want to startle them.

It was a place away from the main camp, a place that was sacred particularly to women and they too were in ceremony now. It was a privilege to be here close to the sound of water and I understood that well. It was also a privilege that might afford me some knowledge into the ways of the women.

It might even be some girls who were my age and although I suspected that watching them now was not entirely right, I knew that I had leave of the Spirits who lived here deep in the bend of the creek, one harbouring a young billabong. Perhaps this would be my consolation for not being chosen.

I'd found the common pleasure in girls, a pleasure we all find in the end I figured. I had heard a lot about women and the guys and I had talked about them often enough but it wasn't until you discovered that your body had its own opinion that it really became a fascination. I had discovered sex and my own body was like having an amusing mate to follow, someone who kept you well entertained.

There were a few amongst the girls who stirred me. A few, who could by a look alone capture my interest almost immediately and there was a sweet pleasure in that. It was almost like hunting I thought. The thrill of the chase and the fun in the catch. It had been Andrew who had pointed out to the guys that the pleasure could have consequence. It was strange to realize that this applied to you though; you always figured things like babies and STD's happened to others.

I hadn't thought seriously about this until one of the guys found spots and little pimples where you really never want to find them. It had been easy to fix but it still wasn't something I ever wanted to find I decided. I was beginning to understand the risks that there were in fooling around with the girls, as pleasant as it was.

When I caught sight of the quick movement of colour through the trees, I froze. It was barely a second though before I realized that it was only kids. It was Jiemba and Deb and another of their friends and they were headed for the creek though this was strange so early in the day. No doubt they were looking for frogs or lizards or on some mission of their own. Maybe even looking for something to eat, though they would have eaten back at the camp before coming here for sure.

Andrew, Jiemba's dad, was leaving the camp early this morning too. I'd heard him say as much and I was surprised that Jem was here, at this place now. It was wrong for him to be here at all. This could be a serious business and if his father knew about this, if the women knew... it would be really bad.

His dad Andrew had been part of my initiation, part of my learning, though he hadn't said much around the fire last night. He and Sean had danced and the story they had told in the dance had fascinated me, as much as we all had enjoyed unravelling the story within the dance.

I knew that not everyone had understood the story, the movement and steps had been different from times before and when I had asked about it, even their answers to my questions had been difficult to understand.

It had been a tale about the serpents, something we knew so little about aside from the stories we were told as kids. Much of it was sacred knowledge and a lot had been lost down through the last generations. So much had changed of our world. We no longer lived as we had for thousands of years, or since the Dreamtime. A lot had never been passed on to the young people of the tribes in the last century.

Andrew and Sean, though they were both strong Shaman, could only tell such a tale as theirs in dance. To speak of it was something you only did when you were given leave to do so. It was spoken of only to those with the understanding and you knew when you were able to talk of such things. So to the uninitiated it was shown only in dance, some in sacred steps rather than the story being told in words.

The dance last night had spoken to me in ways that I didn't understand. It was a mystery and I wanted to know more. I wanted to understand the Lore of the Rainbow Serpents, the serpents of all colours and I wanted to hear the tales of the other spirit animals. It was all part of the shaman's Lore and hearing anything about it was very much stuff I wanted to learn. It was this that drew me towards the mystery of the dance.

What I did know though was that this wasn't sacred business the kids were on now and this place was sacred to the women. Jiemba, even though he was only a boy should not be near here. Again I wondered if I should do anything as I silently watched the kids from the shelter of the bush around me.

I waited quietly, as still as the bush about us as the kids chattered to each other at the water's edge. They seemed to be looking for something and I eased myself carefully into a more comfortable position where I could watch, but not interfere with what little Debbie was up to. She would know that this was a woman's place and that she shouldn't have bought Jem here. Though it might be about business that I didn't know anything of and just maybe it was permissible. So I settled down prepared to wait for them and to see what they were about.

They really shouldn't be here by the creek on their own anyway, not now, not as the spirit hour was still with us and I knew that they needed watching.

The sacred caverns were said to be close by and it was the hour when the Oruncha Spirit men could still be about. If the kids turned towards the caves then I would stop them but for now... perhaps Jiemba's presence was by accident. It might only cause strife if I disturbed them.

Jem and Deb had been friends from the very first. It had been years ago but both of them had arrived into the community about the same time. They were good kids and it wasn't odd that they'd become fast friends. Their world as children was very different from what mine had been, though I doubted if they knew that or even gave it a thought.

They were part of a strong family and within the family there were strong Shaman. Even the women in the family were strong in their ways, the old ways. Jiemba's dad too was strong in the old ways. Andrew led and guided many of the young Shaman now too. He also often took his young son away with him to teach him the things a father does.

It had been like how Taipan had taught me when I had been just a kid, mostly because my own dad wasn't around. I had never met my dad or his family; so much had changed for us in our history. Our world had been fractured with the modern way of things, with colonization. The family no longer held many of the ties we once had, those that had bound us together and to our Country.

It had been a choice many of our people had made, to live closer to the cities where life was often easier. Though we wondered now if it had been a good choice and in many instances it hadn't been. The history of my family had been a cruel history these past two hundred years, but then the colonial times had been a cruel time. Change was often cruel to those who couldn't understand or control it.

It hadn't been easy for many families. The old people had not welcomed the kids whose blood was mixed with the whitefellas. The lighter the shade your skin, the less likely it was that you would be accepted by tribes. The darker the shade, the less likely it was that the new settlers would accept you. That seemed to be most of us these days however and society was moving towards a greater acceptance hopefully. The one thing I didn't doubt was that this was my land and that I belonged to my Country. I belonged to the whole Country; though around these parts would always be my home.

It made it hard when neither whitefellas nor blackfellas seen you as belonging to their people and I was lighter than many of Aboriginal descent. I was too dark for the whitefellas and too light for the blackfella. They were all something of a strange mob to me though and I didn't let it bother me much. After all, I had no say in it and there was nothing I could do about my skin.

It had got me into more than a few fights at school however, but those kids were just idiots. It wasn't so bad now that I had filled out a bit and had learnt to look out for myself.

In the old ways I should have had any number of fathers who would guide me, help me grow to manhood but that too had changed. We had changed, everybody had changed and strong families were rare even in the cities and towns. I had often thought that it was a condition of our time.

The one thing we all had in common was the land. Even the whitefellas were feeling the ties of the land and how it too owned them now. The tribal people had been gone a long time and things had changed. Though some tried to keep the old things alive and I didn't know if it was a good thing or bad. It was something we chose, each differently it seemed.

Andrew was a good dad and I envied Jem that. He was also a law unto himself really and we all knew that he followed a Lore different to that of the Bama people. His ways were different and yet he still lived amongst us mostly because of his kids I think.

I had heard the stories amongst the guys about what he could do and what gifts he had as a Shaman, but you never knew how such things had come to be told. It was spoken of in a way not unlike the story told in dance last night where it was a movement, a hesitation, a whisper even.

It had been an exciting tale last night, one told in a dance full of challenge; a tale of the Shaman dealing with the ancient serpents, the Numereji Serpent they had said. They had hunted him as he had hunted the Spirit Children and it had been a thrilling dance. I only wish that I truly understood it but we didn't talk of these things, the serpent was a sacred business to the men.

Young Deb was something of a storyteller too and I felt a kinship with her ways in this though she was still a child and told her stories in different ways. At times I felt I was almost part of her family, truly a part of Taipan's life.

My place as a young songman and dancer was very different to her place in the community. People spoke quietly about how she had vision, the vision of women even though she was very young yet and her ways were that of a child. At only eight years old she still had to enter her initiations and her world was still very much a kids world.

Disturbing my rambling thoughts suddenly was another unexpected sound in the forest. It was a sound that made me jump. It was the subtle and unexpected sound in the shuffling of light twigs beneath a breath of weight, the subtle movement of leaves. It was a whisper of movement in the dense undergrowth nearby and immediately I swung towards it, my nerves stretched. My senses instinctively reached out into the forest seeking something, anything that should not naturally be there.

In this hour it was a dangerous time, one when the Spirit men would begin to make their way back to the caverns if they were about. It was a time when movement was all about you as the dawn leeched into the forest. When the spirit creatures, which had been drawn into our world by the ceremonies and the dance, would be returning to their own world deep in the caverns. The corroboree after all was about touching the Dreaming, being one with the Dreamtime. The night was a time of learning and you had to move closer to the world of the spirits to learn these things.

The Oruncha men of the sacred caverns would join the Shaman at night; the old Spirit men were a part of our ceremony. They showed themselves to only a few men but you felt their presence and I often had felt it in the steps of the dance.

Tom, Taipan's younger brother had been one of the few who understood these things. We were mates and I'd listened to him many times when he had been here, fascinated to hear what he could see, that which others couldn't.

I was aware of what he could sense. I had learnt to feel the world around me with his help as well as observe it and he had taught me this, but his sight had not been something I could share the knowledge of. He had told me that he could see the world of the Spirit men at times and I couldn't even begin to understand what that would be like.

He had been gone for nearly a year now as he'd been up north but he was due back soon. I was looking forward to hearing hopefully about what he had learnt in his time with the Featherfoot and I knew if I asked him, he would tell me at least something of it.

He was a good few years older than I, but he was also a good mate and we always got on well together. Both of us could sense things around us and we had an awareness that we had found a familiarity in. He had shown me a great deal over the years and I understood his world a bit better than most of the guys my age.

I was also not a child anymore and this would make a difference in our relationship when he returned. As young men together Tom would share more with me than he would with the child I had been and I was really looking forward to that.

Another movement in the undergrowth silenced my thoughts and again I turned towards the sound seeking it out. I could see nothing, but I knew there was something there. I could feel its presence.

Softly, very alert to my senses I began to sing the songs I had only recently been taught. It was the song that Andrew had sung to the serpent in the dance and I had known enough to sound it to my memory.

It was a careful chant, barely a breath in the moist dawn air but I understood that the sound, this song, would call the creature. It would calm it as it had calmed the creature in the story they had told in the dance.

Whatever it was that was now in the bush, I understood that if it were a spirit creature then the song would draw it towards me. The chant would lull it, quieten its movement and hopefully slow it and keep it from the kids down near the creek. I wasn't strong in my skills but I was able to keep the kids safe and that was in part my responsibility as a young man who hoped to be a shaman.

As the sound of movement stilled, I knew that it had heard me and I felt the thrill of knowing that it was a creature of the Spirit world. In that moment Deb looked up, I saw the movement from the corner of my eye as I continued to lull the spirit creature with my song. Even Jem paused and took note of the sound he too must have heard. A movement in the bush they had both heard, or even now felt. Maybe young Debbie could sense something, but I didn't have time for these thoughts, I had to concentrate.

"Come on, we should get back. We can ask your dad about it. I don't think you should be here," Deb said. Her words echoing in a quiet thread along the creek banks as the wall of the bank captured the sound and bent it back into the forest.

Jem paused, then suddenly darted to grab at something he had dropped or perhaps seen. Capturing it he cradled it carefully, winding the cloth he held around it quickly. There was a huge grin of satisfaction spreading across his face as he then turned to follow Deb silently. It was probably a frog or a lizard if I was to guess.

They moved off and I felt the relief of their departure flood through me. I knew that they had moved on down the path as I heard their careless footfalls. Without any apparent concern they made their way back through the forest talking quietly, not a care at all evident. Still I sung my soft song, threading it along my breath in a whisper. It kept the forest quiet around me and I wanted the kids to get away, get back to the camp safely.

I could feel the emptiness of the forest after a time and I knew the kids had gone. It was only then that I silenced my song. I couldn't hold this creature, whatever it was forever and besides I was curious too now.

The moment the low echo of my voice ceased with the sound becoming lost in the forest, the movement about me started up once more. The soft crush of leaves, the subtle noise of a twitched bush and the movement of air, you could feel it. It brushed past me and moved on. I didn't interest it at all and I felt a flood of relief. After all I wasn't even sure of what I was dealing with. My initiation into these ways of the spirit had only been recent and I clung to what little I did instinctively know and what had been taught.

I could see nothing, even though the morning light was strong enough to see fairly clearly now. This was not about sight, but about other senses and as the shadows began to grow shorter more quickly, I remained still.

The birds of the forest had started up their song and it was raucous. They were waking to the brighter dawn of the new day and I listened as the insects too took up a chorus, one that would only last long enough to greet their own before the fresh warmth of the undergrowth sent them out looking for the crisp newness of the day.

I sat there very still for what was an age and listened to the world around me, listening to the songs of other creatures as I noted their subtle melodies. I could still feel the presence of the spirit creature and hear its movement. The rustle of it, the movement of earth beneath its weight and as that sound too changed I felt that it was somewhere down by the creek, nearer to the water and that it was lingering there for some reason.

I had learnt not to fear, that was the first lesson for anyone who wanted to become one amongst the shaman. I had been taught to school my fear and to turn it to other senses, heightening these as I payed attention to the world around me to try and understand it.

For an age I sat still listening, feeling the movement of the forest creatures and then carefully I crept towards where it was brighter, where the daylight had broken over the ground. I was seeking the first rays of the sun as they touched the more open ground. In this light there was a certain level of safety to be found.

As I reached the sheltering edge of the forest, that which gave way to the more open banks and the flow of the creek, I paused. I tried to discover from where my disquiet, my sense of something being present was coming from. It was a pretty scene really as the sunlight began to spill onto the open places beside the creek and then I was suddenly surprised to catch an unexpected glimpse of the creature.

It was a flash of light reflecting against something. It was like a quivering movement in the air, dancing and then flashing. It was the strangest of things and then it happened again. A shape moving or a form of some type, one that seemed to shift in the dawn light as it skittled across my vision in a stroke of sunlight dancing against a form. It was the flick of colour in a movement of brilliant yellow and red in some parts, a bright white in others and it was a flashing dance.

As I tried to train my eyes to the movement it became clearer to me, but it was not a clean or sharp image. Like the movement of water over the ground, water so clear and clean that you can't really see it but you know by the subtle reflection of light that it is there.

I watched fascinated as shifts of yellow and red light danced over a subtle form that was about the same height as I. Then suddenly the creature I could barely sense, reared up. I heard no sound but I knew it screamed as I saw the gaping gnaw of its mouth, the sharp promise of small teeth flash in the light.

Suddenly, swiftly as lightening, the form of this large water dragon like creature bucked when a strong shaft of sunlight glanced off its back. It had a crimson, gold sweep of skin beneath its arms that were serpent wings, as much as they would help it to glide. This was a flap of skin stretched between its forearms and back legs. It was a creature that I realized would be able to glide and leap like a small glider possum only this animal was much, much larger.

What happened next was so fast, so torrid that I jerked back startled when it turned as sharply as it did. The creature, which was a shimmer of light twisted and dived toward the creek water; rapidly submerging in a leap as though to douse the fire of light running over its serpent scale. The water surged and rippled about its sudden movement creating a small wave of rapidly moving turbulence.

I could see the water surge travel, the creature fled before the sunlight and I watched as a surface wave of movement formed to a point, shifting beneath the water showing the clear line of its flight. It couldn't see the far bank... I was sure it was going to collide, smashing itself against the steep earthen wall where a broken rock face barely emerged climbing up the steeper bank on the far side of the creek.

That it didn't collide; that the water surge crashed and then began to surge and ripple to a stillness was surprising. That there was no collision of creature, rock and earth-face confused me. Only the rush of water as it met the bank was witness to its dive.

I climbed to my feet carefully, in shock at the lack of consequence in the flight of the creature. There was nothing... No collision of mass and bank. No turbulent surge in consequence, no torrid movement of a creature in distress. Fascinated I watched as the ripples stilled and died, spreading almost languidly now. The gentler movement in the slow flow of water began to return to the creek and I looked on in wonder.

The far bank was heavily overgrown and in some part the creek had undercut the bank but it looked mostly solid. You could see where the tree roots, rocks and grasses held the bank together. Yet the creature had vanished completely and to my surprise I couldn't grasp what had become of it in that moment.

I couldn't help myself, or stop myself from moving down towards the creek in careful steps. It was a mystery that demanded an answer and I strained to see what had happened, or what had become of the creature. There had to be reason to this I argued in my thoughts.

I felt no threat about me, the morning had regained its peace and the light was now spilling about the bank. I moved over to where the strange creature had been foraging, it was the same place where the kids had been playing. I wondered for a moment what had been the attraction here for them all. It had been almost as though the spirit creature was looking for something yet I could find no clue in the trampled grass and disturbed ground.

The creek water was bubbling quietly in its natural flow. The noise adding to the song of the bush here, the bubbling sound in the motion of water over rock below where I stood. It was where the billabong re-joined the main stream. Perplexed I once more considered what I had seen.

Tucking my thumbs into the belt tabs of my jeans, lending the weight of my hands to my hips I considered the far bank. I recognized that it was something of a mystery and this teased me.

It didn't take much to step into the water lapping the bank. It was cool, fresh and I bent to capture a drink in my hands before I stepped deeper into its gentle movement. I was enjoying the refreshing sensation on my skin as much as I was enjoying pandering to my burning curiosity.

When I reached the bank on the far side I realized that the billabong here was much deeper than I'd thought and I couldn't find a foot grip, or even feel the bottom beneath my toes. I reached for an overhanging root for support from the bush; a root that stretched out towards the water and began to examine what I had thought was only a slight overhang of the bank.

I discovered with surprise that it was much deeper than I had suspected. The bank swept back, supported by something of a ceiling of slippery rock and muddied earth that was held by the tangle of roots and stones barely centimetres above the water line.

The bush that gripped the fine bed of dirt over the rock ceiling gave the illusion of depth and solid bank, but it wasn't solid at all. It was an undercut or even a deeper submerged cave of some sort.

Stretching my arm and hand deep beneath the overhang I gripped the root and balanced myself in the deeper water. I found that it actually travelled well beneath the bank, much further than I could reach. Curious now I ducked below the water surface and stretched deeper into the undercut. It was only then that it occurred to me that the creature could be nestled up under the undercut.

That thought had me surfacing quickly and spluttering a bit as I swiftly moved back and waited. Nothing... thank God! Now though, as I waited I could feel the surge of curiosity tease me again.

I knew there were caves up into the bank and along the creeks flow around here. It was something we all knew about. This was Wollumbin, or what the whitefellas called Mount Warning. It was a sacred mountain, one formed in the Dreamtime and my people had been coming here for thousands of years.

It was a place of spirits and there were many sacred sites, places where the spirit creatures dwelt, sites of ceremony for both men and women around here and some of these were taboo. But we all knew the boundaries and who could visit what places, and when. This one I knew nothing about even though I was aware it was a place special to the women. A place they guarded jealously at times. The serpents however were the Lore of men and this business was Men's Business.

There were no signs either, nothing to tell me that this place was sacred. It was known only as a place of ceremony and I wondered if perhaps this was a site that had been lost through time as so much had been lost. Perhaps those who remain now had never known of it. Perhaps it was a place only the old people who were now gone had known about. Or even a place that only the spirit creatures of the Dreamtime knew of.

Then a thought occurred to me. Perhaps this was something that the Oruncha men had decided to show me. No one after all spoke of the way in which the old Spirits of the Caverns worked. It could be in this way.

On that thought I ducked beneath the surface of the water and kicked off, entering beneath the bank. Venturing beneath the undercut with my outstretched hands to see just how deep it travelled back under the bank and for a moment I was fearless.

I expected that I would meet with a muddy earth or perhaps a tangled tree root. Though I could see barely two feet in front of me in the growing dimness beneath the water I did begin to feel fear as I kept travelling.

Meeting no resistance, no bank or barrier, seeing only plays of light and shadow in the chill water, I began to recognize the slow sense of panic growing within me. It was a panic born of my own stupidity.

This was an ill-considered move I realized as I continued to move forward beneath the water, my breath trapped in my lungs. As the growing panic shifted through me I began to release a breath, easing the pressure on my lungs, looking for a way out in some desperation.

The only thing that kept me going was that I had begun to move towards a lighter reflection in the icy chill of the submerged undercut. As the pressure on my lungs eased I felt the stretch and desperate need for another breath. Panicking I cut quickly forward, up towards the very subtle wall of subterranean light I was approaching. It was almost a desperate reaction to the realization that I was running out of breath and I couldn't get there fast enough.

When I hit the surface it was in pure panic. The reality of how stupid I had been in a moment of madness flooded through me as I reached for a life-giving breath and struggled to control my racing heart. Curiosity about where I was struggled with my fight to control my fear. My eyes adjusting too slowly, my breath reaching and my body screaming in what was the now deeply chilled water as I looked around me, staggered.

It was a cavern, large and dim. The noise of my movement in the water echoing eerily about and bouncing off the walls, amplifying even my reach for breath. The only light here was muted by deep shadows but it was also captured and reflected by the pool, helping to light the cavern. It came in from tangled star-like openings overhead I realized. These had to be holes in the rocky ceiling, some obviously grown over up there, or worn in under rock. The thought that someone could fall through such an opening if it widened, landing into this cavern occurred to me as well. I wondered how long it would be before the whole cavern roof crumbled in as I looked around warily at the waterworn rock and earth.

You would never get out of here; the cavern walls were too concave, too smooth. You would be trapped here likely injured unless you knew about the undercut and from here you just couldn't see it at all. The entrance was deeply hidden in the shadow.

Wanting to get out of the water that was chilling me through to the bone in this eerily deep half-light I reached for the broad land edge of the pool. It was bedded with rocks and slippery with damp earth rarely now disturbed, but hauling myself out of the waters grip I tried to wipe as much water from my skin as I could with my hands. It was growing damn cold and I had begun to shiver.

The light was just enough to see shadows and it seemed to be caught and reflected by the water, though not enough to see clearly. I climbed to my feet and tried to look about into the dim shadows. Moving towards the tangle of dry bracken and tortured branches that at some point had either grown here and died, or perhaps was even litter that had fallen into the cavern from cracks overhead.

It all looked precarious and I shivered involuntarily at the thought of what was inevitably going to happen with this cavern in a time when it would eventually collapse in on itself.

There was dry litter about and small branches of wood or root, which I could barely see. They were mostly roots it seemed and little real green stuff. The few bushes were low and dry, hardy and barely growing if at all in the dimness.

Shivering, it wasn't long before I gathered together some roots and litter to suit me and breaking them to lengths having selected the thinnest and driest of them first I carefully fished about my wet jeans pocket for my small flint. Striking it against the pocketknife that I always carried as with most guys when we went bush, I set about building a small fire. Building embers from the sparks that lit the litter on a gentle breath, the only dry litter that I had been able to gather. I needed light and I could certainly do with the warmth.

Lighting fire with just dry sticks and dry litter was something we had been taught to do, mostly to amuse the tourists when the dance group was asked to perform locally but the wood in here was too light for that. It would have been easier with a match or lighter but I didn't have either of those. They weren't much use when you went swimming a lot and the small flint attached to my pocketknife had served well.

It was a good ten minutes though before I had a small weak flame flickering in the dried grass and litter. There wasn't a great deal of tinder and stick so I needed to be sparing.

The light that the small fire emitted was enough to show me that there was more wood scattered around. It would keep this fire going for a little longer at least, but as I pulled some of that together and carefully nursed the small flame to a fire I couldn't help but pause every now and then. My eyes having adjusted found new things to pause over.

Somehow the flicker of the growing fire made the cavern seem smaller than I had first thought, drawing the walls in around me. But what had me to my feet was the evidence of men in the painted figures and drawn art on the smooth rock walls. I had never seen the like of these drawings. They were stick like figures in distinctive charcoal and with some also painted in white and red clays. The artists had left their marks in the hand spray images that oddly extended in relief to their elbows, which in itself was an unusual thing for me; normally these would only be hand stencils.

Most predominant and staggering in its strength of line was the figure in red ochre and white clay, which was of a serpent. It wound around the walls travelling about me in a powerful form and I recognized a number of the other spirit figures of animals that were much smaller but positioned as though in attendance.

That the serpent also had those distinctive wing flaps surprised me further, they stretched along its body, drawn close to the form. The line was more evident up around the head and shoulders of the creature, tucking in under its forearms, or whatever they were.

The creature was not unlike the one I had seen in the flashes of dawn light this morning. If it hadn't been for my earlier experience I would have dismissed that second tracing of line as likely decorative. These images were recognizable in the flicker and shift of weak firelight across the hand painting and it made me realize that these images were ancient.

The Rainbow Serpent was never drawn with gliding wings like this and this looked to be some type of dragon creature of the spirit world. I would never have believed it if I hadn't seen it myself. This was like no creature in the stories I had been told, nor even the art I had seen.

This was a Serpent's cavern though. I had absolutely no doubt that this was a sacred place now lost to our knowledge. Even the stories had been lost. I had never heard them, nor even heard a hint of the winged serpent drawn here I realized, as my eyes roamed in absolute wonder over the art and story revealed in the flicker of the fire light.

It didn't look as though this place had been used in centuries. No new stories had been told here in a long time and the art had an ancient feel about it, untouched for many, many years. Perhaps even centuries long ago passed.

Pacing around the walls in wonder I was silenced by the beauty of the cavern in the dim and dying light, the colour of the stone and the simple straight line detail in the figures. Detail I could only appreciate and not understand. That the stories of this serpent were lost, as was the knowledge of the men who would have told the ancient stories long ago, was a tragedy that touched me deeply. A loss that was indescribable in the sadness of its passing.

It was then that I noticed the dusty aged wrap of skin left on the small rock shelf towards the reach of the cavern. At first I wondered if it was perhaps a burial place. But there was nothing to indicate this and carefully

I reached for the skin wrap, sweeping away the webs and dust of time.

It was hard, a stiff like skin turned now to a cardboard almost. It too had not been touched in a long time. Carefully I peeled the folds apart and in doing so saw that they were nothing but a bundle of sticks.

True they were solid and they had some kind of decoration carved into their length. When I pulled back the dusty skin wrap fully I knew with certainty that they had been stored here for some reason, perhaps for a purpose to which I had no clue.

The top few were affected by time, they were aged and the wood lightened by the passage of perhaps decades or even centuries. Their tips had once been coated forming a ball of some kind of tar or sap that was now as hard as glass. It had been time weathered and was partially greyed in some parts. It was then that I saw what they were.

The lower sticks in the bundle were darker, their surface and colour more preserved. The dark glassy knob was embedded with some type of nut or black-red seed around the end. This helped me to recognize that they were likely some kind of torch. Sitting back I looked at them in wonder and then I reached for one, holding it as I balanced it in my hand.

These must have been used for light I decided. It was like a giant rough matchstick and I wondered over the knob of near black stuff. It had almost a deep red tinge about the gum or knob of whatever it was and it left me wondering just how these were made. I had never seen the like of them and the gum was now as solid as a dull opaque glass. Surely they wouldn't light? But then I wondered about that too.

Glancing over to the small flickering fire now fighting for its life it occurred to me that I could have a torch in these sticks and this would allow me to better see the walls around me. Without another thought I was at the fire, carefully digging the end of the stick held in my hand deep into the small flame. Fascinated I watched as it caught and burnt with barely a flicker of hesitancy.

It wasn't a high flame; it smouldered within a rich blanket of coloured flame that didn't flicker much at all but glowed steadily. It was fascinating and I once more wondered about the technology, the knowledge that had created such a thing and that which had since been lost to us.

The art seen within the light of the torch however was enough to scatter any curiosity held in so simple a thing as the torch. In wandering around the cavern I came across a small vertical crevice in the rock, one that the drawing of the serpent seemed to emerge from. The serpent figure had wound its way around the cavern but here the lines moved on down into the rock crevice only to disappear along near where the rock face had been gouged in lines as though by claws.

For an age I stood arrested before the invitation of the serpent, contemplating the story here and wondering what it was telling me. Was this what the ceremony of this cavern had been about. A story that lived on in time through the marks made by old people an age long gone? Stories that had been lost, perhaps not retold in centuries. Those whose mystery now seemed to invite me into the caverns to follow the path I knew the serpent was taking.

I had no doubt that this was where the spirit creature had fled earlier. I knew with absolutely no doubt in my mind that the dragon I had witnessed from the world of the Dreamtime had passed this way. That I stood here now before the caverns of the serpent was clearly at the invitation of the Oruncha men, the Spirit Men of the caverns.

Taking up another of the torches as a safeguard, it would be enough to get me back to this cavern when the other one died I decided and I braced myself. Struggling to collect my wits about me along with the courage of those who had stepped here before me, I eased myself into the crevice with the torch held high. Its sombre glow lit the way through the narrow tunnel. In anticipation threaded with uncertainty I drew a deep breath trying to steady my steps.

Others had been this way before me. Others had survived to make the torch I was using now. Others had also followed the path of the serpent. I had to remember these things as I stepped warily on as a man would have, as a warrior would have done making his way into the darkness.

This was an ancient path and perhaps it was time that it was rediscovered. The Oruncha would protect and help me I was sure. I reassured myself of this repeatedly believing I would not have come this far only to be destroyed. I had to trust that they knew how to protect me, how to preserve the knowledge of this secret place having bought me here. So it was that I stepped into my future barely knowing it.

The Caverns

Jeremy:

It was dark and I was glad for the torch that lit my way because the experience was like nothing I had ever had before. The often-cavernous tunnels travelled deep into the earth and along the way I found any number of strange things.

Sometimes I found the walls decorated with drawings, some sketches and depictions of animals and creatures. This was where those who had walked before me had obviously taken time to rest. Other passages and spaces were a tight fit but you could see where others had scraped through also.

I had never seen many of these animals drawn on the walls and I barely recognized others. They were ancient beasts and strange drawings to my eyes. Other times I would come across a tangle of roots deep beneath the ground where no tree could ever grow.

It wasn't a difficult path but it was a dark path to follow as it wound its way deeper into the bowels of the earth. In the dry places I could see that the path had been trodden many times before. I was glad too for the many times I came across a flow or catch of water and was able to at least take a drink.

Often the water would dribble down the rock face or drip from fingers of some kind of calcite. In other places it would be dripping from a fungus like mass and sometimes it would pool or flow, the water dark and mysterious. I even found small light fish, though they were quick but it was a type of small colourless yabby that I lunched on. They were different to the ones on the surface, but they tasted almost the same and they cooked quickly in the heat of the torch.

I noticed the fungus, which grew on the rocks and at times on deep roots now exposed, but I was hesitant about eating these. I didn't recognize them and if I got sick down here, there was no help. It wasn't worth the risk. I wasn't that hungry yet.

The torch was amazing as it diminished barely, burning away happily. Occasionally you could follow the flow of air which made the small steady flame dance and that was reassuring. I marked the passages I took with clay and stone markings of my own, these where I couldn't find other markings left by others who had been here before me. But that someone had taken the time and had marked a way already was also reassuring.

When I was unable to find markings after having taken a fork or passage, I turned back and found that it wasn't long before it was easier to recognize the ancient pointers through the caverns.

After a time I realized I had been missing some of the stone markers, which in some places were gathered into a pile near a particular way, a squeeze or tunnel. I soon worked out that these led to places or caves where subterranean life seemed to live. Small crustaceans and often fish, some blind, could be found there where an ancient hand had left sketches on the wall of these subterranean snacks.

One had such a deep nest of large spiders that it took some time before I would even talk myself into entering the cavern. It was then that I wondered if you could eat these too. Then I saw the drawings on the wall, where others had seemed to indicate that these were considered food.

I could hear the sound of movement; probably bats or snakes, or at least this is what I thought they were. Once I saw a large rat like animal but it was too quick. I wasn't overly hungry after the yabbies but that there was food about living in these dark places was comforting at least.

I wondered at the often-deep pools I came across and the fast flow of water seemed to be always sounding in the air. It was rare to find a completely quiet place. There was always some noise to keep you company and that helped settle my fears as I crept and crawled deeper beneath the surface with each hour seemingly passing so effortlessly.

I had no concept of time and absolutely no idea for how long I moved on through the caverns and passages, moving deeper all the time but it grew surprisingly warm. Having found a defined way curiosity drove me on to discover what it was that had tempted men to forge a path so deep beneath the earth. Some places were warmer than others and the only common thing was that the water was more often than not freezing.

I thought that, until what felt like late in the afternoon after exploring for hours I came across a larger cavern with a small geyser of steaming hot water. It was bubbling out from the ground and spilling into a large dark pool that then flowed through a split in the rock down much further, running deeper down into the rock fissures.

I didn't drink this, it was too soft to touch, too slippery in my fingers and it tasted of something odd when I tested it but it was nice to rest beside its moist warmth for a time.

I was growing tired so I figured that it had to be late in the afternoon. I knew back at camp I would now have been missed and for a moment I wondered who would note my absence. I also knew that it wouldn't raise any concern and that it would be only after three or four days that the men would come searching for me if I didn't return before then. I was no longer a child and it was expected that I could look out for my own safety.

I was able to take care of myself in the bush and the men knew this. I was confident in moving through the forest and good at finding food for myself and I had a fine sense of direction. I knew how to watch the passage of the day and read the heavens at night marked by the Southern Cross.

I knew the seasons and what to expect of the land and the animals. It had all been part of what Taipan and other men and women had been showing me since I was a child. But I had decided that when I felt rested I was going to head back and perhaps bring others back this way next time.

What would I tell them back at camp I wondered? The talk was sure to be that the Oruncha men had taken me down into the caverns to be initiated into the ways of the shaman. This was what had lured me deeper into the caverns, the promise that perhaps I had been led along this ancient route to just such an end. Led by ancient markers and the step of men from another age. You had to trust in these things, there was no telling what the Spirit Men wanted of you until they chose to show you.

There would be a great deal of talk about at the camp, but it was going to be disappointing to tell them that I had been driven by curiosity alone, sure that others had stepped this way before me.

Maybe I should just say nothing. Maybe Taipan would learn of my absence for a time, maybe he would be called back to the community. Then maybe another of the father's would step up to train me or show me a path to becoming a shaman. If anyone was to step up I hoped it would be Taipan, or maybe even Andrew.

These thoughts wound around my head as I felt myself slip into a restful doze beside the steamy warmth of the pool. Comforted by the soft flicker of the torch nearby and the subtle sounds of the cavern about me.

I think I slept, though I have no concept of for how long.

I had lost all sense of time and direction, with only subterranean flows of water along with those ancient markers of clay and stone to give me my sense of place and a promise of escape.

When I finally began to stir it was to a strange awareness and it took a moment for me to remember where I was. It was the steam coming off the pool of water that reminded me. It had kept the air around me moist and warm, comfortable even.

I lay there for a while listening to the sounds about me and then rolled onto my back stretching myself, recognizing once more the cavern but slowly I realized that the light was all wrong.

With barely enough light to see clearly I frowned. The light was dim and shadowy. It was a greenish blue colour making the place look eerie. Surprised by this I sat up looking over at the torch seeing that it was out.

The thing must have burnt out, but the light about me was strange. It filled the cavern and it seemed to emanate from the walls.

I had climbed to my feet curious and wandered over towards the eerie luminance on the walls of the cavern. It was a light, which seemed to be a part of the rocks. Then I realized that it was coming from a fungus or whatever it was that was growing on the walls and some of the strewn rocks. It was really something and it was absolutely fascinating as I carefully touched the strange growth and stood back.

Without conscious thought I rubbed my hand across my belly shifting the light dust and dirt still clinging there. I was hungry and as fascinating as this was, it didn't change things. I didn't really want to have a go at eating this stuff and looking around I wondered what I could find about to eat that would satisfy me for the moment.

In the dim luminance I noticed that up on a rock, not far from the flow of water, there was some kind of bundled cloth or something the like and frowning with surprise I moved over towards it curious. It was a cloth wrapped about something and it had a smell, lost amongst so many other smells. This smell however reminded me of food and I swore it hadn't been there before.

At first I just squatted down to it and looked it over. It had a warm comforting smell but in the damp air of the cavern that had all manner of smells it was hard to discern what it was. Curious I moved closer to sniff it even before I touched it.

The fabric that wrapped around it was soft and fine, delicate even and woven like a neck scarf. Noting it was as slippery as silk to touch I edged the fabric with care as I began to unwrap whatever it was.

What was inside totally surprised me, it was damper, bread of a sort and it was still warm so it must have been recently taken from the coals. It had an inviting shape about it. It was crusty and even light, echoing at my knock. This had to be a type of bread as I knew that smell and yet I had no idea where it had come from.

It smelt good though and as I held it to my nose I glanced around realizing that someone or something had to have put it there for me and that this whole business was getting stranger and stranger.

Tearing a chunk out of the small bread cob I tested it at first, just a taste, but it was good. Sort of mealy with a grain and what was more it was still warm and soft inside.

I couldn't believe that it was so fresh, which meant truly that someone had to know I was here. For a minute I wondered if it was the Oruncha men I had heard so much about. But then, they were spirit men; they didn't eat damper... or did they?

A small subtle sound like a shuffle bought me to my feet and I swung around surprised at the sound. In this strange green-blue light it was hard to see much... everything sort of faded to strange shadows and my eyes searched for anything, any movement. That was when she stood up and stunned I watched.

What did you say to a girl who was watching you like you were some kind of weird thing and I turned to her fully, almost as surprised and even a bit hesitant as she too seemed to be?

"Hey..."

My word echoed between us, and neither of us moved, so I waited. And so did she.

This was ridiculous I decided so I tried again. "Hi there? Did you leave me this?"

Again we waited, watching each other. She was silent and obviously by the look of her she was as curious as I. Undeterred I tore at the bread and popped it in my mouth appreciating it anew as I watched her reaction. Her fingers were restless; constantly busy as they almost played at something but she was silent, not a sound left her lips.

"It's good. Thanks. How did you get down here by the way? I don't know you, you must be one of the mob camped over from us," I offered. Thinking of the few family groups camped around us for the corroboree.

It was an important time of ceremony and there were a few groups but mostly we kept to ourselves. It was only the women who came together really. After all it was their ceremony mostly and an important one for them, a ceremony different from ours.

Still she was silent so I decided to sit down as I watched her. Making use of the same rock where the damper had been I sat and still I kept watching as I continued to eat. Wishing all the time that I had some tea or drink or even some cool water.

I looked around, there was nothing and I wasn't about to drink the water from the pool so I decided my thirst could wait. The bread though was good and I tore off another scrap from the small nob and continued to eat as I watched her.

She was still young I noted as I considered her in the strange light of the cavern. Her hair was a weird colour but it was light and even her skin was a weird colour. Then so was mine, it was what the light made of us but she was much lighter in skin tone than I was. You could see that clearly even in this cavern and she was small, likely about my age I figured, maybe a bit older but certainly not younger. Then again she could be I guessed again. It was the steady line of her eyes, the way she held herself. There was something mature in that.

There was something further about her that was odd though and then I realized, with her colouring and her looks I should have expected to hear about her if she was camped nearby on the edge of Wollumbin. The guys talked about the other women and girls from the different groups and she certainly would have rated a mention. It wasn't only her looks but also that she was so light skinned and this alone would have rated a comment.

"I'm Jeremy by the way."

She frowned, and I smiled as she dropped her hand from the movement that had kept her fingers oddly busy. Then carefully, in a really soft voice she answered me.

"Kirri."

Her smile was fleeting and brilliant, but then it fell away and she was once more wary.

"Hi Kirri. How did you get down here? I didn't know about this place and well... I'm surprised to see you here?"

She shook her head and attempted a small smile as she watched me carefully.

Dressed in a type of loose top and pants of the same soft fabric, which had wrapped the damper, she made an interesting picture. The light lent its colour to her clothes as it did to my own jeans, turning them to an odd shade of blue grey. With her clothes though, they seemed to reflect the colour and they looked almost bright.

"You're from the edge... aren't you?" Kirri asked carefully. "It's been a long time since anyone from the edge was here."

"The edge? No. I'm one of the Wollumbin group, near Nimbin. Locals almost. What about you?"

Fluttering her hand strangely again she paused suddenly and then straightened, as though relaxing a little as her hand dropped back to her side. Then she too moved around the rock carefully and sat across from me on another smaller rock, facing me as I finished devouring the last pieces of the bread. Holding the last mouthful of the small cob I wondered guiltily if I should offer her the final scrap.

My look was apologetic and I followed it with a smile and a small shrug at her stillness as I tucked the last of the bread into my mouth unrepentant.

"Did you want any of that? Sorry... I didn't think you did."

Kirri paused as though considering my words and then suddenly shook her head in what I took to be an answer.

"Thanks for that anyway... the damper, I was hungry. I didn't think to bring anything along with me." The girl just watched me silently in the dim light, not saying a word. "How did you get down here? It might be an easier way out than the way I came?"

Again she shook her head but I could see she was considering it as though she was choosing her words carefully. "I'm going up to the edge, there is only one way that I know." She answered slowly, still watching me as though she thought I would pounce or something.

"Yeah... well. I guess. Do you come here often?" I grinned, it was meant to be a joke but she obviously didn't see that, so I shrugged. Then I was surprised when she suddenly answered my question.

"Only when the light is blue and it is the right time."

I frowned. "Time?" She made no sense.

But she obviously thought she did as she nodded her head in agreement. So I shook mine, "I'm not sure what you're talking about, the time thing." I added smiling, not really caring for an explanation.

Again she used her hands, as though signalling as she waved a delicate wrist, moving her fingers swiftly with purpose and then frowning at me, she answered hesitantly. "When overhead, when it is blue it is time."

She was being funny I realized as I grinned back. Folding my arms about my chest I nodded. "Well that would be just about every day. You get down here that often?"

Kirri suddenly took on a stillness that confused me and my grin slowly died on my lips as I watched her. She seemed to be struggling to say something.

"I have heard that the sky is blue all the time after the dark," she said carefully, watching me as she ventured further. "Where you're from... at the edge."

It was only then that I realized she had a strange accent, clipped and careful and I wondered if she was from New Zealand, or perhaps the islands. "The edge?" I repeated as I considered this and shook my head. "Maybe the rim, or unless you mean the edge of the old mountain... sort of? Strange way to put it..."

"No I mean out, on the edge... I'm not from there, I'm from inland."

I shook my head. "I still don't know what you mean. Where about's inland? I didn't think we would see many from the inland, most are from the coast." I smiled again, she was cute but she was also really hard to talk to.

Kirri just pointed in the direction of the stream flow, watching me all the time as though I would understand her meaning.

I glanced that way and prepared to play the same game I nodded, grinned and then pointed to the small cavern entrance over on the wall where I had come through earlier, much earlier I decided.

I must have slept for about six or eight hours or maybe it was just an hour and it suddenly occurred to me that she would have been away for at least the same length of time as I to even get here. That was unless she had a faster way out of here.

"I'm from that way." I added on a little chuckle as I pointed again, teasing her.

Instead of saying anything she just nodded. "It has been a long time since anyone has been here to meet us. My old mother told me that you once would greet her, when she was very young. I wasn't really expecting... anyone."

I frowned. "OK. That doesn't make sense at all." Shaking my head I was getting a little annoyed, but I continued. "Firstly... you're here and ... well your kinda greeting me. Nice damper by the way." I added at an attempt at teasing her again. "An' this whole greeting business... I have no idea really what you mean by that."

Drawing a deep breath, I felt the growing frustration in my chest swell as I crossed my arms. I was running out of patience with this double talk and sure... she was cute but she was sounding a bit thick now.

Immediately Kirri stood, a little startled at my impatient tone and I frowned as I watched her move. Her step was careful, light and bending to pick up a bundle she moved with a strange intent over to where I had left the 2nd torch, picking it up carefully.

It was only then that I noticed the small ember fire off to the edge barely behind the rocks where she had been sitting. It was obviously where she had cooked the damper because there was a few things scattered about, but she didn't bother with those. She just tipped the torch end into the slow glowing embers and we both watched as the torch began to smoulder, immediately seeming to flatten and douse the strange luminance from the fungus about the wall. The light of the torch killed off the luminance and surprised I looked around curious. How did the women know this and the men not, I wondered.

"We should go then," she announced simply.

I frowned confused. "Go? Where?"

"Down to the edge. I have to prepare for... for... the um..."

I watched as she seemed to struggle for the word and then when she found it ... I was a little stunned.

"... for the equinox." She finished waiting expectantly for something.

"The what?"

"That is the word... isn't it? The equinox?"

I shrugged. "Geez... I don't know. What is it? Some kind of ceremony?"

Kirri looked at me confused. "Yes. Ours!"

Again I frowned. "Ours? Not mine... I don't think."

"No of course not!" She added impatiently though her words were painfully careful. "It is ours', my people. You're just here to help me."

It was my turn to be totally confused now. I had no idea what she was talking about again.

"Listen princess! If you want me to help... you only have to ask you know." I offered, belatedly feeling a touch of resentment at her assumptions. "But it would be nice to know what the hell you're talking about."

Kirri slowly lowered the torch, seemingly confused. "You're here to help. Your mob help... have you forgotten? Isn't that why you're here?"

I shook my head. "You are making no sense. If you wanted help you only had to ask someone. I'm sure..."

"No! It's you. You're supposed to be here to help me. I have to get to the edge, though I've done it before and it is difficult... but I can do it! That was why you are supposed to be here."

"Hang on... hang on... was there anyone here before?"

Kirri frowned. "Hang on to what?"

I stared at her dumbfounded. "Hang on... it's a wait-up. You know... you... you're a bit crazy. Yeah... sure you are. You make no sense." I complained but with a small sudden chuckle softening my words. Then I stopped, she wasn't laughing with me.

Kirri's expression for some reason was now totally without humour and it stopped me in my track, as I stood suddenly, confused and impatient. Having recognised a strange flick of fear in her glance I hesitated.

Raising the torch she looked around seemingly as much at a loss as I was, looking confused as though she expected something of me.

"You are angry with me?" Her question was sudden and completely unexpected. She sounded almost hurt by the suggestion.

I shook my head. "No. No ... Not really. Just confused. You... expect me to go with you somewhere but you don't say... you're not making sense." I protested softly, trying to reason with her.

"You have come here to take me down to the edge. I told you... isn't that why you are here?"

I shook my head slowly. "I don't know why I am here, I was just... just... was led here by a track."

At this, Kirri seemed to pause and consider my words. "It's true, your people haven't been here for a long time. You surprised me... that is all. You used to be here all the time, it was a long time ago... but you stopped coming and we had to go to the edge on our own. We even hoped that it wasn't necessary any more but it was. It is more necessary than ever and we need to know what to expect."

"Look... I don't know anything about that. I mean, I don't even know where the edge... whatever it is... is!"

"It's your place. Can't you see?"

"My place? I live in a community near Nimbin. Sure it's on the edge, the rim of a old caldera but... but no one like you has ever been there before I'm sure."

Kirri strangely looked down at her arm, the one holding the torch and nodded. "We can't go there... not to there... where you say. We would burn; you should know that. That is why you take us to the cavern and we wait until it is darker then we don't burn. We only go out to the edge in the dark. It is only then that we can see what is happening."

I shook my head totally confused. "Look... this is not making any sense. You've been there before?"

"Yes many times, every equinox we come. We can take a sight on what is happening. How fast things are changing."

"You go to the edge?"

"Yes." She answered simply.

"We take... I mean we used to take you to the cavern?" I reiterated again.

"Yes. Once you would feed us there but... well that stopped long ago. So now we bring enough to cook, but... but I gave you mine because you... that is the custom. We fed you and you... well you fed us when we were near the edge."

I frowned not understanding her at all. "How long ago?"

Kirri shrugged. "Long before my time. My old mother told me of it in our stories, we all know about it. You would feed us strange things but we would eat, just like we would feed you here. It is very important that we take a measure, we need to know what to expect, it governs what we plant, how we live and ... many things."

"Here? We would feed you here? Like in this cave."

She nodded. "It helped us both, we would welcome your help again..." Seeing my confusion she continued. "We need to pass through the caverns, the serpent caverns and then you would take us out to the edge, for the ceremony. Sometimes we would trade things, good things. You needed lots of help as well and we... we can help but then it is harder for you too, we know that."

"Hard? How do you mean? You're not making a lot of sense princess."

"Well... you live on the edge, out where the sky burns you. Look at your skin, it is burnt." Her words were patient, as though she was explaining something to a child and it irritated me no end.

Holding up my arm I shrugged. "I'm not burnt, that's just the colour I am. But I can see you would burn, don't you ever get out into the sun?" I argued trying to introduce a breath of amusement to our conversation.

"Well of course not! Look... shouldn't we go. You really are odd; you knew this once you know. How can you not know it now?" She suddenly demanded of me.

I huffed... surprised. "Well yeah... just where is this edge then! That's what I want to know, you still haven't said!" I protested now annoyed openly.

"We go to the edge!"

"The edge of what?" I demanded.

"The edge of this place. Are you an idiot?" Her voice was level, reasonable even.

Stunned I stepped back as though she had slapped me. Then I frowned deeply. "The world doesn't have an edge! And I'm not an idiot... your just stuck up!"

"Stuck up where?" she demanded indignantly after a moment.

I laughed... I couldn't help myself. "Don't you know anything?" I demanded as I moved over towards her and it was she, with some measure of shock, who now took that step back as I reached for and grabbed the torch from her hand. She had moved as though I was going to strike her and that startled me as I stood there now holding the torch.

For a split second I was speechless and then I gathered my wits. "What did you do that for? I'm wasn't going to hit you?" I insisted, still surprised and further annoyed now.

The girl was still wary and fearful. Her eyes wouldn't meet mine as she edged back once more saying softly... hesitantly. "We should go." With that she turned towards the small entrance where I had come through yesterday, or was it today...? I had no idea anymore. She took a step and then she stopped, waiting as though I was to take the lead.

"Jee-zus... what the hell!" I grumbled suddenly, not at all sure what to do... or even where to go. "You want to go back the way I came?" I demanded impatiently but struggling now to stem my temper.

Kirri just nodded and waited with that same certain hesitant fear I had recognized.

"OK then." Confused I moved off holding the torch higher to light the path as I wondered just what I was doing. "We're going back the way I came." I said without preamble, as though explaining something to her. Something she already knew.

As I stalked ahead of her I knew she followed. She was quiet and reticent and I was really annoyed, that was at least for the first few hours.

We had a good few hours ahead of us, a lot of inclines though there were also a number of caverns to get through but I at least had a good idea of what lay ahead and when to take a rest.

The walking was mostly silent and at times I waited for Kirri, waiting in a silence that had become annoying. Any conversation was minimal, singular and curt in its nature and it seemed to me that it became more strained between us as we moved further along.

It was about three hours later that we took a break. I was hungry again and quite thirsty. At least I hoped that there would be something to eat or drink in the next cave. It was more a hollowed area really if I remembered correctly, but it had a water supply that you could use. It dribbled down from something of a glassy wall, more calcite than glass. Last time here it had taken me a while to collect enough to drink. I wasn't too sure about the water in the pool where it had collected. It was just still and running nowhere I could see, too still to chance.

The small fish in the same pool had been difficult to catch on the way down here yesterday leaving me to wonder if I even wanted to try and catch them now. It could as well wait until we got out of the cavern I decided.

As we approached the entrance to the place where I planned to stop, I could feel the strain in my legs in the slow uphill clamber and I wondered if the girl was feeling the same. A few of the lower crawl spaces had been taxing and I was beginning to look forward to this larger cavern.

"We'll take a break here," I offered by way of a suggestion as we reached the much bigger space, seeing the relief in her eyes as she too found a spot to rest. There were seats easily found on the rocks where you could avoid the damp clay of the floor. We had been following a small water flow for some twenty minutes or so but here it pooled with the small dripping streams from the walls and this would allow us a drink.

Propping the slow burning torch into a crack I turned back to the odd girl after we had both had a drink. She was becoming something of an enigma to my mind, one full of odd reactions and diffident comments.

"I'm sorry for growling at you." I said suddenly. "I didn't mean to scare you earlier... I don't know why you thought I would hurt you. That made me angry... pissed me off really. I shouldn't have let it do that."

The moment stretched between us as I watched her. Her expression changing and moulding to her thoughts as they chased each other across her face.

"You did scare me for just a while. I'm sorry too. I was told that once, that the men of your place were angry... well easy to anger. It is where you come from, everyone is angry or... or emotional. I mean I know... I don't mean to offend."

My slow smile grew; I hoped it reassured her as I chewed over her words as odd as they were. I had no real idea what she meant but I didn't want to upset her again and if she had heard something weird... well that had nothing to do with me did it. "So where just is this edge... the one you talk about?"

"It's the edge, outside the cavern. You go underneath the water and then you're there. Only I need to go out further, I don't know if you come with me when I go out onto the edge... I guess you do?"

I shook my head. "You talk crazy talk you know. I know the ledge, under the water. It just goes outside."

"Yes. That's the edge... it is the very edge of the... the world... you call it the world? That is your word?"

I shook my head, trying desperately to grasp at her meaning. "It's a creek." I countered.

It was Kirri's turn to shake her head. "It is the very edge, before the... the... sky."

I frowned, and then it struck me. "You mean the air... it is the edge of the ground and the air... the space? The earth, like the atmosphere comes next?"

Her grin was stunning, her whole face lit up. Her eyes, light blue orbs set in the lightness of her skin, sparkling at my terms of description as her expression came to life on seeing my meaning. "Yes... the edge! I couldn't think what it was you called it. It's the edge between the ground and the air outside."

"Shit!" I exclaimed shocked. "You do talk funny!"

At her frown I stopped... taking a moment to really look at her in the dim light of the torch. "Sorry... excuse the French..."

"French? That isn't French? Is it?"

I chuckled and then shook my head. "No. You know French then?"

"No." She answered shaking her head. "We only learn your language. So... so we would know. But I do know some other languages you might use, we were told that the language had changed a great deal."

It was my turn to frown as I considered her words. "My language? You're not Australian? I could have sworn... I mean you speak funny, sort of Kiwi... But even they speak English?"

"Oh I speak English... as you say. That is its name. Most of us do now but... we learn it very young."

"Where do you come from then?"

At that Kirri frowned. "You don't know?"

I shook my head, looking at her oddly. "How could I know?"

Confused she looked at me. "I come from the inland... you call it that? You are a man of the caverns. You come from the edge... where we are going. You didn't know that?"

"What?" I said confused. "What inland? Like the Outback? I mean what town do you come from?"

"You have never heard of the Inland? But you know the caverns...? How...?"

"I found the caverns... I mean I knew, I know about them. The caves are... are sacred, some of them are, but the in-land? It's pretty big. You must know where you come from... where you were born?" I shook my head confused and surprised at her ignorance.

Kirri took a moment, and then she looked down at her skin gently running a finger along the milky whiteness of it. "I never thought... well that... that you did not know? It is just the Inland. I mean I think we have towns like... like yours but they are Dominions really. They have no name only ..." She signalled swiftly with her fingers and then waited.

"Know what? You're not making a lot of sense. Do you mean you come from the country? Where is the biggest town near you, wherever it is that you live?"

"We thought you knew... I mean I did. I don't know how to answer you. You must know! Your people would meet us, it was knowledge we share... you still must share it in a way or you wouldn't be here. Every equinox when the Edgeland faces the sun equally at this place, ...you call it the sun...? Then the way is clear for us to measure the coming effects for our season. You keep the others away and it is always clear... there is no one to stop us and you leave the way clear. It has been very important to do this for us... for some time now."

I shook my head again. "I don't know what you mean? What do you mean every equinox? That is like every year... we have those every year don't we?"

"Yes, but in your year it is twice, one for the warmer season and one for when it is cooler. We only need to measure it once though and we know."

She answered simply smiling as though I was now teasing her, but she could see the joke was totally lost on me and hesitantly she continued. "The equinox happens twice, once in the cold and once in the hot... the coldest time and the hottest time. Every year we observe when it is the coldest, when the sun is furthest from your half of the Edgeland at this place. Others measure it the second time; they go to the Edgeland on the other side. We look for the stars in the skies, the ones you call the south cross and the emu, and the hunter... you know of these? Those are stories we shared. The colours in the rising and setting sun tell us, we measure the... the light through the stratosphere... that is what it is... the stratosphere? I couldn't think what you called it. Our Elders then know what the coming season will be in the Inland and what measures they need to take. Our world is changing so fast now, too fast."

"Every year... for how long?" I asked even more confused. "I mean you can't be here every year... you're only as old as me and this is the first year for my ceremony here. You are really talking in riddles you know. Not making any sense at all!"

"I've been here many times before, but... but you were not here. No one was here... I am here to make sure the measurement is taken correctly on the equinox. It is your southern equinox for us. It has to be at the same time and it should be clear heavens."

"Many times... on your own?" I questioned with some scepticism. "What two... three... you were just a kid then."

Kirri shook her head. "Maybe fifteen times now... maybe more. I don't know; I don't count. Others did it before me but it is for me to be here, my place to do this... to check what has changed. That is my role until I have another."

"Fifteen?" I looked at her sceptically... the girl was out of her tree and I considered that. Maybe she was on some mushroom trip and a little delusional. "You can't have been here for every year for fifteen years... you're not old enough. You must come here a couple of times a year?"

At this she grinned again, and the light in her eyes sparkled fascinating me. "No. I have not been a child for many of your years... but you...?" and suddenly her smile calmed. "You are not grown fully either?"

"Either?"

She shook her head. "We grow slowly Inland, the sun ages you. You burn and dry out... your skin. You don't live very long really."

She was talking double talk again and I sighed. "That's gabble again. You're nuts you know!"

Kirri smiled a slow intriguing smile and it worried me some for a reason

I couldn't put my finger on, as she continued to speak softly. "As a man from the edge, you sound like what I had thought. You're different than our men you know. You smile more but you are harder in some ways and you anger so easily."

"Is that good or bad?" I challenged. I could enjoy this game I figured, knowing that my anger and frustration had been a large part of our conversation. I considered her words a little repentantly though, deciding to tone it down a bit and really try to listen to her instead. Or at least look as though I was doing so.

She shrugged though. "I don't know. I don't know how you live on the edge like you do. You really don't live long but you don't seem to mind."

"You're crazy! You know that... crazy talk. Come on, I better get you home I think."

Standing suddenly, thinking that she really was a nut I stretched out my hand to help her up regardless. She was a cute nut and I liked to help her but strangely now my actions seem to surprise her in some way. It also pleased her and I could feel that as she took my outstretched hand and stood taking up her bundle. She had carried this the whole time I realized and it didn't look an easy bundle, it looked weighty even though it was small and I caught her eye curious.

"Do you want me to take that for a while?"

"No. Oh no. I... this is very important. I will carry it."

Making a curious face I waited, my expression asking the question on my lips. "You going to tell me what's so important in there."

"It's nothing really. It is the stone, it will take the measure of the light."

I shrugged. That meant nothing to me. "You'll have to tell me about it sometime," I offered as I turned to put her ahead of me. We could travel at her pace for a while I decided as the way here was fairly straightforward.

Pausing at another pool further along we again collected water and it refreshed us both. I decided to have another go at a few simple questions if only to amuse myself. It was here that I learnt from Kirri that she too was hungry.

I wished then that I hadn't eaten the whole bread knob that had obviously been for her. It made me wonder why the hell she had given it to me in the first place and the thought of food made my stomach growl in complaint. I could only hope that there would be something back at the camp. They were gunna be shocked when I turned up with her I thought to myself silently.

Then again, maybe someone knew where she was from. The women seemed to mix freely among the camps more so than the men. After all it was for their ceremony that we mostly had gathered together. For us it was only a few of us who were going through the men's initiation at this time but for the women it was an important ritual ceremony.

What she had said, the strangeness of her words stayed with me for a while before I dismissed them. The Inland... what a strange thing to say I considered; she had to be pulling my leg when she pretended she had no idea of where the nearest town was. There was no place that didn't at least know that. That she wouldn't know was crap... but if she wanted to play this game well I could play it too.

Every now and then we would pause for a rest. I was feeling the weirdness of this whole business over time and becoming impatient. It was while we were resting in one of the caverns again that Kirri inadvertently bought the whole business into our fleeting conversation.

"If you're hungry I could cook some of the fungi. It is quite nice to eat and the flame won't affect it much?"

"Yeah sure... I didn't know if it was eatable or not." I watched as she moved to the wall and stretched to reach the smaller growths there, rather than the larger growths that were lower down.

I joined her after a minute, which seemed to surprise her but after her initial start she smiled. Soon we had what seemed to be enough for both of us of this younger and softer fungus.

Seeing how she prepared the snack was interesting as she delicately peeled the outer skin away and gathered the small fungus in a pile, breaking it up. Then she added a little water to it in the small natural bowl on a rock surface. Bending the smouldering flame from the torch to the edges of the pile of now damp mushrooms she moved them about, slowly heating and softening the fungus. Once she was happy with their state she offered me some.

It wasn't too bad a taste being a rich earthy texture that had some appeal. "This is good." I said as I reached to pinch some more from the pile with a grin.

Kirri smiled. "I wasn't sure if you would eat it. They say that you eat a lot of animals mostly."

I frowned. "Meat... you mean?"

"Yes. That's it. Dead animal carcasses I think they are, those that you burn... you have a great deal of that. It's carrion... we don't eat dead things."

I sat back surprised. "You don't eat meat?"

She shook her head in agreement.

"You're vegetarian then?"

With that suggestion she frowned. No ... we eat fish too, fresh fish. We don't store it. Much like egg, we eat them as well as birds. But mostly we eat vegetables and fruit and sometimes seeds. Once you... your people would bring us grains, unusual grains. It was like a treat for us. My old mother would often talk about it. There was a golden one she particularly liked and I have always wondered what it would be like. We have never been able to grow it like you do."

Grinning I looked at her... "Well that is the same isn't it, almost? If you eat white meat that is, that is meat."

"No... not at all. Dead animals, especially those with red blood and those that eat carrion make you different, they change you. Particularly the large animals unlike the grain eaters ... the carnivores are very different. We eat only the meat from animals that do not eat carrion. These animals mostly eat plants and insects, except for you're... your crocodile and some lizards."

"And where did you get this from?" I countered amused. "Cows don't eat meat and they are red meat."

"You have cows?" she shook her head. "The Edgeland never had those animals before, the animals with hooves. So you have them now? I have heard about them but I haven't seen any."

"Yeah sure." I answered surprised. "Of course we have them."

The girl shook her head strangely, "It has changed then. It's a learning we are taught but... but clearly it has changed now. They teach us this, about your world that is. We all need to know these things."

"My world? Yeah... right."

She looked up oddly and frowned. "Why do you say that?"

"Well your world," I countered. "My world... it is the same thing... come on."

When Kirri shook her head and I paused, wondering what was going through her mind.

"It's not the same at all. Your world is hot and ... and it rains and floods and there is a lot of burning, the sun and fire. Hardly any shelter at all and you use fire a lot. It is dangerous. It is killing your world and ours you know? There are a lot of problems about your world that we don't have. You live very dangerously and die so easily... I don't understand why this doesn't worry you? It is so much carbon that is causing the changes, the ages of ice will return to your world and you do not worry about this."

"Worry... About what ... using fire? What a weird question. Fire is necessary. You can't live without fire. There has always been fire."

"Not at all. We don't use fire like you do; it is not necessary to use it so much. You burn your world, the plants I understand but you burn most of those for no reason, you burn even the earth, especially in recent times. In the Inland we don't use fire so much. We don't burn the earth. We use what is there in the heat of the earth and burn only the things that can renew easily like the dry plant wood when we need to. It would be more than enough if you didn't waste it and if you used it properly."

Looking across at me she must have noticed my incredulous expression as she went on. "It is real, we all live as one and we don't kill each other at all like you do. There is no need to do that; there is plenty of space. You should live as one with your world, you... every creature about you. The forest even, it is all one. Everything is dependent on the survival of this world."

"You can't burn earth... where did you get that idea from?" I demanded still incredulous.

"You dig the earth and burn it, the coal, the ancient beds beneath the ground!" she protested. "You even burn the oils of the earth. You are drying out your world, turning it to desert. You will make it hot quite quickly and this will change everything. This is changing your world too quickly for the creatures to survive the change. Others can't adapt."

"Oh. Yeah... well I guess... I didn't think."

"I don't think you consider what you do much. The Inland people are very different to the Edgelanders. We value our world. You have no sense of value for your world."

"The Inland?" I questioned again, somewhat affronted at her condemnation. "You really have to get real about this Princess... Doesn't anyone say anything to you about this?"

Kirri's expression became inscrutable suddenly and it worried me. I had expected her to be offended, even dismissive or angry but inscrutable was not what I expected.

"You are not taught these things are you?"

"No." I chuckled in a wry response after a time.

She nodded. "We were told that... but I thought after a time that you... your people would have learnt. It is so simple really. If our world dies then you will die... Everything will die."

It was my turn to frown. "My people... your people. You really aren't making much sense. You're like ... delusional!" I tormented her, laughing.

"I told you. But you don't believe me do you?"

I shrugged. "What is there to believe?"

"That I come from inside and you are from the edge. You don't believe that and yet you are here. Your people were always here to take us through the caverns of the serpents until you truly began to burn your world and that began to change our world too. But your people can control the serpent and you can help us in that. It is what is given to you to do. Maybe if we were to work together... if you could see what you're doing."

"You have lost your way," she said continuing in her soft voice. "The Edgelanders are so brutal and cruel. I sometimes think that you don't care at all. Once you would help us to get to the edge through the caverns, we helped each other. Our histories tell us of how much damage a burning world can do and we are thankful for this knowledge but your people do not seem to treasure such things now. Maybe you have forgotten these things. It has been over a hundred of your years since you last were here to greet us... that at least."

"A hundred years? My years?" I questioned confused.

"Yes. We wondered why your people never sent any but the oldest of your Elders for a time. But even they stopped coming almost a hundred or more of your years past."

As I pieced this all together in my mind I watched her, trying to feel my way in her mood. She was serious; I could see that and frowning I tried again to make sense of it all.

"A hundred or more years ago, that would have been the old tribal men. They have passed, we have no Elders of that type around... they... they were killed off by the Whitefellas."

"Who are they?"

"The Whitefellas? Why colonization of course, the English. They are the white fella's. Just like you. Your mob... with your white skin you have to know..."

"Not my people!" Kirri said suddenly. "I mean I know... we knew that the people, others had begun to arrive by sea. I mean we... we... saw it, it happened everywhere and it was to be expected. It was inevitable as your mobs grew in numbers. But you fought like you always have and I guess... it was the same for all! But the burning began well before that. The skin colour is just skin conditioning and the differences customs bring. We are all the same. It isn't anything else and the Edgelanders are the same the world over as we are. We were told of it; the migrations and we were warned. Then when the ... you damaged the air. You damaged it for everyone, for the Inland ... even for your own world. You don't listen anymore to what the earth is telling you."

Shaking my head I had to agree with some of the drivel she talked, but it was all a bit mixed about. "You Whitefellas did a lot of the killing. There was no burning either... come on. Burning is a way of renewing the land. It's traditional Lore. You really are nuts... you don't understand." I added chuckling.

For some reason Kirri shook her head and disagreed and then suddenly looked up. "The traditional ways of managing the land were good, but what you do now is not good at all. You say you don't kill?" she asked with some incredulity. "All the Edgelanders kill... it is what you do. You wage war, you have always done this and this is why we no longer help you. You have become very animal, base' almost. It is as though you have no beliefs anymore."

"You have little left of what makes you a valuable people," she went on. "That which makes you spiritual and this is important. Even in the places where you worship... those where you go to be quiet. You no longer hear or see the world that is truly important. The Edgelanders no longer touch what is inside them. You worship different things now. It seems worthless to us you know? It has no real value and you don't seem to care what you do. It is very hard to understand why you do what you do?"

"Well... yeah. We kill for reason. We needed food and the Whitefellas stopped us, or tried to. I don't know... it was a lot of things."

"The Edgelanders always have killed and there are no white people. None of my people live in your place and yet we are white too. My people only visit the Edgelands rarely; it is not a place that calls to us. We come only in the dark, when the sun cannot burn us.

"We do not need to burn things like you do." She accused almost quietly. "Edgelanders are very violent but I guess it is in your nature or maybe your culture, your way. At least this is what we are told by those who know these things."

"Oh come on..." I chuckled. "I haven't killed anyone! And everyone needs the sun."

"You don't kill?"

"No!" I answered almost shocked that she could think such a thing. And then I realized I was beginning to sound as weird as she and the oddity of it struck me suddenly, disturbing my line of thought.

"But you do," she protested. "They tell us how you do... and these things are true. We know you do, you are lying to me now! You even kill those who are like yourself. You even kill your own. We don't often see your children; I have thought that you must hide them to keep them safe. When our people, those from the Inland come to the Edgeland we rarely see the children and yet your numbers grow more and you damage the world so much. I could never understand it... why you do that and yet you can reason, but you can understand and easily see these things."

"I don't do anything!" I protested and then the oddity of my own protest struck me. "So you really say you're from some inner land? Is that what your going on about." Then I laughed even at myself for the suggestion.

Kirri nodded her head in agreement; obviously pleased I seemingly understood the silly things she said.

"OK... OK... so what is your world like?" I challenged her amused in part at her audacity and the threads of her imagination.

"It is much gentler than your world. We don't fight like you... we don't have wars and kill and there is plenty for everyone. But we don't have as many people as you do. We know there are limits to what is sustainable... we don't hurt our world like you do. Your world is truly very violent."

"No it's not!" I protested with rancour.

"It is."

"Oh... so there is nothing in your world that hurts you. Come on... no spiders or snakes or crocs? No sun!" I added with incredulity.

"Oh yes. We have those... though we don't have a sun, or days, and no darkness or... or night, it is always the same. We do have dangerous things though and much worse than those that live on the Edgelands, they are there but we leave them to their own. We don't try to kill them. We just don't go where they are; every thing must have a place to live. It is a balance that you need to go on living. We don't want to disturb our world... it is precious to us and it has taken an eternity to bring it into a balance. We only have one world you know... you should know that. You should tell everyone else."

"Yeah right!" I chuckled.

"You should!"

She was serious. Watching her I could see that and it confounded me. "You really are nuts."

But Kirri just shook her head and smiled that inscrutable smile once more. As though I was some idiot who could not see what was obvious. It confounded and annoyed me.

"We should keep going. I need to reach the edge before the day burn ends or I will have to wait until just before it begins again."

"The day burn?" I questioned amused and in some way annoyed.

"Yes. You call it daytime, but you have other day words too I think?"

"So you only come out in the night? Like some vampire hey...?" I asked laughing.

"It isn't a joke. You burn! Look at you... and this ages you, you die so young because of it."

"Not me. I am going to live until I am at least... ohhh seventy I guess."

"Seventy is so young." Kirri said, surprising me.

"Oh it is? Are you planning on being around longer then?

She shook her head patiently. "We live until we are about... ohhh... three hundred and fifty at least... maybe four hundred years in your year count or your season cycles. But your years are so often and they are shorter... I think that is right. You count the daylight times... we don't have that, we don't have the day times."

"In your dreams Princess." I protested, impatient with her fantasies now as I stood reaching for the torch. Waiting while Kirri again picked up her package and settle it about her shoulders in the type of sling arrangement she used.

"We don't you know. We don't need it, it is light all the time with a crystalline sky," she said quietly.

"And how old are you now... in Edgeland years...?" I added laughing at her strange terminology.

"About eighty five I think, maybe ninety of your season cycles, we don't count years, your years, they are only cycles you know and you are changing them anyway. They pass so quickly those years you count. We can only measure them by the succession of your seasons within the equinox and watching the change is important."

"We have about five of your years to one of our cycles," she explained patiently. "This is in your way of counting your time. You age a lot quicker but it's an odd thing to do really, count like that. We use a balance of our world and its changes and it is all linked. It all has a life. Everything has a time span of its own and you have unbalanced this. This is what is important. Our way is the old way and much better."

"A what? Balance...?"

"Yes. I don't know what you would call it, in your language. I wasn't very good at some of your words. There is no word for it I think." With that she flicked her fingers strangely and then seeing I had no understanding, dropped her hand and quietly continued.

"They say that Edgelanders age five times faster than we do because of the lives you live... in the sun all the time on the edge where you are. Plus you kill yourself all the time and die much quicker. You force change on your world out there and it unbalances the things that are important. You destroy everything about your world, which is really stupid."

"Yeah right! Suck it up Princess." I said carelessly, becoming impatient with her criticisms and now I wanted to just annoy her. She spoke a lot of rubbish I decided and she was beginning to get on my nerves. I turned to lead the way again and tried, determined to pick her prattle apart.

"So... according to you, you're... say one to our five, that makes you just under a hundred or something. You look really good for your age." I added laughing at her. "What are you? Eighteen, maybe nineteen?"

"How old do you think I look?" she asked strangely.

"Oh... I don't know... Maybe that, not much older than me I think. You look a bit younger maybe than that."

"I do...? I guess I do," she added softly as she chuckled to herself.

I was impatient with her game now and I led us back through the caverns silent for a time. I began to wonder about why she would make up such a story. There had to be holes in her imaginary world, they wouldn't be hard to find but did I really want to bother with it.

Sure she was cute in a petite sort of way, but such light skin as hers didn't do much for me. I liked to be out in the air, a more active or sporty type of girl suited me better and she was way too cosseted by the looks of her. But it was her expressions, her eyes that held a fascination.

Somehow she was in part believable and I realized it was the knowing expression in her eyes. It left me wondering what her family was like and what her home life was all about. You didn't get that knowing look without experience and that intrigued me.

As we moved up through the crevices and cracks, following the ancient markers I tried picking at her tale. Worrying the details in wanting to find flaws and it wasn't as easy as I had thought it would be. She had really thought this through and it was in part fascinating to hear how she told it. How she countered each of my questions and suggestions as often as they were based in tripping her up.

Her world, the one she had built in her imagination was in its own way interesting. As I sank back into what I found could be believable I also found myself adjusting more to this game of hers. It passed the time and gave you something to occupy yourself with other than the path.

It was hard to visualise but it appeared her world didn't have a sun, nor day and night. They simply had a sort of seasonal variations of colour in the sky or whatever it was overhead and it was in some way important to her... or rather to her imaginary world.

This sky colour governed the ground conditions, or maybe it was the seasons... if they even had seasons. When I asked about that, her explanation seemed to indicate that seasons were non-existent. What they had was a world with tropic pockets within the earth, with constantly humid climate patterns that varied with our passage of seasons in what she thought of as our surface world.

With subterranean heat, came life for her and it was a strange thing to consider that they would get heat from inside the earth rather than the sky.

For us the sun was the kernel of life and according to her it was killing us instead.

What amused me more was that she was really pissy about my world. She imagined that the Edgeland, as she insisted on calling it, was responsible for the changes in the season or weather variations at times in her world. Everything was affected by what came down to them from the Edgelands. It polluted their water, their air, even their light. This seemed to affect other places but it was hard to pin her down about what she meant by these other places. It all had something to do with chlorine clouds over the Antarctic in winter.

It took a while for me to realize she was talking about the ozone layer and that hole that builds in the Antarctic winter. Where there is no sun to destroy the clouds that cause the gaping great seasonal hole in the ozone layer, high in the stratosphere. It had a lot to do with the CFC's and carbon, it was all-important it seemed.

I realized after a time that this was about all the stuff in the news on how we were building a global warming pattern, which threatened to bring on an ice age. That to me just didn't make sense.

It also amazed me that she had built this link between the two worlds and seemed to have a scientific grip on stuff that I didn't know a lot about. She prattled it all off and seemed to grow more confident with her explanations as we went on.

At school we had looked at that in science once and I remembered it, well bits of it. But it seemed she reckoned this ozone hole was chilling the water and poisoning the inner world or worlds, as well as ours. It seemed it was changing their pattern of life down there somehow. In some way it related to what came down to them in the water. Particularly where their lands were nearer the Poles.

That the worlds she spoke of were pockets of land somehow joined like bubbles in the earth was weird. It was an interesting story but you would have to be nuts to believe it I decided after a while. It all seemed like some science fiction model, even if that was entertaining.

What really did interest me though was her imaginative description of the things in her world. I really enjoyed hearing her talk about the animals and other creatures, they sounded to be really prehistoric.

The little that we had been taught at school about prehistory had more to do with the Northern Hemisphere and their dinosaurs. It was more about the history they had up there. As a kid it had been years before I realized that Australia had its own breed of dinosaurs and mega-fauna unique to us.

We also had our own history but school didn't teach us Australian stuff even though it was the oldest continuous history on Earth. So it was our Elders who we relied on for our history, that of our land and our Country.

I wasn't much interested in the history they tried to teach at school. Who wanted to know about stuff that just didn't relate anyway? It was all pretty irrelevant to Aussies really, that stuff they taught at school. It was about another world, another place even. It had nothing to do with Australia or Australian history.

She also spoke of ages past, as though it was stuff I should know and I didn't say that I knew none of it. She talked about battles that seemed to be important to her even though they were very old and it all sounded a bit like old legends. She even expected me to think they were important, like they were my history too. She was nuts.

Taipan and Sean had taught us a lot about our mega-fauna, which was our prehistory that I knew. Then there's the Dreamtime histories and stories. I guess because it was said that the brothers were both shape-shifters, these creatures were something they knew a great deal about.

Sean had once said that skills drew often from the Kadimakara of the Dreamtime, those ancient dinosaurs and mega-fauna that no longer walked the forest and wilderness of Australia.

Of course we didn't talk much about shape shifting to anyone, it was forbidden knowledge even though most of us knew about it or had heard bits and pieces. It was all part of the Shaman Lore and not spoken about openly so I couldn't speak of the comparisons with her.

Listening to her though, as she described the animals that ranged through her imaginary world, I wondered if she might be storyteller. Jenna would love to talk to her, she had an interest in these things and it occurred to me that I should introduce the two of them. But then... I dismissed it. Kirri was clearly a nut and Jenna might not thank me for the introduction and I didn't want to put Sean off side.

When I asked her for the second time about how she got to the cavern where we met, she actually answered me this time and that story was also more complex to me than the one about her imaginary world.

It seemed that she approached the cavern in the same way I did, via a water flow. An ancient track was the common thing between our paths.

It boggled the mind though because it wasn't as though her water flow or stream was upside down. It was right side up for her, as it was for me, even though she was upside down, or rather on the inner side or was she? She made her way through the caverns to reach a common ground where I met her in much the same way it had been for me.

I got a headache thinking about that. Just who was upside down and who was right side up and how had we come to be the same. I was too tired to really sort it out and it made me irritable as well. So I let that go and instead immersed myself in the stories of her world as though I was listening to a good sci-fi.

Later we were arguing over food of all things when I first heard the strange shuffling. Then with a louder sound of stone fall and grating sand I shushed her suddenly with my hand held high and straight in an imperious gesture, one she surprisingly obeyed.

"Did you hear that? I whispered flicking my glance to capture hers.

"What?"

"That sound. We aren't that far off the first cavern, but I am sure no one else should be down here. It had to be getting late now outside."

"Yes. It should be getting towards sunset, it is a good time for..."

"Shut up!" I spat impatient as my ears strained to any sound.

"What?"

I just glared at her and then carefully moved my head to pick up any slight sound that might echo through the passages. Kirri thankfully remained quiet as she looked about and then watched me intently.

The cavern was quiet, and then I heard it again only it was different. It was the shift or the shuffle of sand grinding against the surface, perhaps a rock face or platform.

"That! Can you hear it?" I whispered.

Kirri looked around nervously. "Perhaps it is the serpent, we should go!"

I looked at her a little surprised. No one ever spoke of the serpents and while she had used the description before, this was very different. Dealing with the serpent was a skill for men, not women. "It can't be." I protested uncertain and a little incredulous even though I knew well it could be. Women never spoke of these things to men.

"Let's just go. It's the serpent... and.... and I don't want to meet it."

The fear in her eyes had me reaching for her hand to tug her along as we moved off. She was really afraid and it unsettled me as I braced my hand around hers and stepped ahead.

The entrance cavern was only perhaps ten minutes away so silent now we moved quickly along the path, both battling with our own thoughts. It was good to leave the threat of the serpent behind. I wasted no time in putting distance between the odd cavern noise and us.

When we reached the entrance cavern it was with a certain relief. Immediately both of us looked up to the cavern ceiling, each for our own reasons trying to assess the hour. The light was darker and dull in the high ceiling reaches and it had a feel of dusk about it, where the air is chilling around you and the light growing feeble.

"I need to get out into the edge quickly, the sunset is near and I can use that." Kirri said strangely.

"The sunset?"

"Yes, to take my measure. So near to the equinox it will be clear. It is only sunset and sunrise I can do this. Hopefully there will be no cloud."

"You really are set on this aren't you?" I asked impatiently. I had thought that once we reached the surface she would give it up, but it seemed not.

"Of course I am! Why else would I be here?"

Shrugging with some impatience I moved down towards the deep pool and then stood quietly waiting for her.

Kirri approached warily for some reason. "I hate this part," she said softly. "I never know what is going to be outside."

"The forest of course." But my words didn't seem to soothe her so instead I left her to her emotions and eased myself down into the chill of the water. I was breathless with the bite of it as I pushed out into the deep pool and turned again to wait for her.

Kirri just looked at me fearfully as she too eased herself reluctantly into the chill pool, her sash fixed carefully about her shoulders still carrying her small burden.

She stayed close to me as we ducked beneath the surface and occasionally she would reach and touch my foot or brush against my jeans and I knew she was still near as I surged forward underwater beneath the overhang, moving toward the light outside as it grew. It was a relief to reach the outer stream and cutting up quickly I knew she followed me.

All was as I expected it to be, it was the same as it had always been. It was my world and it was familiar in all its sights, smells and sounds. As I stretched for breath Kirri surfaced beside me and flicked her head around fearful but I could only smile and laugh at the apparent fear in her. She was a good actress at this sort of thing I decided.

"There is nothing to eat you." I teased her laughing, having listened to the stories of hers about the monsters in her own imaginary forest and then I moved quickly to the bank as she struggled to stay near me.

We were both dripping as we emerged from the water. I was quick to wipe myself down with my hands, sweeping as much water as I could off my skin and skating my fingers through my hair. Kirri instead was wringing her clothes carelessly as her eyes searched the growing cast of the late afternoon light in the forest with what looked to be a fearful look still.

"Come on... we had better get back."

She looked at me confused. "What? No ... No I have to go up to the ceremonial ground."

I frowned. "Look, this game is over. We really should get back, your family will be wondering where you are... my family will be too. It has to have been a day since..."

"My family!" She repeated disbelievingly. "You don't believe me do you!" she then demanded. "Go then! You go... I know what to do and I can do this."

"Kirri... ! Come on... this is stupid. I can take you home."

Glaring at me in some frustration she just turned, leaving me looking after her as she stalked off following the streams path, flicking me a single glance of anger.

"Kirri!" I yelled after her. She didn't stop, nor even look back again and so I paced off after her trying to reason. "Come on... cut this out. It's over, it was fun sure but it's over Princess. Your being bloody stupid now, it's getting dark. It will be dark in ten minutes."

"Yes. I have to hurry," she tossed back, stepping up the pace as I followed, wondering just what I was supposed to do in this situation. "Do as you choose. Come or not... I don't care. I can do this on my own and I have done so before."

"Bloody hell!" I mumbled to myself as I stepped up my pace, making my feelings more than clear but following in her wake none the less. I couldn't let her wander about. I wouldn't know where to find her again and I had no idea how well she knew this place.

It was as I trailed in her wake I began to realize how fantastically unlikely my own story was going to be. A strange girl, from a strange world, someone I found in a cavern that no one knew about. How I had lost her, abandoned her... geez... it didn't sound so good even to me.

"Hey... wait up woman. There is no bloody hurry!" I called as I reached her but her flashing glance was impatient with me. It was almost as though she was now choosing to ignore me.

Kirri mumbled something under her breath and it took a minute for me to interpret what she had said.

"It's just like an Edgelander to make it all *bloody*."

"What!" The look she had tossed me over her shoulder was full of impatience and annoyance and it silenced me. However it still didn't answer the question.

Together we wove through the bush quickly, following the flow of the stream even as its path began to climb. I struggled to keep up with her. It was a struggle and she had set a bruising pace despite her diminutive size but I was determined to keep up even though she seemed to easily weave through the bush, more so than I could, as small as she was.

Luckily it wasn't too far and despite the sudden climbs we reached a small mountainside clearing where a flow of spring water spilled and pooled for a moment before going on its way.

It was a tiny area really, one edged by growth but the rock carvings ahead on the rock-face had me frozen in my stride along the track. I knew immediately this was a woman's ceremonial place and that the women had used it in the last few days. For all I knew they could be planning to use it again soon. This place was taboo to me and as Kirri broke into the small intimate clearing I remained frozen, unsure of what to do, stopping at the edge of the clearing as I then moved back away from it hesitantly.

For a moment she glanced back impatient, then dismissed me in that same moment. It was as though she had no time for my presence or even my fear and reluctance at finding myself where I was.

Kirri stepped quickly towards the sacred shelter of the rock, swinging the bundle from about her shoulders. Working surely she unwrapped the swath of cloth and took something from the bundle. Abandoning the rest in a pile she headed to the rock where the ancient carvings of the spirits forms were sketched onto the stone. These were a warning to me, to others and one that we would not ignore. I looked around nervously.

I watched on though as she clambered up the stone. I was unsure about what to do and every muscle screamed to be given ease. I wanted to leave this place and leave it quickly.

Standing steady Kirri braced herself against the falling dusk light in the sky. Holding high whatever it was she had carried in the bundle of cloth, seemingly measuring the dying light reflecting through what looked to be a clear crystal. She moved it about catching certain angles. It had smooth shiny planes on its surface that caught the light and yet it also had its own soft bluish fluorescence, which was like a dancing light growing in the deepening dusk.

I watched fascinated as the dying light flicked over it while she studied it carefully, as though she was taking care to position it in a pertinent way to catch a certain light or measure.

Kirri waited for the dusk at the point where the light turns to gold. The few short moments of glorious sunset before the dying light faded. That was when she too froze in the face of the light.

I had always loved those few seconds of golden light, as this light found the reflections of the world in the dawn and dusk. It was a beautiful crimson to golden glow, tempered by where ever you were. It seemed to weigh the day by the dust in the air and the reflections of our world.

Once this moment in the setting of the sun had passed, Kirri climbed down from her perch heading back to her bundle. I watched silent as she busied herself for a moment and curious I wondered just what it was she was doing with this odd-looking crystal.

Pulling out a small stick of some type she took care to mark a measure on it. Wanting to join her, to see what she was about, I found that all I could really do was wait. I wanted desperately to leave. I needed to get away from this place; this was not a place I could be.

I watched on and after a moment I was relieved to see her wrap her bundle about her shoulders again, having ordered it and with what was a brilliant and very satisfied grin she looked up and then moved to join me.

"We can go now. It is done." Was all she said leaving me somewhat at a loss as she stepped passed me, expecting me to turn and follow.

I scrambled after her again confused and at odds with my thoughts. Just what was going on here? I had no idea really. The things she had said couldn't be true but she was beginning to spook me some. She was so sure of herself, of what she was doing and she looked to have no intention of returning to camp. This was crazy stuff.

"Look! Hey Kirri hang on a bit."

"What?" she answered impatiently. "And stop asking me to hang on. Just what does that mean?"

Catching up with her at last and able to walk abreast at her pace finally, I drew an unsteady breath. "Hang on? It means just that."

"Hang on to what?"

I laughed at the absurdity of her question. "Nothing really I guess... maybe the moment. You have to have heard that before?"

She flicked me an impatient look. "No."

Surprised I shrugged, at a loss now. "Come on..."

"I am. Can't you see?"

I laughed again. This was getting absurd but my curiosity was demanding answers. "What was that? That thing you have, that crystal and stuff?"

Kirri flicked me a strange look. "It's a measure stone, I told you this. It's... I think you call it amber, something like that but it isn't like your stone. This one is very precious, very ancient. It is a special amber."

"Amber? Amber is yellow isn't it, that is why they call it amber? That stone was almost blue."

Again she flicked me a look. "Yes. I just told you that it was a precious stone. It is blue amber. It is only yellow when light shines through it. I don't think you listen much!"

"OK... We'll do it your way if you want then." I retorted after a moment, irritated again suddenly. "But... but we do have to get back."

"Yes."

"Well then... where is your camp? I mean I can take you there." I said answering her once more with a impatient look.

She stopped suddenly and glared at me. "You are taking me back through the caverns? ... Aren't you?" She demanded suddenly.

"What!"

"The caverns. I have to get back and you said you're taking me back?"

At my confusion she released a long drawn breath and then continued. "Are you taking me back, or... or...? I can go on my own you know. I can do it on my own, I have before."

"You want to go back?" I was incredulous at the very thought. After spending the whole day weaving through those damn caverns, and with the threat of the serpent, the girl wanted to go back in there! It was unbelievable!

"Well of course I want to go back. This is your world not mine... I hate it here. I have to go back and take back the measures of what I have found, don't you see! Don't you understand anything we have been talking about?" She demanded, now somewhat incredulous herself.

"You're crazy!"

Kirri shrugged suddenly, and then turned away continuing to follow the path of the stream we had stepped along only a short time ago.

She was really going back I suddenly realized. This silly girl was seriously going to be going back into the caverns at the time when the Spirit men were about. That was the very least of it!

It took two seconds before I stepped up to follow her... two seconds... and in that two seconds I had to reposition all my thoughts. She was crazy! But what if she wasn't?

That very thought argued with my common sense. What if she wasn't?

The question was something that I had to know the answer too. What if she wasn't crazy? What if what she had been telling me all day was real?

I was at a loss and it was a breathless sensation to deal with. It sent my imagination spiralling into the unknown as I tried to remember the detail in all the things she has said. Struggling with my thoughts I followed her along the trail we had stepped earlier; the same trail that took us back towards the undercut and which would take us on into the caverns.

Kirri walked with a determined tread as though she had done what she had come here to do. As though it was all a reality to her. She was now going to make her way back to her home and there was nothing I could possibly do to stop her or even distract her. This all was so very real to her and I felt compelled to follow. I wanted to discover the truth of it.

As we walked, the forest about us fell to darkness and when we reached the undercut the night was blanketing the forest, leaving it in a growing night shadow. Kirri was set on her path and with only a small glance back at me she stepped into the stream once more.

I had to follow her; I had no other choice, I couldn't abandon her to this. My conscience wasn't about to let me and my curiosity was waring with my common sense and winning.

"Look. OK. I believe you." I reassured her as I too stepped reluctantly into the chill of the water once more and struck out to join her as she prepared to duck beneath the surface and take on the undercut. "You can't go back on your own, wait up a bit will you."

Turning back to me as she reached for the support of the same roots and branches, those that I had held onto an eon ago, then she nodded. But it was a reassurance without conviction or care. She didn't care what I felt I realized.

"Jeremy, you don't have to come. I have done this before but... but I would welcome your help. I don't like to walk through the serpent caverns on my own. I never have..."

"Well then I can help." I added trying to reassure her though I wasn't entirely sure what I was agreeing to.

"Thank you," and with that she slipped beneath the surface, moving under the undercut and leaving me breathless again. She really was frustratingly sure of herself I realized as I prepared to follow her.

The Eyes of the Serpent

Jeremy:

When I broke the surface of the water back in the cavern once more I had a whole new mindset to settle with. Kirri was pulling herself from the water lit by the deep dimness of what little shadowed light was available in the cavern. I could barely see her form ahead of me.

Her clothes stuck to her body and for a minute I could think of little else. It was like I was seeing her for the first time in a dark silhouette.

I struck out towards the shallow reach of the bank and she was within seconds shaking the fabric of her clothing out. It left off clinging to her skin, releasing the form of her to once more hang in the loose folds of the fabric. It was something that was incredibly distracting but by then I was busy trying to deal with my own stiff and wet jeans which were not so easy to climb from the water in, having taken on more weight with the water. Or perhaps it was the chill of the air that helped me realize their added weight now made me feel clumsy.

It was growing cold and the cavern was no longer comfortable with the deep evening shadows making it a strange and lonely place. I thought of the relative warmth in some of the caverns ahead and that was at least welcome.

"Do you want me to light a fire before we head off, dry our gear a bit?" I commented, still distracted by the chill pertness of her body in places.

"No. I don't like fire, I told you that. My clothes are pretty dry but you…" Her eyes ran over me in the dimness and she grimaced unsettling me. "Maybe if we moved down to a warmer cave."

"Sure." I mumbled disconcerted.

"Yes, that would be best." She added simply as she finished shaking out the water from her top. "We need to get some rest too, if we are going to climb down through the caverns. We need to be alert."

"Yeah…" I agreed. Yet I had no real care for the word. Grabbing at another two of the torches from the bundle still high on the ledge, which I had found earlier, I looked across at her curious. "Who makes these?"

Kirri was surprised at the question and for a moment she frowned, paused confused and then answered. "You do."

I shook my head. "We have nothing like this… maybe it was something we did once?"

"You don't use these anymore?"

"No. We have torches, real torches."

"They are real torches," she answered simply.

"No. I mean we have batteries and better torches."

The wooden torch we had carried earlier had been discarded on the ground, though it still smouldered in a muted fashion barely casting a light where it glowed with the very last of its life. The remnant of the glowing tip was however thankfully enough to fire the new torch.

With a bit of care and steady working the new torch was soon burning with a solid steady glow and I settled it in my hand moving ahead to lead the way with somewhat reluctant steps.

"Well maybe you will need to leave a few of those other torches here for next time."

"Next time?"

"Yes, a year from now... one of your years. I will be back again in the next equinox, we always come back to take the measure of light."

"What do you do with that... the measurement?"

"I told you. We plan our forest and ocean harvest. It tells us where to find food and when to plant others. It is a good measurement this year, the damage is not so bad."

"Damage?"

"Yes... to the... the stratosphere, remember. The measurement tells us that, so it will be a better harvest. Not so cold. The water currents will not shift as they do when it is dryer or cooler."

"You really are a strange one you know." I added, though it was more to reassure myself in some way than it was a question. I turned to move off carefully towards the now darker corners of the cavern while I held the torch high adding light to the gloom.

My clothes were still stiff, but that would dry in time if only from my body heat. Kirri on the other hand seemed barely to be wet at all now. The light fabric of her pants and top seemed to have dried and she looked more comfortable than I. So without further comment I led the way back down into the caverns, wondering just what the hell I was doing here.

I knew it would take us maybe an hour to reach the warmer caves, where the water heated the air in the closeness of the smaller spaces. Kirri stopped every now and then to collect fungus when we finally began to encounter it but it wasn't the mushroom like growth we had collected before. It was more a layer like fungus that she pulled carefully at and I wasn't too sure that I was going to join her in eating it.

It amazed me just what she stopped to collect along the way, tucking it into her sash each time. The odd moth I could understand and the occasional piece of root was to me acceptable but when I suggested we try for a snake or listen for the high chirp of bats, she dismissed me with an impatient look. We both agreed on catching the blind yabby like shrimps when we saw them and it was here we settled on stopping for a feed of a type.

She wouldn't allow me to light any fires again, even though there was a tangled collection of dry litter about. Instead I watched as she used the heat from the torch we carried to soften and cook the food she had gathered along the way.

"Can you do this also, with those other torches of yours?" She asked as she carefully turned the mixed pile of gathered foods to the heat.

I grinned and realized that these old type of torch did have other values which a battery torch wouldn't have. "No. But I am sure we can think of something."

"Humph. You will have to... though it seems to me that I might have to carry more food. Perhaps you could bring some yourself next time?"

"Next time?" I contemplated the thought. "Do you really need us here next time? You seem to manage."

The look Kirri gave me was intriguing. A mix of confusion and even hesitancy and then she said the oddest thing.

"Do you not know how to keep the serpent away anymore?"

This confounded me. Women never spoke of the serpents to men, never raised the stories even. "I guess I do." I answered, knowing that it was only by the grace of Andrews dance and the chant I had heard only recently that it might even be possible. This was something I had to talk to the men about, I needed to ask advice and I wasn't sure that even Andrew and Sean, or even Taipan or the Elders could answer such questions for me. But for some reason I couldn't tell her that.

We sat in silence for a while as we ate and then feeling full for the first time in what seemed like an age. I eventually rested back against the rocks and closed my eyes for barely a moment. Or that is what it seemed to be to me.

It was Kirri's vicious and sudden grip on my arm that disturbed me and immediately I knew there was something wrong... even before I had reacted, opening my eyes properly.

Startled by the sudden bite of nails into my arm the first thing I noticed was the strangeness in the light in the cavern when I lurched to awareness, reacting to the unexpected pain. It was that blue green glow and I reasoned quickly that the torch had gone out already.

Kirri, though silent, had a death grip on my arm. Her fingers digging into my skin in fear but it was the glowing orb that startled us both as it whipped about the cavern in sudden, sporadic movement.

Immediately I pulled myself up in surprise, a surprise threaded with a tempered fear.

I reached for her and held her still under the shelter of my arm pulling her into my side, even as she clutched at me. Neither of us said a word to break the silence of the small cavern while the orb of light, a low glow, barely a fistful, moved about the cavern rapidly for a few bare seconds equally as silently. Then the orb suddenly shot off at speed as though on some errand which had little to do with either of us.

"It's the Min Min." I whispered tersely, pulling my thoughts together.

Kirri's grip had not eased, nor had mine about her arms, but she needed some explanation.

"What?"

"The Min Min light, I have heard them tell of it. Some of... the Shaman talk of these things. It is something of an amusement really I think. I'm not sure. I once heard a story of how they used the Min Min light to keep the women in line." I whispered trying to reassure her. A slow growing and cheeky grin easing my own fears as I remembered the tales Andrew had told around the campfires.

Forcing my grip about her to ease, I sat back with relief. I waited while my eyes once more adjusted to the now much dimmer light of the cavern. "It's OK. I know... I've been told it won't hurt you. It can't hurt you." And then I gave a low chuckle in relief, unbelieving that I had seen it.

Kirri sat still looking at me strangely. She didn't seem afraid now and for some reason she was looking at me with a type of calm confidence. I was a little amazed that she hadn't screamed or even yelled. Most of the girls I knew would have freaked out but this one; this strange girl just watched me carefully with the large, clear blue cast of her eyes. She was so strangely silent it spooked me.

"It's OK really." I tried again to reassure her. "It's just looking for something and we aren't it. The Shaman send them out when they need to find something," I shrugged; even I wasn't sure of the source of the tales but I knew them well and for some reason I felt in control.

She nodded slowly.

"Are you OK?" I asked, not sure what to expect. I expected something at least but again she just nodded.

"Maybe we should just move on. I guess we can rest at the other end, it's warmer there." Again she nodded and began to collect up her wrapped bundle and arrange it about her. It was almost as though she would have done anything I would have suggested and there was something about that which I liked.

Leaving the cave silently, we walked on for a time. Negotiating our way down through the caverns we followed the ancient markers and I was feeling more and more confident with myself. Then all that was shattered in a few steps.

We had been talking, for some reason keeping our voices low which likely had more to do with the echo of the spaces we moved through. Kirri was telling me more about the animals of her world. I wanted to hear what she would come out with and I was beginning to believe her I think.

As strange as it seemed I really was beginning to consider that her stories just might be true. I was even contemplating challenging her to take me there with her and that very idea filled my mind.

That was why when we had stepped into one of the larger caverns that the shocking noise hit us like a blow.

There was a thunderous crash against the rock face and the flash of light, the brilliant orb, as the Min Min light suddenly shot up through the cavern and danced again before our shocked faces.

Then this creature lunged at it. The movement was so swift that we scarcely had time to acknowledge that there was a serpent in the cavern. The Min Min seemed to travel all about us as we ducked in surprise and fear. Kirri diving behind the shelter of my own body as I too crouched scuffling towards the shelter of the rock cavern wall before the swift body of movement. Not too sure about where to dive and avoid the melee in the violent dance between the Min Min and the serpent.

The Min Min quickly shot high into the corner of the cavern and seemed to take on a higher glow, lighting the cavern in a soft coloured yellow light that flooded into the corners. It was in this glow that I recognized the dance of light over the serpent form.

It was the same serpent that I had seen out by the stream, the same outraged flash in its movements and the same angry whip of its small vicious teeth bright in the brilliant hues of blue and crimson scale. It moved like lightning about the cavern as though trapped, unable to find an exit. It seemed to be blinded by the Min Min orb and outraged by its presence but the bright little orb still sat high in the cavernous ceiling almost as though it was laughing at it, its light shimmering in challenge.

Kirri had screamed this time and had scrambled to push back as though to disappear into the wall of the cave. I had never seen anyone so afraid and that she had abandoned me for some reason made me angry.

I lunged towards her as we both cowered beneath the outraged movement of the serpent.

The thing was barely larger than I, but more mobile like a lizard. This animal had the wing like flaps of skin down its side like a glider. It didn't fly but it lunged and leapt from its grip on the ancient walls of the cavern. Flying and leaping from one grip to another in its outrage at the glowing light of the earth orb overhead. Each time the serpent moved, shards of light seem to dance about it, like spears bent on their own path. They were flashing around the head of the creature as though they were a weapon or a defence of some sort.

It's scream was high pitched and while I could barely hear the edge of its scream Kirri was forced to cover her ears as though in some pain and I found myself trying to cover her with my body, shelter her from the sound with the breadth of my shoulders and what bulk I had.

I wanted to hide her from the creatures scream, which I could barely hear but which I could see bought her a lot of discomfit if not outright pain. It was however the flash of fire, those spears glancing around the cavern walls that really worried me. These shards continued to splash against the cavern walls on a deadly mission of their own, all but blinding us. They flicked dangerously close at times and splintered almost as though it was the serpent showering us in a venomous flame.

The outraged serpent leapt again and this time I felt the race of air across my back as it swung by closer. I found myself turning towards Kirri, hiding her from its breath, which seemed to scorch the air as it swept down past us again.

Flinging myself against Kirri in an attempt to shield her, I felt the burn of the breath across my back and it was like a brush of heat. Then unexpectedly I felt claws sink into my skin as the serpent took a grip about me, riding my back. The weight was not at all what I expected.

In its clawing grip the serpent held me in its embrace. The claws of its feet dug into the skin of my hips and upper arms. I felt it move violently, struggling to dislodge me. I could feel its pull with the movement in the shift of weight, as though trying to rip me from my brace against the wall.

I knew not to fight it even as the pain of its claws bit savagely into my body. Instead I threw myself back into its own weight, off balancing it. It was a trick I had learnt from the men. To follow the flow in any force, go with it, use it to dislodge or disarm any assailant. It worked and I felt the serpent lose its grip as it tried to counter my unexpected move but then to counter balance the shift, I felt the animal sink its teeth about my shoulder and the pull of muscle as it struggled to balance itself.

The pain was excruciating and I bellowed, lurching back into the creature in the agony of it. Trying to free myself until it felt as though only the nail of its teeth held me by my shoulder.

Reaching up as I lay back with my weight pinning the winded animal against the ground, I grabbed at its rough skinned snout where the teeth were biting into my shoulder. Feeling the heat of its mouth at my touch, my fingers fiercely worked to force free the grip of fangs from my skin and then suddenly in a roll I was free.

It was Kirri's scream that focused me again as I tried to struggle to my feet, fighting through the mist of pain in the serpents bite as my weight had pinned it. My hand was wet and burning with the saliva of the serpent, my head swimming with pain in my shoulder making nonsense of the discomfit of where claws had dug into my body.

What I saw as my eyes swam with pain was amazing to me and I couldn't focus, couldn't believe what was swimming in front of me. Andrew... it was Andrew and then in the shimmer of movement seemingly all about us Sean rose suddenly beside him as my mind grappled with the sight.

My head seemed suddenly too heavy for my body to hold up. Then I felt myself sink into a weird warm silence as my body buckled to the floor of the cavern. It was a place without pain that I fell into and a silence born of being deep within caverns of darkness, it was blissful and oh so very welcome.

Caverns of the Dreamtime

Sean:

We had come searching for the Serpent, the Kajoora; she was a creature of the caverns that had lost what is most precious in the world of the Dreamtime. The baby serpent the kids had found from the caverns. The same serpent that Andrew had discovered in the bathroom where Jiemba had left it, thinking it was merely a lizard to be played with.

The tiny thing was the promise of the future and it was now tucked inside Andrew's shirt. To ensure its survival we both knew that it had to be returned to the caverns, the one place it could thrive. We had to find its mother or in a sure knowledge we knew it would die.

It was not an easy thing to do this and we both understood the risks in trying to return this serpent to its parent. But that the risks would have been Jeremy's, a young dancer before us now and a songman of the community, had never occurred to us.

We hadn't expected to find him here deep in the caverns, nothing had prepared us let alone that he had a girl with him. A strange girl who was now cowering in the corners of the caverns as both Andrew and I stood there struggling to understand the scene we had swept into.

These caverns were the place of the Oruncha men and the Serpents who guarded the caverns. The spirit men of the Dreamtime who fought so hard to control what they could of our world from the depths of the caverns. Yet despite our efforts they did control a great deal is seemed.

As I watched Jeremy writhe in pain and then lose it. When he slipped into darkness, losing awareness, I knew that the Oruncha had bought this about. I was left wondering if their own ceremony would be an echo of ours in the two worlds that merged more often than we cared to realize.

It was a birth and ceremony of the Shaman and I knew that young Jeremy had truly only begun his journey as it registered with me that he could be here only at the bidding of the Oruncha.

I was left in awe that the Oruncha Men could achieve their want so easily and without anyone knowing about it apparently.

That a woman cowered in against the rocks still sheltering her ears was a surprise. I watched Andrew's fingers dance in the language of silence and she too noted the same movements with evident relief as she eased herself up.

I understood immediately that she was not such a surprise to him but then he knew these caverns better than I ever could and it was not the time to question him about her, that could wait. I watched Andrew move quickly to the young songman and realized that he and the woman were still in conversation of a type, their fingers dancing.

I had never learnt the fast movements of the fingers and the swift talk of the mind but I knew enough to play with it occasionally and to recognize its dance.

The woman spoke nothing, she was silent in her words yet apparently obedient and she remained exactly where she was. She didn't move, or she moved barely a sketch as she watched us, her eyes never truly leaving Andrew. She was less afraid now, no longer cowering but still pressed up against the rock.

We would have to physically move her I thought and I was regretful that our sudden arrival had caused such apprehension in her eyes. Though at least the fear was receding. This talk between Andrew and her kept her silent and that was a good thing with women, especially now with the serpents about. The serpents and women had a strange relationship one that I had never understood.

While Andrew checked Jeremy over I moved silently over towards the serpent that lay still stunned up against the rock. Jeremy had handled it well. He had near squashed it likely in trying to dislodge it from his back. This we had seen on our arrival. It was still moving with each breath though and there was the occasional twitch of life. You could easily see the subtle movements, which indicated life and I didn't particularly want to be around when it came back to consciousness.

Looking up, I noticed the Min Min orb and then glanced over to Andrew. It was dying and we needed light so moving back towards where Jeremy still lay I joined Andrew silently. He would know what to do, how to deal with what we had at last found.

Andrew looked up, frowning as he ran his hands over young Jeremy's limbs. "He's been bitten."

"Is that bad?"

"Yes. It's way too deep a bite." His words were clipped and I realized as I saw his frown deepen that this was serious.

"What can we do?"

Andrew drew a breath and considered the question noting at last the dying light. With a look, the orb took new strength from Moongunn and then he flicked his eyes across to the woman and considered her.

"We need to get him out of here. How is the serpent? Is it dead?"

"No. Just stunned I think."

Nodding in understanding he took a further moment as I continued. "Who is she?" I asked quietly.

"No idea... though she belongs elsewhere. It seems young Jeremy was taking her home, that much I know from what she has said. She would have been what the serpent was after, her kind smell and taste sweeter than we do I understand. The woman is a natural prey to the serpents."

That surprised me, the whole lot of it. That the serpent was hunting the girl for food was surprising, but that young Jeremy was protecting her, perhaps it seemed escorting her somewhere was even more surprising. I knew that there had been no talk of any such task for Jeremy, or even one remotely such as this in the dance and ceremony of barely two days ago and yet here he was.

I was at a loss to understand how Jeremy came to be here and then I recalled how he had been so curious about the serpents. Had he perhaps this task in mind, had he known of it then I wondered? But there was no time for these questions I suddenly realized when I heard the careful movement behind me.

The serpent stirred.

Immediately Andrew was on his feet and shifting his shirt about I knew what he was looking for. We had been caring for this thing, the baby Kajoora serpent for two days and I was over the whole baby-nursing bit. Finding food for it in here was no easy task and that alone had taken more time than we could spare.

Andrew flicked his eyes to the Min Min and immediately it dimmed, seemingly struggling for life high in the ceiling where it had remained. Carefully he bought the small baby Kajoora from the nest of his shirt and making his way over towards the serpent he settled it against the shiny scale of its parents belly, then stood back, stepping carefully.

Immediately the infant serpent began to cry, a small high mew that I hadn't heard before. It was a strange high tone and at this sound the woman still over against the wall once more covered her ears in some obvious discomfit. Andrew moved quickly in his step then, though careful moving towards her, his fingers dancing.

Fascinated I watched as the serpent stirred, moving at first as though groggy as it struggled to force itself back from wherever it's senses had retreated. I flicked a glance across to Andrew but he held up his hand as though to quieten me while he nodded towards the serpent and its baby.

The serpent shifted and then slowly seemed to move as though to surround the baby with its body. In a quick flick and flash of reflected light against its scales, in a movement way too fast for me to follow with my eyes, it fled in that second with its infant. Leaving in a curt shuffle of dust and air just as the Min Min orb suddenly died.

The silence was deafening and the light from their dull torch like brand was barely stretching to Jeremy as the woman reached for the brand. She stood up slowly, almost reluctantly holding the torch high and moving it about seeming to fire it up as she continued to watch Andrew with something that looked like awe.

I knew that look, it was one I saw occasionally in my experience with Andrew and women and I smiled a small grin at the evidence of it. It was a grin that faded as my eyes dropped down to Jeremy. I checked the marks of the serpent's fangs, testing the wound on his shoulder carefully with my fingers and watched him flinch involuntarily.

There was little blood but then the serpents venom saw to that, and it looked as though Jeremy had got a fair dose of the stuff.

Andrew squatted down beside me once more leaving the woman to hold the torch high as she too moved over towards us. Still hesitant, still silent, I looked up noting the paleness of her for the first time. She was fairly young, barely a woman I thought. Her hair looked to be white, well almost but it could be a trick of the light. I had never seen anyone so pale as she seemed to be in this light.

"We have to get him out of here. We can't do anything for him in these caverns and we can only wait until the venom rides it's way through his body."

"Will it kill him?" I asked afraid to hear the answer.

"No. I don't think so but I'm not sure. He needs the attention of a healer, perhaps Taipan. Maybe the Elders..."

"What about her?" I nodded towards the woman.

"We will need to get her back too." At that Andrew looked up, the dance of his fingers asking questions I couldn't understand. Then he looked across at me after she had apparently answered him in kind. "I will need to take her back through the caverns, the Kajoora serpent is still about and the Oruncha Men will take exception to a woman wandering the caverns alone. Do you think you can manage to support him back up towards the surface?"

"Jeremy... yeah sure." Moving to test his weight, Andrew jumped in to help and together we eased Jeremy up against the rock. The movement seem to rouse him and that was a good sign but he was still off with the pixies... or perhaps the Oruncha men. But he also seemed to know what I wanted of him.

He was able to help me support his weight as I shifted him across my shoulders in something of a fireman's hold despite his grunts of half realized protest. Once he gained a few more senses he would have to walk on his own but for now I could help as he recovered more.

Andrew helped me to adjust his weight as he commented. "You have a few hours before you get him to the surface, you will likely have to carry him for the first of it, you know that. Just follow the markers they'll be there. He should begin to come around a bit more and the exercise will help move the venom through him though he is not going to be really present or even with you in his senses."

"Yeah... OK. I'll manage. My body is still riding high with the transitions."

"I'll probably meet up with you soon hopefully or I wont be long behind you. It isn't far to where the girl needs to go and I will be able to travel quicker than you."

"Where is she going?" I asked curious as I again adjusted young Jeremy's weight.

Andrew just grinned. "I told you. I am a gatekeeper of a sort; I'll take her down to her gate. See you soon OK?"

I nodded and watched as Andrew signalled the woman and they moved off together. She was still silent and I guessed that it was gunna be that way for the entire time they were together. Andrew knew how to keep his secrets, that much I understood. He was well versed in the secrets of this world. I had yet to understand anything of the truth to be found in the caverns of the Dreamtime.

Birth of a Shaman

Jeremy:

I knew what was happening, on some level I knew but it was difficult to hold the reality together. It was liked being in the grip of some kind of evasive madness that teased my mind, drawing my thoughts into dark caverns deep within the bowels of the earth. A place where strange men and odd creatures lived and their songs kept my mind reeling.

It was not unlike where Sean was trying to take me it seemed. I was being pulled into two directions within the darkness of my mind. He was dragging me at times and shoving me at others, this darkness and the sometime putrid smells that we found in some of the caverns invaded my senses, rousing me. It was a path different to what I would choose to take and it was difficult to separate his need for me to help myself and my need to preserve what sanity I could find in the dark recesses of my thoughts.

At times I thought he was leading me into places I didn't wish to go and yet he was impatient with my feeble protest, insistent that I go with him and I had to trust him. I knew I could trust him, but why then did I not wish to? The madness that gripped me at times left me with no desire to give in to him.

Sanity was mine for a few moments though when we finally reached the last cavern, one where ahead of us the light of day seeped into its darkness in some way. I was suffering with a foul taste in my mouth and I could do little about this. It was an almost metallic taste but I couldn't seem to speak well, nothing made sense.

An ancient hand had decorated the walls in the cavern here too, in the same way it had been decorated in the cavern Kirri and I had passed through. I knew then that this was what marked the entrance of such places and I would remember that next time I decided in a lucid moment.

It too had the serpent winding about its walls and there was something about the art of this ancient serpent drawn on these cavern walls that trained my thoughts. Something about the still rich red colours and it was a song that the serpent was trying to teach me.

It had taken hours to climb up through the caverns. Hours where my thoughts had wandered, where shadows had become men and ancient things. Sean though never stopped harassing me to keep moving, he kept insisting I drink where we could and that did help to soothe my mouth.

He harangued me at every turn about going forward, not stopping or delaying, as I wanted to. I was as exhausted as he when we finally reached that last cave, the last bastion of the Oruncha Men. I realized then that this was what had kept us moving, it was the need to escape the caverns.

The water pooling here from some unknown source seemed icy, chilling me to the bone as he dragged me into it. Wading through the silted bed covered by the pool of water, he dragged me into places that were chest deep and thick with weed and bracken. I realized I must have been running a temperature because the shock of the cold water bit at my skin causing me to shiver suddenly.

It felt good though and my thoughts cleared for the moment giving me a few seconds of what was becoming a scarce reach into the reality around me, even though it made my shoulder and body ache painfully.

We had no need to duck beneath the surface here. The pool flowed easily joining the gentle rush of water outside as we scraped through the brush mostly concealing the entrance.

It was a simpler path than the one I had taken but I hadn't much cared for the caverns through which we had passed. They had held the stench of rotting things and to my mind there were reminders of death in that awful smell which had lingered in some places.

Once on the outside of the cave, out in the Edgelands as the girl Kirri had called it, Sean didn't bother going down off the side of the mountain. It became apparent that he didn't want to return to the camp even though he would know it had to be closer than home. Instead he dragged me through the forest and higher onto a bush fire track, which eventually led surprisingly to Andrew's station wagon. They must have parked it here at some time I realized and it was only then that I wondered what had bought them into the caverns.

Too exhausted to ask, or even to really care I just collapsed onto the back seat where he bundled me and eased my head back against the seat. My shoulder was throbbing mercilessly and my mouth was dry and uncomfortable. Reality was slipping away again; leaving me to the war that was going on in my mind.

I was winning this war though, I could feel the grip of something releasing me but still the darkness of madness sat heavily in the recesses of my mind. It lurked like a promise, like an ominous shadow.

I didn't remember much of the drive, nor when it was that we arrived back at the community but I did recognize the growing light of day. It was another day and I was confused as to just how many days it had been now.

How many days had it really been since I first woke to the whisper of dawn in what seemed a lifetime ago?

I felt the ease of the bed give beneath my weight and felt the cool hands moving about me. Then there were the voices of women murmuring in the room, voices that coaxed me to drink some kind of salty gruel, which they insisted on.

They were interrupting my thoughts and I had to hang onto the threads to stay conscious. I heard Old Granny asking questions and the mention of Taipan. There were so many questions and I knew when Sean left, he had stopped answering the women. I was glad I didn't have to answer any of their questions and that Andrew could tell them what the women needed to know.

I knew when he arrived, when the women began to tax him. I heard his voice through the fog in my mind and then Andrew too left. I felt his impatience for some reason and that unsettled me. The only savings grace of listening to what went on around me was that no one taxed me with questions. I had too many questions of my own as my mind drifted in and out of strange new places.

It was around this thought when my world tipped into madness. The women left me to the touch of old men, a strength I could feel both in mind and in body and I felt safe under their hands. Something was keeping me safe and I could feel that sense of security when it came.

Sanity eventually returned after a lifetime it seemed and it was with a strange awareness, to find myself again in the full light of the day. The shock of seeing Taipan seated patiently beside my bed was sobering and for a moment I just lay there watching him, desperately trying to draw the threads of memories, those that I couldn't find.

"Welcome back." He said simply, for all that I had been on a long journey.

I was confused for a moment, and then more so when an elderly man appeared behind him, stepping lightly through the door. The shock of seeing him killed the questions forming on my lips and in my mind. The old bloke was a Kadaitcha Man, an old man of such a strength that I felt the threads of fear and shock before I realized Taipan had simply turned to welcome him warmly with his glance. He cast him a smile and then settled his eyes back onto me.

"This is Apari, he has been tending to you."

"I've been sick?" The question formed before the others, though I knew the answer to it before the words had even left my lips. I knew it in the ache of my body, the burn I still felt in my shoulder and the strange taste lingering in my mouth.

"No young Jeremy." Taipan said carefully as though speaking to a child I thought, something I didn't much like. "You have been through an initiation of a kind, you have been with the Oruncha. Apari has been leading you through the trials of the Shaman."

"The Shaman?" Suddenly struggling to sit up more I felt the pain stretch through my body, arresting me.

"Be still," the old man Apari suddenly insisted. His hand moving quickly to my shoulder stilling me but the heat in his touch seemed to scorch my skin. I noticed then that I was painted about heavily in ceremonial clays. "Open your mouth... wide." He suddenly insisted and reluctantly I complied.

The old Kadaitcha man peered frowning over what seemed to be my tongue and then he grunted and stood back. "The mark is there Taipan, it is finished."

Confused I stared up at him, testing my mouth carefully as Taipan nodded speaking softly. "It is done, you carry the mark of the Oruncha."

"I do? I mean my mouth feels... kinda' strange. Like my tongue is big and I keep having to swallow."

"The women have been giving you a gruel to strengthen you. Your tongue carries the cut of the ceremony. It is a piercing and it should not be allowed to heal. If it does you will loose your strengths young Jeremy. I'll get some lozenges for you, that will help and cold water is good too. I'll also get you a barb to help keep the hole open, it will settle down quickly just give it enough time. This is the path of the Kadaitcha that you have been chosen for, it is a mark you should wear proudly young man."

As he had spoken I had been testing my body, noting the strangeness of the painted clay and ash markings I now wore. My fingers found the fine black ash and fat as they traced the dark line running down the centre of my chest, a marking in deep charcoal dividing my body. It was a heavy line edged by other designs all about my chest and shoulders. As my glance flew amongst the two men I also recognized that I was covered in a grease of some sort, which was keeping me surprisingly warm.

"You have been through ceremony young Kintji-iruka, these are the marks of your initiation." The words of the old man echoed about the room as I felt the Spirit name settle on me. "The eagle-hawk will protect you and Taipan has been asked to guide you. Soon you will leave with him, both you and Ariaka will be under his care until such time that he decides you can care for yourself. You will find your way in time."

"Kintji-iruka?" I tested the sound on my tongue carefully, hesitantly and with a certain discomfit.

"Yes. By this name you will be known to me. I have marked you with the Orunchilcha, these marks will protect you but they are not for the eyes of the women. So you will remain here and only the men will come here for the time. Taipan will tell you when you may wash the marks away. He will be able to tell you a great deal young Kintji and you must hear him."

At his words, I felt the thrill of them skip through my body. A thrill born of the look in the eyes of the old Kadaitcha and he too must have known the path of my thoughts. He smiled at me, drawing me into his mind.

"You have been chosen young Kintji and soon I will return. I am going to prepare the sacred weapons for my Grandson; and for you I will gift the ililika. For this you have been chosen also. You must guard these things well Kintji-iruka. Do you promise me this?"

"Yes." It was a breathless answer, one breathless with anticipation and fear. That it was I who had been chosen as a Shaman by the Oruncha men stunned me. Restlessly the knowledge settled on my mind in some amazement but it was the last of his words that had shattered my concentration.

The old Kadaitcha nodded, accepting my simple pledge and then he turned to Taipan. "I will find you by the time of the new moon. Thank you Taipan for all your help. My time is coming and I must settle this sacred business. I am pleased with this choice and that the churinga is to go into good hands."

"Thank you Apari." Taipan answered climbing to his feet out of respect as he continued. "I'll walk with you back to your camp. There are things I would ask you."

The old Kadaitcha man nodded and I watched as they left. Their step was almost silent, melding with the sounds lingering of the day. For a moment I wondered if I had truly heard what I had heard, or could it be a part of what was the flights of my mind?

I was stunned, still struggling to come to grips with what had come about and my thoughts reeled trying to order this knowledge that I had been given. I struggled to accept it but I couldn't get past the thought that I was to be trained as a Shaman, by the Kadaitcha no less. Trained in the sacred dance, trained in the skill and I would be gifted the stories.

I was to be given one of the great treasures of the Kadaitcha, the ililika. I had heard of these, yet I didn't know what form it would take. A weapon of the Kadaitcha, the ililika was held in great esteem and reverence. It was a powerful and ancient weapon, one endowed with great strength, great spirit-magic, that which had been born of the Dreamtime. It was an ancient tool. Not even Taipan had anything the like as this I thought... though perhaps he did and others had failed to recognize it or perhaps it had remained hidden as were many such weapons.

The ililika was a gift given between Sorcerers and Shaman, passing on their strengths down through time. I knew of no one who held the weapon of the Spirit Men for those so gifted never spoke of such things, not amongst those who were ignorant. Yet this now was to be mine. A gift from a powerful man of the Kadaitcha and the reality of it stunned me.

Then something else occurred to me. The old sorcerer had spoken of his Grandson, spoken of another named Ariaka. I knew of no one of that Spirit name, a name sacred and secret. But for the old sorcerer to speak of it meant that to me it was not to be a secret. I wondered who this Ariaka was that he was to share my training?

As I settled back into the comfort of the bed, exhaustion once more overtook me; I was left to wonder about the question of my companion and what he was to be in my life.

My body was still very weak though and I must have fallen again into the darkness for it was the dark of night when I next woke. I was no longer in the bed where I had been, instead I found myself stirring to the sound of the motor and the sense of movement.

I was stretched out in the back of a car and it was a moment before I realized that it was Taipan's vehicle, the cruiser, and Taipan was driving.

Propping myself up slowly I realized also that his younger brother Tom, my friend who was a few years older than I, was in the car too and this reassured me though I still wondered at it. I hadn't known that he had even returned to the community and yet he was here. He sat in the front passenger seat watching the play of light along the highway mindlessly. Then he tossed a glance back at me, likely having noticed my movements.

Tom had been away up north for over a year or near that, learning the ways of the Featherfoot and I was pleased at this time to see his return even if I felt like crap. But I wondered where we were going and why was I even here in the cruiser? Had I been out to it so long?

"Hey… you're awake." Tom suddenly said, swinging towards me more fully as I struggled to ease myself up further.

"Where are we?" It was difficult to talk and I continually wanted to swallow which was growing annoying as I struggled with the demands of talking. Noticing this Tom handed me a water bottle and I took a deep swig, pulling myself up in the dimness of the back seat. Still feeling the stiffness of my body and the discomfit of my tongue, which seemed to have stayed with me. I wished for a moment that I had some way to check my mouth out as the thoughts of what the old Kadaitcha had said came back to me.

"We're on our way to Sydney. It's Ty's solution to keeping us away from the women." Tom answered, teasing Taipan with his glance as his older brother snorted in amusement.

"What?"

"Yeah… the women. It is one of the tenets my Grandfather has insisted on. No women."

I struggled to sit up, trying to make sense of his words and instead Taipan interrupted my thoughts.

"Tom's right. No women to distract you, at least until you have passed through your initiate. There is a lot you need to understand, both of you." Ty caught my glance in the rear vision mirror and I could feel the testing of his eyes as he continued.

"I've decided that it is best if you and Tom stay with me and Aine down in Sydney, at least until you are fully fit and that could take some time. How do you feel?"

I tested my limbs slowly. "Like shit!" I exclaimed, realizing that was exactly how I did feel. "What is it?"

"It's the venom I expect that is causing much of your problem, you were drifting in and out of consciousness. The women gave you a draught to make you rest, but it should improve now. I suspect that it's the Oruncha that are fighting to draw you back towards them. Not many escape the bite of the serpent and live to tell of it young Jeremy. Sean did well to get you out of the caverns so quickly."

"The Oruncha?" Suddenly realizing that I was no longer wearing the ceremonial markings of ash and clay I ran my hand about my hair and body uneasily. I felt clean, refreshed but strangely divorced from the natural knowledge you have of yourself. As my hand swept up to the discomfit of my shoulder I winced, feeling the bandages and padding over the wound and curiosity swept through me.

"Yes. It's another of the reasons we wanted to get you away from Wollumbin. Your shoulder wound is still weeping and while you are conscious, or seemed to have been this last few days, you are absent in your mind. Your consciousness isn't with us but elsewhere. Apari thought the Oruncha perhaps had too great an interest in you and Andrew felt the same. He has given you something to help also…"

"Andrew? I can remember something… there was something…?"

Tom swung to me suddenly curious. "What do you remember?"

"Something about the Kadaitcha man, a Grandson?"

"Ariaka?" Tom asked grinning.

"Yeah…"

"Yeah that's me. Apari is my Grandfather. He is off in ceremony preparing. He'll be some weeks." Suddenly Tom thoughts grew dark, almost secretive and he turned to settle his eyes ahead into the stretch of darkness cloaking the road. His silence suddenly striking as his thoughts captured him.

Taipan then took up the telling with carefully spoken tone. "Apari is preparing to retire into the caverns with the Spirit Men of the Kadaitcha and he has decided to gift his strengths to yourself and Tom. This is what he is preparing to do now. It is something he must do on his own and it will take a lot of preparation."

"The ililika?" I questioned curious, remembering suddenly some of the old Sorcerer's words despite Tom's apparent reticence, which now had settled resolutely about him.

"Yes. This is something Apari has been planning for some time now. Tom, as his Grandson will naturally inherit considerable strengths. But this inheritance comes with... prerequisites." The sudden grin that flitted across his face warned me. "Part of this, is that in acquiring these gifts there are tenets you must also abide by or the gifts will be lost to you."

"No women." Tom interjected suddenly, emerging from his dark stillness as Taipan hooted softly in quick response as though to draw him from his thoughts and mood.

"It's not as bad as that, this is only for a time. There are some food restrictions I would like you both to observe also and certain behaviours. This is a serious business Jeremy, to Apari it is his legacy, his life."

"What is the ililika that he spoke of?" I asked curious to learn as much as I could. "I have heard about it but I really know nothing of it?"

"What form it will take I can't say. That is for Apari to decide but it will be endowed with his strengths, in much the same way as the Shaman's band Sean and I wear on our arms. These carry the strengths of our fathers, fathers; and yours will carry some of the strengths of Apari and the power of the Kadaitcha. It is a considerable power and you will need to learn how to wield it, and how to protect it."

"I am to be trained as a Kadaitcha?" I asked stunned.

"No and yes. As a Shaman most certainly, though your training is not wholly of Tom's creed. The Kadaitcha, or the Shadow Walker is a blood Lore that is Tom's alone, as you will learn. What Apari is planning on gifting you is within the power and the skill of a Featherfoot, one who manages the concerns of the Kadaitcha. They are the same creed though the Kadaitcha is a spiritual man. No man is an island young Jeremy. You will become Tom's keeper and Tom, yours. You will be brothers under the Lore, even though you may spend an age apart in life at times."

"Apari has chosen this path because the Serpent has left his mark on you, the bite on your shoulder. Because of this bite you will be hunted, the serpent will sense you are about and seek you out. It is an odd sense of something that calls the serpent to you that you now carry in your blood. You will feel his nearness as he can feel yours. You will need weapons to deal with the Serpent and Apari has decided that you will be his emissary when it comes to controlling the serpent."

"It's likely that the ability to control the serpent is what you will be gifted but only Apari can tell you of this and what form it will take. You are a danger to the Spirit Creatures; you will be taught to control them and it is a control that the creatures of the Spirit would choose to destroy. Apari has not just gifted you just a weapon and knowledge Kintji, he has gifted you a future path as well as something to keep you safe from the Spirit creatures who will hunt you."

"Is... is he... the serpent; is he going to try and kill me?"

"Not if we can stop it and we have to means to do so. Have you ever heard of the Sky Stones young Jeremy?"

"No."

"These are opals, spirit gems of the earth and they are endowed with the means to protect you from the Spirit creatures. Such stones as these will stop others from finding you. The Oruncha or the creatures, the other spirit creatures of the caverns are blinded by the Skystones. They gift their owners with the means to walk through the world unseen by the men and creatures of the spirit world and they are very powerful stones. They are sacred and secret stones."

"Andrew has given one to my care for you and you will wear this once we can organize a means for you to do so. It's something we will see too in Sydney and it will blind the serpent and the Oruncha Men in both our world and theirs. It will hide you from them; they will be unable to find you. In our world they can only see you as though you were a natural thing, a tree or a part of the natural order, their other senses are blinded."

"What of the girl? What happened to Kirri?" I asked suddenly as the thoughts raced through my mind trying to understand what I was being told. It was slowly returning to me, the things that had happened in the last days. I realized there was so much I needed to know, so much to understand. This whole experience was daunting and it was beginning to overwhelm me.

"Kirri?" Taipan echoed, a question on his lips. "I have no idea? I will have to ask Sean or Andrew about that."

"She was in the caverns, an Inlander...?"

"Inlander?" Ty echoed strangely, his glance catching mine in the mirror again as Tom too turned to me, flicking his eyes between us before he interjected.

"You met an Inlander?"

"Yes. I mean I don't know? She was a case... really strange girl with some really weird idea's about things."

Both Ty and Tom shared a glance and then settled back, watching the road ahead in the beam of the light, strangely silent.

"Come on..." I asked laughing on a small curious sound. Though they were both silent, strangely so.

"Are there...? Is there really such a place?" I questioned stunned.

"Yes." Taipan answered me, leaving no room for doubt. "But this is something we can explore at another time Jeremy, not now. We will find someone who can answer your questions in time. Not at the moment though, there is too much else going on. In time... and now is not the time. If the Oruncha have gifted this knowledge to you then there are also other things you need to know. It is a secret and sacred knowledge and there is a great deal to it. Give us time, I will need to rethink some aspects of your training Kintji, you will need guidance in this."

The use of my spirit name on Taipan's lips silenced me. He was according me a certain privileged respect and I was a bit in awe of that. It was going to take some getting used to.

We travelled through most of the night, arriving into Sydney just before the break of dawn. I had never travelled through the city before, as I had never really left the caldera of Wollumbin, which was my Country. I was now transfixed however by what I saw.

Taipan took a path across the Sydney Harbour Bridge, an icon of the city. It was like entering into a new world as we drove through the streets bleeding away from the bridge. This was a world that it seemed was now to be mine and I was as curious as hell. What I saw of the city as we wound through the back blocks really shocked me though.

I had no real experience of the homelessness that inflicts itself on some people in the larger cities. People huddled in the fading dark, standing around burning drums and bins, or spread out up against the walls of the tall city buildings leaning into the morning light. They blended into the landscape as they were trying desperately to find oblivion in now quiet streets and alleys.

As the bright lights of the city began to die in the dawn the city seemed to be taking on other aspects of its character that I had never even heard of. I listened intently to what Taipan said in answer to my curious questions about the strangeness of the things I was now seeing.

"The city has many sides to it Jeremy. I bought you this way to show you this harsher world in particular. It is a world you need to be aware of. Don't be deluded into thinking that everyone has a comfortable place. Toms father, he ended up here... or around near here and it killed him."

"It was a slow death of the human spirit. Many of the city people end up fighting for an existence on the edge of these places and it is a hard life, but they don't know much different. There are those too who are not interested in other ways of living as there is an uncertain security in familiarity. They are bound by their own particular addiction."

My eyes flicked to Tom, but he was silent as Ty went on. "He's not dead, Tom's father, but he is like the living dead in our world. He has lost his spirit. This is what draws Apari into the caverns. The want to care for his son's shadow, that which remains deep in the caverns now. You need to know this also because Apari will return from where he goes at times, to show and teach you the things you need to know."

"Geeze... I thought Sydney was where a lot of the rich people lived."

"Wealth is here, but not everyone sees this seedier side for the despair wealth creates for others, even though it is in front of them. Every city has places such as these... some people actually prefer this life. In some ways it's exciting, the nightlife but during the day it is a harsh reality."

"The city has lots of attractions," Ty went on to explain. "Sex, drugs and a certain companionship and challenges. But there aren't many people here who do not carry dreadful scars, even a few kids. You can always assess the merit of the worlds you brush through by how they treat their elders, their young, as well as their sick and people in need."

"Where there is an obvious absence of elders, there is early death and usually suffering, these things go hand in hand. You should think about that. Where there are not many women evident, there is usually abuse. Where there are few children, there is high infant mortality or abuse. Balance, young Jeremy is the right measure of everything."

Considering his words they reminded me of Kirri's comment about how she thought we hid our kids. I wondered if this was the world she and the others from the Inland saw. Looking about with newer comparisons in my mind I was silenced by the things I saw.

Many of the seemingly homeless people were men, a few women but all looked in a bad way. They looked hungry, not just for food but for life as though they had exhausted or muddied their pool of life.

They were sleeping in corners and looking for the first rays of sunshine cutting through the streets, perhaps looking for warmth of the sun. It was a relief when Taipan drove the car out of the inner city back streets as the dawn broke over the more industrial and industrious type cityscape.

Here there were shops. People bustling about getting on with the day and they appeared blind to the poverty of spirit I had just witnessed.

"Is it very far?" I asked, wondering if these sights were something I would see every day.

Tom stirred and glanced back, as though waking from a silent reverie. "Yep. That is the City; we are a good way from there. Where we're going is in The Shire, the Sutherland Shire on the southern edge of the city and before the Royal National Park. It's a lot different from this. I'll have to take you into the city some time and show you around. It's different again at other times to what you just saw. We will be living on the Wanny... the Woronora River, well south of the city."

"How long will we stay?"

Taipan took up the answer. "Hopefully you will finish your senior schooling here, maybe the best of twelve months if you get your finger out. There is a local Secondary School and Aine and I will look to enrol you there. Tom will get a job or I will keep him busy. He won't like what I have planned as an alternative. There will be no sitting around on the dole!"

Ty chuckled as Tom now huffed at the light threat he had made, and then he went on. "I am hoping we will be able to leave you boys from time to time. We are planning on returning to the community but can drop down here occasionally to check up on you both. You should be responsible enough to be trusted."

"On my own... just Tom and I? What did my mum say?"

"She thought it was a good chance for you, though Aine will be speaking with her over the next few days. That seem OK with you?"

"Yes... Yeah sure. I always wanted to find out what the city was like. Do I have to go to school though... can't I just go to TAFE or something?"

"We can look into that if you like. It will take a few weeks to settle you both in and we will be around till then. You will need to share a room for a while but then one of you can take the main bedroom once we sort out what we're doing. I've suggested to Aine that we move back and forth for a while and maybe permanently back to the community in a couple of months and she seems keen. We can talk about it this week."

Sorting our new life out became epic. The quaint riverside cottage perched on the steep hill over the water was really something. Though all I really wanted to do was to try out the little dinghy Tom pointed out as we moved down the pathway. This led to what Tom described as the old fishing cottage clinging to the side of the ridge on the edge of the river. Fishing looked a real promise but there was gear to bring down from the cruiser.

After only the first load though I was over it and my shoulder had begun to ache badly.

Aine soon had me stretched out on the lounge while she checked the dressing on my shoulder. I could see how much it had apparently healed, though it still wept some. The stuff she put on it stung like buggery but Ty reassured me it would help it heal and it was only a light dressing Aine used when she patched me up again.

All I wanted to do was to get up and explore but I knew I wasn't going to be allowed to do that for the moment. So instead I helped settle into the room that Tom and I were to share. It wasn't overly large but enough for two beds and a cupboard with a dresser in the corner. It was larger than my old room at home, which was really part of a lean-too and it was odd to have so much comparative space and yet be told that it might be a squeeze.

In the next days Aine, Taipan and I visited the local school and even found the college, which while being a much further distance to travel each day, look like a place more suited to me. After a lot of discussion I was enrolled here on a completion course of Senior study with a prevocational stream into forestry. This was my choice and for the first time I really considered what my life was now to be like in the big city.

My shoulder was healing at last and after checking out my tongue in those first days and the small slit I had found there, Ty had me treating it regularly. I found that it was tiresome and at times difficult to keep the cut open as I had been told to do.

It was Tom who suggested we look into some type of tongue jewellery. This to help keep the slit open and it would also make the management of it easier and more acceptable to others in time.

It was a mark of my ceremony and it was important to keep it open, but the barb I was using was uncomfortable even when I used ice to chill the area. At first intrigued at the possibilities of a simpler solution we both went off to discover just what we could find out.

The adventure of the tattooing and body art shop we found was something else again and I really found it fascinating. A lot of the art was after my own taste and as I poured over what they had on offer I was tempted to get a tattoo as well. The idea was forming in my mind but I wasn't so sure if Taipan and Aine would let me get away with it. So instead we bought a small stainless steel stud and ball for my tongue and I spent the next few hours getting used to it.

"What do they use these things for?" I asked as Tom and I made our way back to the car park and I was playing with the feel of the stud in my mouth. Tom just grinned instead of answering me and despite my curiosity declined to answer. In the end, after my badgering, his comment raised more questions than solving any answers and it really got me thinking.

"If you don't know that, then your too young to have one. I found out about them when I was about your age, even considered getting one but I chickened out. You never know… might even rethink it maybe."

It was enough to stir me to later spend some time on the internet and it was a revelation. It was one I was keen to try but with Taipan and Apari's dictum that we stay away from girls it didn't look much like I was going to get the opportunity any time soon.

This whole business of staying away from girls was a trial for both Tom and I. There are boundaries to these things and neither of us knew where they lay. At night we would often talk about it as we sat out and watched the endless flow of the river from the balcony under the star lit sky.

"Did Ty say anything about what he really meant about staying away from girls?" I asked, hopeful that Tom could give me answers from his own experience.

"Why? You got plans?" His tone was curious, amused even.

"Yeah… well… I mean its good to know what he meant."

"How's TAFE going anyway? Sounds like you've found it interesting."

I grinned contented. I had only been going to TAFE for a few weeks now and I found it a whole new experience. It was much more independent than school had ever been. I felt the weight of responsibility and the need to learn and listen instead of the push for mere entertainment. It was odd getting use to that.

"It's great, they are hard though. There isn't a lot of mucking about."

"So… there is someone there you like?"

"Well, yeah. A couple of girls I wouldn't mind getting to know, it's not like school though."

"No it wouldn't be." Turning back to the night skies Tom eased into one of the old camp chairs we had found in the boat shed.

"What about you, how is the site going?" I asked, knowing it had been only the first few days on the construction site where Tom was now working. It was a small build and Tom had found a casual position as a labourer. Although I knew that it was physically demanding work I don't think he thought it too demanding.

"Yeah… good. Good team."

"You working tomorra'?"

"Yeah."

"I thought we might go out maybe. Head into town and see what the place has to offer. Saturday night and all, see what there is about."

He flashed a quick grin, but then his words were contradictory. "Nah... not tomorra' I'm staying away from town for a bit. Maybe another time."

"Girls too?" I asked curious. It was his tone. It was settled and almost diffident in a way. Not at all like the Tom I had thought I knew well.

He sighed softly. "That too... Why go there when you can't eat at the table?" He chuckled and then looked up catching my eyes. "Things change you know... when you get older. Your view of women changes that is," again he sighed. "Well you kinda start looking for things different to what you would imagine."

"How do you mean? It's not like they change or anything."

"Yeah they do, and you change. You look for different things. It's not just about having a good time, though when I was your age I thought so."

"Did you meet a girl up north? I heard some talk back at home. It must have been serious?"

I didn't think he was going to answer for a moment, but then he looked up. "It was," he said simply. "But she isn't mine, she belongs to someone else now and that... well that is a good thing. I mean, I am happy for her... for them both."

I didn't know what to say and I didn't think Tom wanted to say more. He cast his eyes out into the night and there was no invitation in them. It was as though he wanted to keep his secrets, but something in his thoughts touched him deeply.

"So what can we do? About girls I mean. Can we still mess around with them but not do... well... anything?"

Again his quick grin bought him back to my company. "You could ask Ty?"

"Yeah... I know. But I'm asking you. Ty'll give me a lecture. I mean he's good and I appreciate everything he's done but... I don't know. I don't want a lecture. I thought you might know as much?"

"Well... I figure you can mess around a bit. I mean it is about not giving something of yourself... physically. That commits you like... like giving of your body to a woman."

"Really! How do you mean?" I asked chuckling in disbelief.

"When you take a woman in that way it really ties you to her. Sean once explained it like a thread, a link that commits you to her. I never saw it really until... until I realized that it does just that. It focuses your attention, your strengths and it's like a pull that you can't control no matter what. You have to actively fight to resist it or ignore it. It's an instinct maybe. You can become accustomed to ignoring it but that doesn't make it any the less real. There is more to it than just how good it feels, it's a tie like that... it builds.

It has a spiritual component that lingers... lurks around really without you realizing it."

"Like with any girls I ever slept with? Is that what you mean?"

"In a way. You give of yourself whether you want to or not and it is what it makes of you. It's how you see yourself in your own worth an in your own estimation. A lot of guys don't see it that way and it's like... easy they think. But its not really, when you get older you see the cost. When you look back. I'm only seeing it now, seeing the cost and how it changed me. I sometimes think that a good woman would save me somehow, make me a better person. I can see now too, that being without a woman in my life may not be the best thing."

"I hadn't thought I could be with just one, I mean one woman, constantly." He went on to explain carefully. "I don't know how to have both worlds and when I thought I had it sorted out... I think now that I let something really good go, because I didn't understand it when it was all about me. I gave what I had away and didn't even realise how valuable a good woman was."

Tom's quick grin flashed in an ironic fashion as I too smiled "You've had lots of women, well the guys say anyways. I guess you would know but I don't know what you mean... not really. I've known a few girls but no one really serious. More foolin' around really."

For a moment he considered me. "Yeah it's been good but I think the party is over for me. The thought of chasing women doesn't feel the same. I think something has changed for me. Then you never know do you? Maybe it is a different party, maybe I've grown up and there is something different out there?"

"What was it like being with your Grandfather, with the Kadaitcha Men. I've been wanting to ask?"

"Awesome." Again he grinned as he continued, casting his glance out to the skies. "The caverns... they are a different place. From here, it's like it's a place for men though there are some women there but they have their own place I'm told, away from the Men. It's a place like none other I know of. I wonder though...? When you mentioned the other day about meeting an Inlander it was a shock. I mean I have only ever heard talk of them in the caverns and I thought that they were maybe of the spirit world but ... maybe not."

Tom went on, his voice low. "My Grandfather once said that a long time ago we were connected in a close way, but no more. It's not like that now. It was a surprise that you had met one of them. I thought they were a secret knowledge of the Kadaitcha. Though Ty said that it wasn't the case, we were all one once. The world has an ancient history that has been largely lost, it's not taught now. Things have changed and I think the truth and these histories live in legend mostly. He's going to ask you about what you learnt you know."

"You mean like that girl? Kirri."

"Yeah. Tell me about her." Tom asked, surprising me. "Apari asked about her when I mentioned it but I knew nothing. He will ask me again for sure."

"I didn't know your Grandfather had been here?"

Tom just smiled. "He hasn't, I visit him on occasion. We stay in close contact since my training began. It is a thing of the spirit that we share."

"Well... she's a girl. I didn't believe her at all though she was really strange. She said some weird things, told me some really weird things."

"I've not been to the Inland. I've only heard about it. The Inland and other places I mean. They are like islands in the earth and there are a few of them. Sorta' like caverns... huge ones, so huge that in some you can't see their extremities. They are all underground... like communities or whole countries I believe."

"The Inland? Just where is it?" I asked curious.

"It's a world like ours I've been told, though not at all like ours. Their entrance into the caverns would be like ours. To them their world is not unusual at all; it is our world that is strange. Our world is harsher I think than theirs, I don't know really. I have only heard of it from amongst the Kadaitcha. They speak of those places and others around the fire at night. The Kadaitcha will tell you stories, legends of places and ancient times where we were more one-people, but then things changed. Worlds divided long before we built other civilizations that grew out of what was left, after things went pear-shaped. There were great battles back then in the stories told and I guess it is much the same as today really. We destroy and rebuild forgetting the old ways. We forget the old knowledge that we have destroyed. Things change."

"Other worlds? Like what?"

Tom's grin held secrets and he teased me with them, enjoying it. "Others... like the Mimi, the Oruncha, the Dreamtime. Even the old traditional lives of our people, that has now all gone. What we build is new. It is for the future... our future. My Grandfather has taught me how important it is to look forward and not forget, but to also continue to build. There are many other worlds and places I hear of, many strange things in our world that we don't see. Most people don't see what is there in front of them. The world of the Inlander is one of them, and who or what we are too. To an Inlander, to the Mimi we are the strange ones."

"Apari says that."

"Yeah. Taipan too. He listens; he hears the voices. Secret things."

"He does?"

"Yeah. It is a gift he was given, a gift of the Karadji."

"Is that why you can sometimes see him sort of thinking deep like, on his own."

"Hmm... took me ages to realize it and then I saw it for myself and I understood it then."

"You see them, you said once that you see the spirit men... do you still see them?"

"Yes, and women sometimes. I used to get confused about who was real and who wasn't but it is easier now. I have sat around the fire with the Elders, the Kadaitcha, and seen the spirit men talk to my brother. Seen things that others couldn't see. Even Ty couldn't see and I never knew it. I thought that what I saw, everyone saw. That everyone was seeing the same as I did. I thought it was all part of what was normal. You never know what is real to others and what isn't sometimes."

"I wondered what that would be like? I saw the serpent, outside the caverns but it wasn't clear. That was why I followed it in."

"The Serpents are not easily seen. If you are of the Rainbow Serpent Lore she will show herself sometimes, but the other Serpents... some can be seen and some can't. It's like the Skystone, with the Skystone the Serpents and Spirit Men can't feel you even if you are in front of them. But they can see you. Never forget that they can still see you there even if it confuses them. Just like when you feel there is something there. To them it is as though their lizard type brain registers you're there. They won't recognize your form as they would recognize a Shaman's form or the presence of any other person though. You would be like part of the furniture really in our world," he added chuckling.

I fingered the heavy pewter ring, which now held the Skystone safely. It was an intricately carved ring that sheltered the soft stone, almost hiding it, as it held the stone firmly. Aine had designed the ring and given it to me only recently and as I fingered it now I considered his words.

I liked the weight of the ring and I knew I was still growing accustomed to its presence but it was becoming more settled with me. It too held its own secrets, the secret of the Skystones and their power though I wasn't sure of exactly what it's power meant for me.

"I don't think I mind that they won't feel me about. Those big lizards can bite and it stings like the buggery. I've been thinking about getting a tattoo over the fang marks. Do you think Ty will let me?"

"Wait 'till he's gone, they are talking about going in a few weeks though he'll be back again for sure… checking up on us. Hold off till then."

I grinned. "I might do that."

"The Skystone will be a great help to you, it blinds Taipan though. Did you know that?"

"How do you mean?"

"Well we, the Shaman, and the Kadaitcha too can see you like normal but can't sense you. While you wear the stone I can't find you with my other senses, anymore than Ty can, or Sean or even Andrew. It was a constant problem for Andrew and why he found it hard to let Jiemba from his sight while his son had the stone. If the Shaman want to sense you about them, they must have other than just their skills."

He continued after a moment. "Sean also had to hold close to Jenna who got a stone given to her by her father. He could see her and feel her only because of their closeness. It was because of the links they shared as a man and woman. Like what I said earlier. Others though could not sense Jenna's presence. The Quinkin shaman couldn't find her because of the Skystone she wore."

"Did he tell you this?"

"No, it was Andrew. His… baby daughter, Ellie also has a stone. She has the other stone and it was Jenna who gave up hers to keep Ellie safe when she was born. Jen no longer needs it now. It is the partner to yours. Ellie too was marked by the Serpent."

"Ellie? Andrew & his woman Alex…? Their new baby you mean. She has been marked by the Serpent too?"

"Yes."

I watched as Tom closed his eyes as though tired and I wondered at the weariness in his face. It was as though he was in some pain but he couldn't have been. Perhaps it was thoughts of his father that came to mind. Speaking of fathers and kids seemed to disturb him I had noticed.

I knew Tom had recently been to see the shadow of the man who still lived amongst us while his spirit dwelt in the caverns with the Kadaitcha Men. I knew his father lived in the nursing home not far from here and I wondered if I might even meet him one day.

I had not known that a man could exist without the spirit of himself but this explained a great deal. The man at the nursing home that was the shell of Toms father, seemed not to really live. Although Tom would visit every now and then, he would not speak as though he was visiting his dad. It was more that he was attending to the welfare of a stranger, while his

Grandfather attended to what was his father deep in the caverns.

Perhaps though, this was something that Tom would not want to speak much about it seemed to me. I had only begun to piece together the story that was behind the man that Tom's father had become and the promise of what he could have been.

The Mark of the Serpent

Jeremy

Settling into TAFE over the next months was at times easy, though at other times I missed the simple companionship of the friends from my old school. It took time to travel to TAFE and it would have been simpler to go to the local school instead. I preferred however the freedoms of the TAFE classes and I soon settled into that, rather than the stuff of Secondary School. My world had changed even in my eyes and I needed new beginnings, new challenges and new friends.

My subjects were similar to what I had started back at home but the approach of the teachers was very different. If you didn't do the work, that was your worry not theirs. You were also expected to behave with a sort of maturity, which easily dealt with the idiots you often had to contend with in Secondary School. Excluding you from classes, if the teacher's want to, seemed to be an easy process as well.

That I had been one of those idiots in class previously, became obvious to me now. For me TAFE was a very different environment and a different way of approaching education. Even the kids here were different; they looked at life differently from me so mostly I just kept my mouth shut until I could figure them out more.

The first few days were the hardest but I was making friends as I grew to know and recognize faces. What began with simple acknowledgments as we passed each other became easy friendships quickly. I didn't look for deeper friendships than that, I didn't know how long I would be in Sydney but I did become friendly with some of the kids easily. Plus there was my training to consider and that was happening outside the concerns of TAFE.

Taipan often would talk with us in the small backyard when we gathered around the BBQ of an evening, usually with something light to drink while we toasted light snacks on the barby. Here we could talk what was our business away from the hearing of Aine.

Any fat of the red meat kind was forbidden to both Tom and I. Instead Aine had taught us how to roast vegetables and other white meats like fish, which were mostly free of the worst fats.

Best of all were the bush foods, which usually gave us few worries in breaking the taboo of our training. That fish was good eating gave us an excuse to spend hours at the end of the old wharf fishing and talking about many things.

This diet often reminded me of Kirri, the strange girl I had met in the caverns. It was as though in meeting her my life had changed and that came to mind more often than I would have wanted. Though I rarely spoke to the others about her these days.

There was a small group of students who I commonly met in the cafeteria at college and amongst these were some who shared classes with me. It was with these kids that I found friendship.

After a while it became apparent that we were in general, more serious about our studies. Perhaps because the teachers didn't have to put up with us if our behaviour was anything other than reasonably mature or if our attendance was poor.

During the long Christmas break I spent time working with Tom as a 'go-for-it' person and general dog's body but the pay was good. Getting back to TAFE in the new-year was a more settled process than I had imagined that it would be. We met with a new round of students and got back in with the old groups again with ease.

It was during a break session in the cafeteria that I met my first interesting challenge, a girl who got my attention. I was talking amongst my new friends, sitting around when I first noticed her at the end of the table busily ignoring us. She looked deep in her own world of girls and mostly busied herself with those sitting nearby.

While I had seen her about before, it was for the first time I had really noticed her. She was drawing in a sketchbook and it was that her sketching was giving her so much pleasure that it caught my attention. I was curious and for a time my glance kept finding her despite the conversation I was sharing with others.

Her name was Kelly, we hadn't been introduced but I had heard the other girls call her that and she was really easy on the eyes to look at. She had a mousy, blonde hair and the delicate tan that white girls get when they get into the sun often enough. It was also her quiet playful glances towards others, hints to her character that attracted me most along with the quick smile that flashed occasionally when she heard something that amused her.

A little taller than many of the other girls she was a build that couldn't be called slim, but more curvy than most. I had let my thoughts wander more than they should have before I drew myself up short. For the moment I had forgotten Ty's advice, this was not the time in my training to allow a girl to get in my way.

Dismissing her though was more difficult than I had thought it would be. She often arrived at the train station for the walk up to TAFE about the same time as I did and I noticed her sometimes on the return trek back to the station, though not as often as in the mornings. We came in from different directions so I never saw her on my platform but that made waiting for her easier as I could stand around the general exit and watch the commuters pass by without attracting much attention.

It was in the following week that I decided that trying to ignore her was only making me more interested than if I were to approach her. It was this that had me deciding to deal with my curiosity about this girl. Approaching her was perhaps a better way than my daytime fantasies which were harder to ignore. So I made the effort to catch up when I saw her sitting at one of the outside tables at TAFE one afternoon, those tables and seats scattered about the courtyard.

"Hi." Surprising her I threw my leg over the low bench stool that was fixed to the table as I took a seat. "Mind if I join you?"

Kelly had looked up curious as I settled, her eyes sweeping me, recognizing me while she barely smiled a welcome acceptance.

"No. Go for it." She quipped, inviting me to the table easily even though I was already seated.

"I've been meaning to say Hi when I've seen you down at the station."

"Yeah. I noticed."

"You waiting for someone?" Feeling as though I was going to have to work at this conversation I wondered why, but I persisted. I had thought that she'd have been friendlier than she was.

"Yeah. My boyfriend. He picks me up here on Fridays."

"Oh. OK then." I added, thinking that perhaps I should leave.

"No, its OK. He won't mind. Stay and talk, he'll be a while yet."

I smiled back. Things seemed to be improving at least. "I was going to suggest walking with you to the station, I guess not hey?"

Kelly just smiled and nodded in agreement before she added. "I'm going into town with my boyfriend Pete."

"Your boyfriend, have I met him?"

"No, he doesn't go to TAFE. He works in the city."

"Oh well. Friends is good place to be, I've got to stay away from girls for the time being anyways." I quipped back, hoping it would make chat between us easier.

Kelly looked up curious and then her smile reached her eyes. "What have you done then... that your not supposed to mix with girls? Did you catch something?" She added chuckling gamely.

"No. Nuthin' like that really," I answered, laughing myself. "It's a training discipline." I added, desperate for any other explanation.

"Training?"

The flash of interest in her glance amused me as I nodded. Then I wondered how I was going to hold her interest and balance my reality with her own, without upsetting Taipan or even the old sorcerer Apari. I was fairly new at finding that balance and it was all very odd to me still.

"What's the training for?" Kelly asked again after a moment, her curiosity surfacing easily.

"It is a discipline for guys really. It's hard to explain."

"You could try? Is it like… like kung-fu or something?"

I grinned. "Well yes, sorta. Only it is not just that, it's a way of life. For us blackfellas, the Shaman."

"Shaman? Aren't they like magic stuff… all that new age type crowd?"

I hesitated, regretting for a moment that I had got into this so quickly. "Sort of, but not like tricks or anything. It's an old discipline for us. A lifestyle really that is about the bush and stuff like that."

"Mmm…"

Kelly considered me with tolerant amusement and I wondered how I could avoid any more questions. Usually the girls I spoke with knew this stuff from the community. They knew not to question but she was asking stuff with a fine curiosity. I realized then that I should have left well enough alone.

"Do you do this on your own?"

"No. No I have a mate who does this with me and we have… teachers, trainers if you like."

"A mate?"

"Yes. Tom, he lives with me. We live together like; I mean… he doesn't live with me. We live in the same place, flatmates. Along with another friend, well with one of our teachers."

Kelly chuckled and it was a nice sound I thought. Then she added in a teasing tone. "I didn't think you had a boyfriend."

"No. Definitely don't have a boyfriend," I added as I laughed easily. Then suddenly Kelly broke into another amused chuckle as though she had just thought of something she found really funny.

At first I smiled but then as she continued to chuckle trying to control herself, her amusement seemed to be getting deeper and I grew curious. Frowning I eventually felt I had to say something.

"What? What's so funny…?"

She shook her head, trying to gain control as her eyes glistened. "It's nothing really… sorry," she said struggling and as she kept looking up catching my eye and going off into her giggling fit again.

Finally she gained some control while I watched her in her efforts. I was amused but curious and when she drew a breath, still fighting to hold onto that control, she looked over at me. Her eyes still alight with entertainment. "I'm sorry... really... it is just ... well really funny."

"What?"

"You. Really... Tom and Jerry... living together...?" and then she broke into another peel of giggles.

At first I didn't catch on but then it registered with me and I grinned remembering the old cartoon tales. I hadn't seen it before, hadn't even thought of it. "Its Jeremy!" I protested, myself struggling to contain a grin. "Jeremy! Not Jerry!"

"I know... I know really. It just occurred to me!" She answered, her words buried in another uncontrolled giggle. "Sorry... really I... it's silly."

"Yeah."

"Sorry..." Drawing a ragged breath Kelly struggled for control again and then began to settle. "That was rude of me. I'm sorry." She added on an errant smile, which broke the more serious tone she was aiming for.

I just shook my head, seeing the funny side as I wondered if Tom would find it just as funny.

"So tell me about this training?" She offered after a moment, having regained some control.

Shrugging I tried to think quickly. "It's like... like a vocation I guess. A lifestyle. A way of looking at things and living life accordingly, there's nothing flash about it ... just a way of life."

"Do you do anything? Like competitions or... or Shaman meets' an stuff?"

"We have corroborees. I guess that is the same."

"And your teachers, where do they learn? I mean... I haven't heard of anything like this really?" She shrugged. "Sounds sorta odd."

"Well they kinda' learn from the Elders. It is a Lore, a tradition."

"I have heard of Elders, you don't call them chiefs do you?

"No, we have lots of names though. The Karadji and... and others."

"Others?"

"Yeah... We have rules and things. Disciplines I think... stuff we learn."

"Like... from these Karadji people?"

"... and others." I added.

"That's an odd name, what others, are there?"

Her smile was friendly and curious and I searched to answer her question. "Oh... the Oruncha I guess. The spiritual leaders and men like..."

"Oruncha? What are they?"

I frowned seeing my mistake, it was something I couldn't explain. This was dangerous ground and for a moment I wondered if I had overstepped the boundaries of what should be her knowledge.

I knew some men were known by that name, but it was also the name the spirit men were known and that was a dangerous knowledge. But then I realized that this was just a light curiosity on her part. I had heard Ty talk of these things to others who were not following the Lore and there were ways of saying things. Ways that he used to avoid what was mummoo or too spiritual or perhaps frightening for some to talk about openly.

I thought quickly back over conversations I had heard trying to find an explanation that would not cause problems with the Spirit men, or get me into strife.

"You have another name for them, umm... I think you call them gargoyles, those things... the old figures on buildings like on the big church in town. I saw them at Sydney Uni' as well. It can be a tribal name too, sort of like a group. Do you know what I mean?"

"Gargoyles? You're kidding!"

I grinned seeing the teasing in her eyes, relieved that this conversation had now taken an amusing turn and looking for answers quickly I went on. "No. They are in your own stories." Then I shrugged, "Well that is what I understand. Your gargoyles are those creatures that guard great buildings and libraries and even knowledge, your buildings. I mean not yours personally but those in history from the... your mobs in your old world. Where you whitefellas come from. The gargoyles are creatures of power and knowledge and well ... that is what the Oruncha are for us. It is from where knowledge comes often."

"Really?" She questioned. "This is my world, just like yours, so I guess it's our world. I don't like all this racist stuff. I have never heard that before though, about the gargoyles. But it's not real is it?"

"Isn't it? It is the same thing for my mob. I guess people forget... too much else going on maybe. They guard knowledge and it's what we are taught. It's history and it could be real too. Taipan, one of my teachers was pointing the gargoyles out on the buildings when we went into town to have a look around. Yours... well the European ones are more animal-like where as ours are more people like, but I guess it is what the artist imagines."

"It sounds interesting but I don't believe it all. Is this just knowledge then... that is written about like at school? Is it like a bible or something you use to learn, a text book maybe?"

"No. We don't have books in our Aboriginal histories only stories, not in the old times. We do now and it is slowly getting into books too I guess. We have other things. It is other things too... not a lot is written but we have rock carvings and drawings, dance and stories. We teach a lot in stories and then there is training like your kung-fu I guess."

I grinned seeing the analogy I had partly earlier denied. "We learn how to hunt, and fight too and to live as blackfellas... like how it was with the old people. We learn lots of things, how to feed ourselves and look after others and ourselves in the bush and stories... old people skills and the old stories that tell you about things. Like a moral code really and law."

I knew I was searching for things to say. Things to try and impress her with and as I realized it, I stopped myself quite suddenly.

"You know how to do that?"

"What?"

"Camping and eating bush stuff... Aboriginal stuff? Bush stuff, like living off the land."

I nodded. It was my life and I had never really considered it a special talent but I supposed from Kelly's point of view it was. "You have never gone fishing? Or... or camping?"

Kelly shook her head. "Never. I would love to go fishing and bush walking maybe one day. Don't know how I would go though. I like the city life, going out and well... partying."

Grinning I nodded. "I maybe can take you fishing sometime, that can be arranged." I offered as she looked up and then she cast her eyes towards the car park, suddenly frowning and yet it was a frown with an apologetic smile.

"Pete's here." She said as she stood immediately to gather her books and bag. "I betta' go."

I too climbed to my feet, my glance finding the high-powered sleek black vehicle pulled up as near to where we were as he could get.

"It was nice talking... maybe I can catch you Monday then. At the train station."

"Yeah sure." Kelly slung back with a smile as she headed towards the car and made her way quickly across the space between him and us.

My thoughts stayed with Kelly as I was making my way down to the station a short time later. I had enjoyed talking to her, seeing her eyes light up with entertainment and laughter though I wished we had spoken more of her life than mine. That was something we could fix I thought as I walked along steadily. It would be something we could talk about on Monday.

It felt good to have a friend, a female friend and for some reason it nice to know that our friendship was not going to be complicated between us. Somehow we had found a place that was absent of the normal stresses between the sexes for the moment and it was a pleasant thought. A friend was good for me now and Kelly looked to be entertaining in her own way.

Not that I didn't think along other lines when with her, but what was important was that she didn't make me think about it as she didn't seem to think about the question herself. That was nice and I considered for a time that perhaps I could have a friend who was a girl and that this boy-girl stuff wouldn't be a big problem, particularly if she had a boyfriend anyway. It gave me hope somehow and I knew I was going to enjoy this light friendship.

I was later than usual when I finally got back home, but I was just ahead of the sunset and at least Aine wouldn't be worrying. She had enough to worry about with little Kiahan and they had only recently mentioned the idea that we might be responsible enough to be left on our own for longer periods. Particularly now that I was settled in TAFE and Tom was working solidly.

I knew Aine was hoping to move back north to the community soon, though Taipan was not yet ready, but the move was definitely on the table. Ty however wanted to wait until Apari, the old Kadaitcha man, had returned and I figured it would be only then that he would feel at ease with us looking after ourselves.

We just had to wait, even if the waiting was hard. It was something we lived in daily expectation of and while we waited, we explored the bush and river around us over the months that passed. We spent time fishing and learning about the bush, those places which Tom was keen to share and that which Ty had discovered on his own in his time here. It had been anything but a restless time for me, as I would have expected it to be. I knew it was because I was enjoying TAFE, enjoying my new friends and the city had a buzz about it that was entertaining.

It was Sunday morning some weeks later when Tom crawled out of bed and announced that things had changed. It was time and he knew it. He understood somehow from his Dreaming that it was time for us to gather with the other men. Over breakfast he raised the issue of Apari, his Grandfather and immediately he had our full attention.

"Apari wants us to meet him north of here, at some place that they call the place of the emu up Kuring-Gai Chase way I think. We should head out there tonight maybe. It is time."

"I know the place." Taipan added, glancing across at Aine to further explain. "It's a men's ceremonial place and as it's a time of ceremony for the boys it seems. You can't come Kitten." He suddenly added as his glance returned almost apologetically to his wife.

Aine pouted playfully and then sighed, accepting what Ty was saying easily almost as if she had been expecting it. It left Ty with a slow growing, yet intimate smile between them as Aine juggled little Kiahan on her hip.

"Is it far? I mean how do we get there?" I asked my excitement showing at this new turn of events.

Tom never ceased to surprise me and I knew that his Grandfather had been instrumental in this. It was knowledge given in the dreaming that they sometimes shared during the spirit hours of the night. It was the only time I truly longed for the links between grandfather, father and son. Links I had lost without ever really understanding it. It was like a penance I paid for my cross-cultural heritage in having a whitefella for a father.

"We can drive up there this morning. Did Apari indicate when we were expected?" Ty asked of his younger brother.

"Yep, he wants us camping off from the ceremonial grounds by tomorrow I think."

Ty nodded. "This is an important time for you both. I will need to ring the TAFE, or perhaps Aine...?" he added glancing her way again.

"I can do that." Aine agreed readily. "How long will you be away?"

"Maybe the week... I wont know until I speak to Apari. I will ring you as soon as I know Kitten."

A week! I was shocked, as I hadn't imagined it would be so long.

Our drive later that day took us through the city and on into the northern suburbs towards a place in the cities northern National park. We then walked through the bush and into an old ceremonial site.

It left me with a deep respect for Ty's knowledge as he spoke to us of these things, explaining some of the Lore and stories we would hear and should know.

It was a site that was marked by public signs and while I found that strange, I soon realized that the crowds who made their way to the site during the day soon left as the dusk fell and the old world seemed to move in about us.

We embarked on our week of learning and ceremony away from the well-trodden paths, deep in the bush with the old sorcerer and others. It was a quiet and secret thing for the men involved, including us. I began to realize then that a week would be scarcely enough time as others began to gather. This thing was bigger than I had even imagined.

The night skies held stories about which the Elders spoke. Stories that I hadn't heard before. It fascinated me, these ancient legends of Lore. The weather was cooling but this didn't bother us at all as the grease on bodies kept us warm and there was little time to feel the chill.

Being in the bush and in ceremony with the men was all that I thought about. Hearing the songs, the stories of our histories and stepping along the path given us. This was a major turning point in my life.

It changed me, this time we shared in the bush. This was the business of men. I learnt the songs and sacred steps in the dance, beating a tempo against the earth, a beat that bought the worlds together. I too began to realize just how much these things were to continue to change me as I moved towards the promise of my future. That of becoming a man.

The night skies overhead told of these stories, which the Kadaitcha Men spoke off and these stayed with me like the ancient art of the caverns. The subtle meanings not of the brilliant stars but of the dark places and things whispered in the heavens. We were told of the secrets of the Lore in the Emu Dreaming, which echoed in the shadows in the night skies.

The emu from the skies was also carved deep into the rocks at our feet. The pound of our feet in the dance linking the earth with the heavens bringing the worlds together with the clack beat of the sticks. The deep vibrations of the didgeridoo or Yidaka as Ty called it. This became part of you, melding with the song of men, making us all part of one body. These night skies that remained forever overhead telling of these things drawn down through time, even since the Dreamtime.

When Apari gifted Tom his hair belt amongst the other things he was surrendering from life, the words he spoke were for both of us and it was a sacred moment. I too received a gift of the same and it sat around my hips easily. The decorated hair tassels plaited at the front beating against my legs as I stepped in the dance. I was told how to sit the weapons that hung into my belt; those I would need to hone the use of. But I was left wondering just what these weapons were for and just what it was I would be hunting. Our world had changed and we no longer hunted to survive.

Apari's words echoed in the chant of the men as though from another time, or perhaps time immortal as he turned to Tom.

"This, young Ariaka will guard you. It has the strengths of those who have gone before you, of your fathers and your mob. It will travel with you when you hunt and when you step the path of the Shadow Walkers. It is the hand of your mob who will lead you and give you wisdom and strength when you wear it."

Then turning to me having fixed the belt about Tom with the help of others, Apari smiled confident in his seriousness. The mark of ceremony was on us both, as he lay down a long threaded whip on the rock hollow between us.

"This Kintji-iruka is yours. It will bring you the strengths of your fathers who are here and as your totem is now the emu, so is your strength that of the emu. You will guard what is good and guide that which is in need. This is your ililika and it will tame and kill the serpent. It is a serpent killer, my gift to you."

Apari then took up the dance and chant that we were to join him in, as others also joined us. I knew then that important amongst us was the man Badjimala who stepped the sacred steps of the emu with Apari, Tom and I, guiding me.

Big Jim, as I then also knew him, joined us and I was glad of his company and his guidance. When he took up the whip and wound it about me I knew that it was he who would follow and guide my training and I wondered at that. In time I would know these things though, nothing would be hidden from me. I was with the Kadaitcha and I was to become a man of the Featherfoot and the sacred Lore this night.

As Ariaka took on the mantle of Shadow Walker, I joined him in this time. I was to step in his shadow, his brother in the Lore and we both felt the strengths grow within us as we stepped about the sacred engraving etched in stone, our totem.

Later we were told of things that we should know as we sat with Taipan and Big Jim discussing the Lore while Apari and the others rested. It was Big Jim who spoke also of the things we needed to know.

"You have learnt to control your fear, learnt the ways of the Shaman. Now you will know the ways of the Kadaitcha. The Kadaitcha control not only their fear, but it is that they must learn to control their anger. This must never control you, for then you will be the wrong side of the Lore."

Turning to Tom, he continued, his eyes careful in their serious intent. "Ariaka, you have learnt much in dealing with the man who was your father. You have learnt to temper your anger but now you must temper your hate. This is your added burden also as you go on to master schooling your anger to leave you."

I could see the hard line of Tom's jaw form and I realized that Big Jim, perhaps somehow knew more of what was in Tom's heart than any of us. He saw more and he sensed more and it was then that I realized that he was to be a father to us both. As he turned back to me I wondered at what he would now see in me.

"Kintji; for you your journey with the Featherfoot has only just begun and while you have mastered your fear, it is anger that is your weakness. You will be tested on this as Ariaka has been tested. Only then you might be taught to master your hate also but it will mark you a Featherfoot, one within reach of the Kadaitcha Spirit Men."

I drew an uncertain breath and wondered at his words. I knew I had mastered fear but anger? Hate? What were these to me I questioned silently. But Badjimala just nodded as though understanding.

"You will recognize this in time, as Ariaka has done. It is the way and has always been the way. The spirit men of the Oruncha will know what it is that will test you. I too am a man of the whip, the snake killer, and I will teach you this. I will train you in its use and its strength. You will learn what you need to know and how to use this thing."

Fingering the tight weave of the ililika which lay laced about my shoulders I looked up at him pleased, you could feel the strength of the man. He was a powerful build, more so than Taipan but darker and much heavier in the shoulders and around his body. Perhaps slower to move but then he would not need speed if he used the snake whip wound about his own shoulders. He looked to be a man of the stone country, hard and strong and as he glanced over at Taipan I wondered if I would ever be like these men, as Ty added.

"Big Jim, Badjimala will be spending a lot of time with you both. I have invited him to make use of the boat-shed when needed. It will be his place when he is with you both. I think now that it is time that Aine and I returned to the community but I'll be back though. There is a great deal you need to learn in the coming months before you step out as Kadaitcha initiates. Your gifts can't be used until you know how to use them and this we will teach you both. It will take time; much of the year and then it will take experience. This only you can learn but not before you have learnt your earlier lessons. You will not use your gifts without our guidance until such time that you have moved through your initiations."

His words were a dictum; a law and we had no choice in that we were to follow them. To take any other choice ourselves about when to use these things Apari had given us, we understood would mean that we would then lose the gifts. They were not ours, but they belonged to the Kadaitcha and it was that we had merely been lent their power.

Returning to my studies a week later was like returning to a different world for me. I now had responsibilities to my Lore, more than I had known before and it took a while before I stopped losing patience easily with the TAFE lessons I had to also learn.

The flow of my friends around me was the same, but I felt different and it was odd. It wasn't until the Tuesday that I saw Kelly again and she seemed quietly distracted, paying little attention to any of my attempts to catch her glance.

When I considered it, she seemed to be at one moment hyper and the next almost compliant, yet full of nervous energy which left her fidgeting. I soon dismissed the idea of her strange behaviour as fanciful, but I would keep an eye on her none the less. Something was bothering her and it could even be just a girl thing in the end I figured.

Big Jim arrived by the close of the week. I got home from TAFE Friday to find that he had moved easily into the boat-shed. Aine had set it up as a small studio and he was obviously more than happy with the arrangement. It seemed that in no time he had dumped his old bag and settled in with a quick word that this weekend I would begin learning how to handle the small whip Apari had given me.

It was that weekend also that Aine and Ty made plans to head north back to the community, making no bones about Big Jim being in charge. Tom came and went, sometimes heading to work and others he headed out on his own mission. He had heard from Andrew through the week and this seemed to affect him in some way, it seemed to leave him with a sense of disquiet and he was restless.

I never knew where he went, or when he would be home. He was truly his own man. He didn't confide in me often about his movements though I knew enough to respect his privacy and what was his business alone particularly with his Grandfather Apari. Tom was after all a good few years older than I.

I felt the keen interest that Big Jim showed me as we moved on through the weeks. An interest not unlike that which Taipan had shown and I felt that being the youngest here had its disadvantages as well as its privileges, as few as they seemed to be at times.

Learning to handle the small light whip that was barely the full stretch of my arms in length was something again. Big Jim kept me hard at practice and I enjoyed it I must admit.

Of an evening you could often hear the crack of our whips in the crisp air of the winter as it moved in around us. I came to understand the discipline of the whip, never having appreciated it before.

I learnt to lay it before me at ease, to bring it to life with a flick as though it was an extension of my arm in the movement of the wrist. The most difficult was to learn its pace and its coil. I had to learn how to know exactly where to lay the tip in a target needing precision.

My whip was made of subtle and furless kangaroo hide and plaited tightly and carefully, requiring breaking-in on my part. The handle was weighted at times and it changed the balance of the whip. Big Jim showed me how to weight it with small spears of wood or bone that were carefully worked and even sharpened to a dangerous point. It stiffened the handle when needed, but he didn't say why I would need to do this, even when I asked.

I learnt all about the whip and when I wasn't practicing I was working on a targeted challenge that Big Jim would set me. I learnt that the snake whips come in many sizes, made of different things and each had its purpose and place. Big Jim's favourite whip was longer and sleeker than mine and he could touch a target with the lightest caress or the quickest bite of leather. He was a master of control and it was a control that I aspired to.

He also tried to get me to move the control between my arms and hands but I found that right-handed, I could handle the whip best. The scars from the serpent bite on my left shoulder would often give me trouble and it didn't help to exercise them too much. They were scars, two puncture marks that I realized I would carry for life but I wondered how long it would take before they gave me no problem at all.

Unsightly marks, I wanted to find a solution in making the scored skin barely noticeable, much in the same way that I now wore the tongue stud in my mouth. For those who had even noticed it, it was a simple thing to dismiss but for my shoulder scars I had other plans.

I had hit on the idea of tattooing the marks, making them part of a design. Fittingly I was thinking about a serpent design, though was undecided on whether to wind the serpent about my shoulder and arm, or along my back with the design running around my side and beneath my chest. It was an idea I often played with in my mind and one I kept to myself for a long time before I even gave the idea voice.

It helped that Big Jim also wore a tattoo about his arm, one he told me he had done many years ago for reasons he wouldn't say. I didn't doubt that it held some kind of meaning for him but he said it had little to do with anything that I would need to know about. It was more an expression of experiences he had when he served in the Army in the years warring with North Vietnam.

We had any number of great discussions, Big Jim and I. Usually around the campfire that had its place on the small lawn beside the cottage. The least of these informal chats were about women and while he took a mentors role, he didn't expect us to behave as he did.

This came about after he had entertained a visitor the night before. It had been a Friday on the edge of the spring and Tom was home. We had been inside and had got into the usual discussion about eating. We were thinking about using the BBQ. When we heard Big Jim arrive outside in the company of a woman we for some reason found it amusing.

I had not thought of him in that light, though it was no surprise that he had a woman with him. He hadn't announced his arrival at all and didn't even make a move to join us or introduce us. He didn't even acknowledge our presence in the house, though he would have known we were there.

It was clear right from the start that he and his woman had plans. They shut the door to the boat-shed, though the light still spilt out onto the river from the boat-ramp double doors. It was more than obvious from the sounds they made and then didn't make that this was not a social occasion for all of us.

He made no apologies and gave no explanations the next morning. It was as though he had never even entertained his houseguest and she had left by the time we got up.

I couldn't leave it at that though and the following afternoon, I bought it up.

"You have a good night last night?" I commented to Big Jim as we sat around the BBQ table leaving Tom to toast our dinner. I was waiting for the reaction I was expecting, a cheeky grin playing around my mouth.

His look smacked me, amused at my audacity but he wore a small grin. "And you care why?" He asked, waiting expectantly.

I shrugged. Not sure how to respond and thinking maybe that my cheek was not such a good idea. "Just sayin'"

"My woman is none of your business. I'll have none of your cheek." Tipping his evening stubbie to his lips he dismissed me easily. Then thought better of it."

"You're not fooling with the girls at your TAFE are you?" he asked suddenly.

"No." Again I shrugged. "Just a few friends really."

"Good." Short and sweet, he again dismissed me as Tom quipped in.

"Yeah, I have been meaning to ask you about that. There is a girl I wouldn't mind getting to know better. She lives down near where I am working at the moment at Caringbah. I want to ask her out."

Tom gathered up the now cooked meal off the grill and headed over to join us at the table, settling it between us as he continued. "Apari said I would be soon out of my initiation period, maybe a couple of weeks more. Does that mean I can start messing with girls again too?"

You could see Big Jim consider the question for the moment. "Well I'm not sure, seems to me you should wait for your trials. That could take time."

"Trials?" Tom echoed in a question.

"Yeah. Though it may be that you're ahead of young Kintji here. You're older, more responsible, maybe? Jeremy is not ready yet but maybe for you it is good."

"But for me it's not?" I added affronted.

"No. For you its not a good thing yet." Big Jim answered dispassionately.

"Great." Tom said elated, you could see it in his whole body and for me, I felt really hard done by but there wasn't a lot I could do about it.

I had arranged with some friends to head down to Cronulla Beach after TAFE in the following week. The weather was warming up and the surf still carried the warm spring currents down from the equator. Those the whales rode with their young calves after their winter birthing in the warmer waters. They were now on their way back to the Great Southern Ocean.

I was keen to learn to surf, a talent I had heard a lot of from my friends and I was also keen to find a sport of some kind to keep me entertained.

With the coming summer months I was looking forward to spending time at the beach as well and with any luck I could learn to surf before the long summer break over Christmas. I hadn't made plans about what I would do once TAFE was done with and the thought of travelling about attracted me after I had listened to many of Big Jims tales.

"How long are you working around near Cronulla way?" I suddenly asked Tom, realizing that this was something that could be handy.

"Maybe a few months, they have a couple of jobs lined up. A reno' at the moment but there is a big build coming up. Why?"

"Just that I wanted to learn to surf, can you put a board in the back of the ute do you think? We could maybe meet up at Cronulla and pick it up after TAFE."

"Yeah I guess I could. Might come for a swim myself, after work."

"You could pick me up after an we could come home together?" I suggested hopefully.

"Yeah. I could. You chip in for petrol."

I grinned. It seemed a good arrangement and it lifted my mood I must admit. Nodding easily I glanced across at Big Jim who was mostly just listening to us.

"Mind you stay away from women. I know what the city girls are like." Big Jim suddenly said, giving me a hard look as he finished off the last of his meal. "I'm going out again tonight. I'll see you both tomorra'."

We watched him head over to the boat-shed in a companionable silence. It seemed unfair to me that while Tom could move on I was judged not ready to emerge from the restrictions our training placed on us.

Then, I wondered about those trials Big Jim had mentioned. They would mark the ending of our initial training period and recognition as men of Lore. But I didn't think either of us had any idea what it really meant and we were not expected to ask.

As the warmer months crept over the city with the spring, for me there came a settling into city life. Living on the southern edge of the city was good. You didn't get involved in the frenetic pace of the central district unless you headed into the city, but you could choose to involve yourself or not.

Kelly from TAFE often headed into the city with her boyfriend on the weekends. Even though we were friends, it really wasn't so bad a thing to be able to mix with others as well.

The guys and I could get out onto the beaches with a couple of girls in tow for entertainment sometimes. It was a young crowd and a fun group. Though we got up to a bit when the crowd got big. Sometimes getting into trouble and this I didn't share with either Tom or Big Jim. It was a good time and I was enjoying my mates from TAFE without the constraints of others looking on.

I soon found that Kelly who lived out towards Cronulla would often share the train ride to the beach with me after TAFE during the week and occasionally even share the beach.

Tom had met her on more than one occasion when I had collected the board from where he was working in Cronulla. At first he was sceptical of our relationship but then Kelly began to flirt with him playfully after I made a comment to her when he was teasing me about our friendship. After that he seemed to back off some and he mostly stopped tormenting me. I wasn't sure if it was because of Kelly's playfulness or because he had other things on his mind.

I found it amusing to watch her influence him in her own way, as easy as it was for her to do this. It left me off the hook and he stopped annoying me about the relationship Kelly and I shared. In time we all settled into an easy friendship, if not a mateship that Tom, Kelly and I all enjoyed.

As for Kelly and I it was an easy alliance where once or twice a week she would join me down at the beach often without the others from TAFE.

I had found that in escaping to the beach after TAFE, spending my time fooling around at Cronulla rather than trying to make the commute back to Shackles Estate, often found me arriving home around the same time of day as Tom. Sometimes though Tom would join me at the beach for a swim and we would muck around on our boards. At these times it would be dark when we got home together, though this I didn't mind at all.

Life at TAFE was also good but at the beach it was just great. I was learning to surf after a fashion and it was fun. Kelly and I were at times joined by Tom and sometimes not.

When it was just the two of us, we spent time in the mall and in the beachside park where we finished off classwork. I found her company entertaining. Sometimes we would just head out for a walk along the shoreline together to enjoy the late afternoon.

Kelly lived around Gunnamatta Bay way, the bay around from Cronulla that ran off the surf side into a safe harbour. It was something of a short walk for her, though she never invited me back to her place and I never asked. I didn't particularly want to meet her Aunt or family, there was way too much else to do.

It was not that our friendship was particularly platonic, nor was it demanding. Playful would have better described it. After all she did have her boyfriend and she seemed fairly intense about him. He was a bit older than she was and that kept me from asking any more of her, not that she would have willingly told me much it seemed at times.

We were sharing some hot chips as we often did down at the southern end of the beach. Sitting back relaxing after an earlier swim and we had been slowly been making our way towards her place as had become our custom. We were in no hurry and it was an easy afternoon.

I had already sent Tom a text about where we were and it would be a half hour or more before he would be meeting me, when together we would head back home as usual. It was one of those great afternoons and the sunset was shifting slowly more into the evenings, turning the sky from a pink through to a full and rich blinding crimson.

Kelly was in a playful mood as we settled back with our backs to the sand enjoying its warmth before the shadows of the dusk reached across the beach. It was a quiet companionship and I was enjoying her light female chatter.

"You should come into the city sometime, there is this great place where we go to eat. It serves really good sushi, you would love that."

"Nup... eating out in town isn't my thing."

Kelly pouted playfully and then slowly relaxed back against the sand beside me. "I suppose not."

I watched as she considered me, her mind ticking over as it often did with her thoughts. Then she sighed. "You're not the city type."

I chuckled. "I'm not?"

"No. Your more the country type."

"I get into the city sometimes with the guys. It's not so bad. It's just that there is only one type of entertainment, spending money that I haven't got."

Again she pouted and then started ratting through her shoulder bag for something. Finding it, she held up the small tin cache of weed she carried occasionally. "Want some?"

Kelly didn't wait, she took out one of the small tight joints putting it to her lips as she flicked the tiny lighter she carried in the same tin. Her eyes testing me, waiting as she settled into appreciating the ease the grass bought her.

"OK. Just a drag, thanks."

It was light enough and I drew back deeply, handing the joint back afterwards. I didn't want or need more than that, she was welcome to the rest. It was a thin tight roll and it wouldn't last very long. Kelly I knew often mixed it with dead heads. I didn't normally smoke but I occasionally joined the others in their habits more to be a party to the fun than any real enjoyment in the light effects it had.

It was a moment in which she watched me and then her brows settled together in a question. "Where did you get that from?"

Indicating the small scars on my left shoulder now exposed to the sun after our swim, I knew she meant the fang marks the serpent had left me with. I shrugged reluctant to involve myself in the question. "It's just a bite I got once, an animal bite. I am thinking of putting a tat' over it."

"Looks like angry sort of fangs. It's a snakebite isn't it? It's really too big for that though ... it must have been something big?" Reaching up she touched the two puncture wounds softly and sent my skin tighten to goose bumps.

I grinned enjoying the sensation. "Yeah. Maybe a snake tat'. What do you reckon?"

"How would you do that? I mean... how?"

"I was thinking making them eyes sort of. Maybe...? I don't know? Can't decide."

Suddenly Kelly's eyes lit up. "A snake. I've got an idea... let me draw it."

It was only for a second that I hesitated. "Yeah sure."

Rummaging through her bag Kelly came out with a small felt pen. "I can use this, it is a bit thin but... here."

Shuffling up to my shoulder in the sand she scuttled partially around behind me and stretched over from the back to better see the two small scars. It was only then that I realized she had plans to draw on me, not on some sheet of notepaper.

"Hey... what!"

"Oh stop whining, sit still. This wont hurt."

"I don't know about this."

"It isn't permanent, it isn't even thick. Shut up will you and let me do this."

I watched as she sketched about the marks. It was a thin weedy line, not at all what I had in mind. "I don't know about this."

"Oh it wont hurt. It's just a sketch. We can see what works and then you can decide if it is really what you want. It'll wash off."

I watched as she played at drawing around the scars, it tickled a little but more pleasant was her closeness and the light touch she had. "Something like that do you think?" She asked after a time.

"I don't know? It is hard to see."

I considered the light lines, barely noticeable against my skin. It looked like nothing to me.

"You really need a mirror, and... and I need a darker pen. Maybe some colour. We could sort of do a snake winding around here?"

As she made the light marks on my skin of my back I grinned, enjoying the playfulness of her mood. "I was thinking down my back maybe and a tail winding around my chest a bit, or my side maybe?"

"You think so? Maybe we should do different designs. When did you plan on getting it done?"

"I haven't decided. Maybe at the end of the year or next year."

"Do you have a design? Maybe I can help? I have a friend..."

"Just a serpent, something sort of going over my shoulder, not on my chest at all, much."

"Let me see what I can find, there are lots of designs. We could get it done temporary like. They do them in a vegetable ink and if you like it... well you could make it permanent."

I thought about it for a moment. "Yeah. Sounds a good idea, I might do that."

"Well I think you should," she laughed, agreeing with me. Her mood echoing in the brightness of her eyes.

"I could help draw some designs in texta maybe," she offered playfully. "Or in a more permanent ink, it would last a few days. That could be fun."

Those designs grew in the following weeks and few enough people even noticed Kelly's artwork on my shoulder to my surprise. The permanent ink that we took to using was easily worn light after a few days and it became something of an entertainment for Kelly and I to work at the design on my shoulder.

We tried a number of different things, even occasionally taking to having a design we liked spray-painted by an artist we found in the mall who Kelly seemed to know. The design sometimes winding about my back and others twisted about my arm. I preferred the arm design, though I found people noticed that more and I wasn't sure if I liked that. In the end a design on my back and chest sat more easily with me. The mall artist was great, I liked his suggestions and he help develop the idea's in my mind.

Working from Kelly's designs he built up templates we could put together for different things and it all became something of a project. The temporary tat's only last a week, two at the most though they were much more prominent than the texta touch ups and designs. In all though, it was fun. Tom gave up commenting on the art exercise after a while. Though every now and then he would look over the growing and changing art as amusing as he seemed to find it all.

Kelly seemed to get a great deal of enjoyment in sketching about my shoulder and I would admit to enjoying the activity almost as much as she did. She had a light feminine touch and I loved the warm closeness of her skin near mine. It was a lot of fun even when I had to listen to her complaining when I moved while she worked on the different designs.

Taipan was the first to notice it amongst the men aside from Tom. He was down on a visit to take Tom and I bushwhacking into the Blue Mountains. We were to make our way along the thin tracking trails or songlines towards one of the many gorges hidden deep in the high bush plateau of the Great Dividing Range west of Sydney. It was somewhere that he had promised to take us more than once and it was something that we both had been very much looking forward to.

He had mentioned that Andrew had hoped to go with us but it seemed that his woman Alex was expecting again. It was a wonder to me that he could even consider getting away for a few weeks with the three kids and another now on the way.

Ty had mentioned to Tom that the eldest boy, Jiemba was now living with his Grandfather in the Territory up North, not far from where Sean and Jenna had now apparently moved to at about the same time I had left the Community.

He and Big Jim who walked with us made little fuss of the artwork on my shoulder, they were more interested in the detail even though there were more important things to take-in on that hike into the mountains.

It was in that weekend that we took on an important part of our ceremony though we didn't know it as we headed out into the wilderness deep behind Sydney.

Trials of the Kadaitcha

Jeremy

The Blue Mountains still sat silently at the back of the Greater Sydney; they have sat there for thousands upon thousands of years, even before Sydney was ever imagined or before time was ever conceived. These mountains go way back into the Dreamtime and our stories have followed their very creation.

At one time they had marked the very edge of the continent, at another they were a distant haze on the horizon a great distance from the same ocean as the world changed through its ages. They always have been a place from where life is given, from where the rivers of life are born.

These rivers flow out across the land as they always have, bringing life to the Great Western Plains, looking for the oceans that have long since buried themselves beneath the ground as did the Great Spirits of the land. These rivers also flow down onto the coastal rim and spread their fingers into the sea's feeding and renewing them. All things change.

The silence of the mountains is testimony to change, the only testimony that is offered. These mountains have looked out across the land as the land was born, died and was born again while it danced the ageless step with the great oceans. It was the silence of something that is truly timeless I thought as we began our trek into the mountains with Taipan and Big Jim that weekend.

The clans, the mountain men and tribes once of this land had ranged freely through the mountains long before the whitefellas came. Taipan had told me that those old tribal people had walked this land since the Dreamtime. They had even left their mark some 40,000 years, long before others in the Northern Hemisphere had even settled to sow the first crops in other more distant worlds.

We didn't sow crops in our histories, instead we nurtured and managed the land with fire and careful management of the animals that we hunted, which in turn usually nurtured and fed us well. But that had now changed and no one kept the fire trails or the water holes clear. The animals no longer followed the hunting trails we had set over thousands of years to feed the mobs in what was a seasonal turn.

The forest men of our history had been fearless amongst the forest quiet, knowing the secrets of the Dreaming Times and even of the land itself. They had been aware of the dangers and they knew of the Spirit places, places I knew little of.

So many places had been lost to us, largely with the disruption to tribal movements and the disbandment of the tribes. Colonization of the country had changed the land, as well as feeding our own curiosity for new ways and different things. Thing of the world that mostly hadn't served us well at all, this we had come to realize in the end. But no one can keep the world at bay for long, even if you choose to try, and the world had overtaken the tribes and mobs in the end.

Our world had been destined to change as it had changed the world over, regardless of us. It had been an inevitable thing.

For a moment my thoughts turned to the caverns, those I had found by myself. Those which had set me on my path and I wondered how Kirri fared even now. I still thought occasionally about that strange girl from the Inlands and my curiosity fired at times over the whole adventure we had shared.

Now though we stepped quietly as we always had and I tore my thoughts away from distracting memories knowing that there were creatures in the bush about me that you don't want to disturb. I knew that if you stepped carefully the land would embrace you and take you to its own. You become part of this land. You became a creature moving with a natural pace across mother earth, across country.

I had learnt that you don't disturb her, this country, not if you want to survive. There are things still unknown deep in the shade of the forest.

We had been told many of these things as children while we sat around campfires and listening to our Elders. Paying attention to our mothers and fathers in the community. We knew of the Jongorrie, the small spirit men of the forest. We had heard tell of the Dreaming creatures that had become part of the rocks and rivers. Those that flowed across the land once they had done with the Dreamtime creations and lessons.

So you were aware of the tree spirits, the rocks as well as the shadows of another time and place. Children were told the stories as you moved across the land since time immemorial, stories told by those who knew about these things and to whom it had been given to tell such histories.

We had left the cruiser behind hours ago and even though it was dark now, we still moved along the paths following the old songlines and trade tracks, those that even the creatures of the forest still used. It seemed Taipan and Big Jim knew this way well. They were men of knowledge and I knew and trusted them implicitly.

We trusted them with our lives as we stepped in places we had never known or seen. Places we might step many times more perhaps, as Big Jim and Taipan had. One day with younger men, we too would step here and show them the way, as we were now being shown. The path we trod was a lesson to learn. Tom and I both knew this and drew the lessons to our memory with the songs that were spoken along the way.

The bush about us wasn't dark even in this time of the full moon. The stars in the night sky lit the bush about us brilliantly. It was far from silent and even the moon cast its own shadow in certain times as it did now. Many creatures and native animals moved and foraged through the shade of the forests as the night was their precinct. This was their world, now our world, which we stepped carefully through.

When the moon was high the older men stopped and rested for a time. I managed to sleep for a bit, not caring to eat much. The forest wasn't too cold so we didn't concern ourselves with a fire. The spring warmth had begun to wake the bush around us and I was glad that it wasn't yet the time of bush fires.

That season would inevitably come in the months ahead. Now though was the time of feasting and bush food was plentiful. I had already snacked along the way, encouraged by the men.

Big Jim woke me later into the early hours and I knew to be silent. This was the bush world and the hours of darkness were a time that was not ours. Spirits and other creatures would be about as it was their time. Because we didn't have a fire we had little to ward them off, but I had realized that we were about the business of the Spirits so we should be safe enough.

I had come to understand that in the first hours of our trek that this was no simple bushwhacking trek the men had planned for us and both Tom and I welcomed that knowledge. This was the business of men and it was good to be about such business. It was good to be counted as a man amongst such men as the fathers and hunters of our mob had been down through time.

We walked well into the morning. When we had stopped to rest and eat we were instructed unexpectedly to settle down to sleep in preparation for the coming gathering.

A man had approached, he had stood sentinel and had come down to greet us as he guarded the way. We heard that the ceremonial grounds were nearby, though we wouldn't be gathering until the night hours and that we should wait for now. Not until the others had arrived would we continue to join the camp as initiates.

Taipan had gone on ahead and I was impatient to hear what he could tell us when he finally arrived back. Big Jim was quieter than usual and it left me wondering what the ceremony was to be all about. It was almost as though he was preparing himself.

As we gathered around a small campfire late in the afternoon after Ty returned, the excitement of it all was growing within me. The time of waiting seemed finally to be over.

"We'll get ready for the corroboree before we approach Baiame's cavern. You need to dress your skin heavily. There is a pool nearby that has what we will need and then once we're ready we can join the others."

"The others?" Tom asked as curious as I.

"Yes, the Elders have already gathered while they wait for the initiates, they will all arrive soon. You and Kintji will be amongst those gathered. It will be that Wolgaru serpent will be testing you both. Though Badjimala will be standing with young Jeremy while I will stay by you Tom."

I looked across at Big Jim. I would be addressing him by his Spirit name, as would be expected. I moved to raise the question that sprang to my lips but Badjimala instead answered what was uppermost in my mind.

"I hope young Kintji that you have learnt your lessons well with the serpent whip, your skill and mine will be put to the test."

"What, will we use the snake whips against?"

"Wolgaru, the death serpent of the caverns will be testing the initiates but it will be the Djaranin that will test you and I. While Ariaka stands with the other initiates we will need to guard them from the fangs of the black dogs, the Djaranin."

I felt the tension hit my gut and for the first time I was truly afraid of the trial ahead. Wolgaru was to test and judge the initiates and he would judge Ariaka. This we had been taught of the many stories told by the men. He was the serpent of the shades and he judged men for both their strengths and weaknesses. I would have rather stood before him than before the Djaranin. I had nothing to fear in Wolgaru's judgement but I had heard a great deal about the dogs of death.

Dark dogs of the caverns the Djaranin travelled with the Wolgaru Serpent and we had all heard the tales of his path through the Dreamtime. I remembered well the stories of how they judged men before the Lore and when men were found wanting they tore at the Shadows of men from our own world. Ripped at them, tossing them into the fires. There they roasted, seared by the flames that purified them of their evil so that they may be bought again back into the sun, so they could walk across their Country once more.

It was only barely a year or so ago since Tom and his brothers had danced with another serpent and the memory of the story they had told gave me courage.

They had told us of the tale when they had returned to the community.

It was the story in the dance that had scared the children and many of the men and women into careful obedience for weeks afterwards.

It was the story of the trials, which they as shaman had faced in Far North Queensland and of later, here at the cities edge where they had danced again with the Numereji Serpent. An account the Elders had asked Taipan and his brothers to tell so that they may understand what had come about in those months that had kept the Shaman and the Karadji busy. It was a story that others had a need to hear, one to warn them and draw the people to account.

We really knew little of what had kept the men away from the community, as it was only in dance that they would speak about these things. While we knew of the tales of the Dreamtime creatures we understood that shaman never spoke of their own experience, it was a tale only for the dance.

That time had been when Tom had truly taken on the ways of the Featherfoot and the first time he had truly also taken me into his confidence. It was when we had become mates and confidants, we were both men of the dance.

Even back then as Tom had walked amongst the spirits and shades seeing them, he had no need to face the Djaranin or even the Wolgaru Serpent but now it seemed it was time. The Dreamtime Spirit of the Kadaitcha awaited us.

It wasn't the Serpent however that I feared as I knew I could stand before him and he would have no need to call me to account, but the Djaranin... that was a different matter. They acted without reason and on any instinct and I would be holding the one thing that could threaten their serpent master. I would hold the serpent killer, the ililika and I knew that it was a powerful weapon against the spirit creatures.

Badjimala nodded watching my thoughts race across my mind. "You will stand well Kintji, I have taught you well. We need only to keep the dark dogs from the Bora rings where the initiates will be tested. You and I will dance with the serpent killers in our hands and it will be a great honour for us to see this thing. It is the birth of the Kadaitcha men. This is not a hunt young Kintji-iruka. This is not a killing to test you, that will come in time when Ariaka and you are ready."

It was as though we had stepped back into an age that I had thought no longer lived. It was a time never to be forgotten. It was to be an experience that stays with you through out your life, one lurking in the back of your mind always. It was as though it was a dream and in parts a story born of the Dreamtime. One that would be told in the dance and it would be danced again down the years for other men to wonder at.

We coated our bodies in the thick ooze of mud and clay slurry born of the fine crushed sandstone and ground mud we found along the edges and banks of the clear, running creek. We wore only our hair belts as men of the serpent have done since a time forgotten.

The mud kept the insects at bay but it gave us the look of wild creatures shifting along the canyon floor, weaving about the green forest hidden deep in the mountains. I felt a part of the world too old to recount, older even than the country through which we stepped.

I didn't doubt that where the men led us was a place not often visited. It was a quiet place without the mark of man. A place that was the preserve and knowledge of only a few and sat timeless this cavern at the end of the gorge.

Tucked up into the corner where the sheer rock walls of the canyon met was the mouth of a cave. Here the creek spilled into the open from a mouth gaping wide like a deep cut. The cavern ceiling hung low into the canyon in a wide and open face. There was a higher bank of stone and scree to one side and it dribbled down into the flow of the creek forming a broad bank.

The scree that had gathered on the bank had been there forever it seemed, as in places there were heavy boulders that had been shifted there by the force of a water flow. That volume of water would have been something that would be awesome to see and I wondered at how often this bank was awash with the sheer force in the power of nature.

High on the wall just inside the shelter where the rock had fallen away in the open-mouth of the cavern, you could see evidence of the ancient stories of men. Much lower, spread out at the feet of the hand-stencils and sketching's from ages past was also fashioned a ceremonial ring and it was about this stone and sand Bora ground that the men were now mostly gathered.

Tom was welcomed immediately. As an initiate his role was more important than mine and Badjimala took me aside, his tone low as he explained what was expected of me.

"It will be some time before the initiates are ready but when it is time we, you and I, will dance within the outer ring of the Bora. We will keep the dark dogs from the initiates while Wolgaru tests them. They will not leave the inner ring or they will be torn apart and it is only the serpent killers, our whips, that will be able to help them should this happen.

The Djaranin will not enter the inner Bora rings unless they see their chance. We will not give them such a chance with an initiate."

I nodded, understanding now what it was that was required of me.

"You have another weapon Kintji, one the others know little of. The Djaranin can only see you, but not with all their senses. Taipan has told me of the Skystone as I wondered why I was unable to sense your presence. They too can only see your presence in our world but you are like the forest animals to them so their senses are blind. All that they know of in your approach is that which is in their sight. They are blinded to any other sense of you and the flick of your whip will bite them unexpectedly. If you have need too, approach them from where they do not have a line of sight to you."

I smiled; glad that Badjimala knew of the Skystone I always wore encased in its own cage on my finger. Then as I saw his frown, he nodded knowingly as I realized he was seeing the complacency I thought I had hidden well.

"Kintji, you don't realise that because they will see you yet be unable to sense you, some of the shadow dogs who feel your whip may particularly seek out what they don't quite understand. It will be that I will likely spend most of my time protecting your hide as well as that of the initiates. The whip is not to punish the dogs of death but to control them, so don't lay it too often across their hide. You need to raise their fear in the sound and the movement of the whip. This is the whips greatest strength, the fear it can work in others."

Those words grounded me and I swallowed nervously watching the others move about me. I had felt I held the trump card in this but it seemed that it was one that could bring me more attention than I wanted.

"Would it be better if I took the stone off?"

"No." Big Jim answered almost affronted. "If you did, you will come to the attention of the Wolgaru Serpent and distracted, he will hunt you because you have been bitten. See that wallaby over there, the one the Kadaitcha have killed?"

I nodded seeing the kill clearly, which was against the wall in readiness for what I thought had been a feast to be eaten during or after the night.

"That is Wolgaru's reward for his time. Once the initiates have spilt their blood to the ground and given back to the earth, this will be given to him and he will leave contented with his reward. The dark dogs will leave with him also. Without the Skystone the serpent could well think that you are his reward because you will smell right to him. Always remember Kintji that you will be hunted by the serpents, it is now in your blood this thing and if it wasn't for the Skystone that blinds him in our world, Wolgaru would hunt you."

That grounded me too, making me more aware of the things that were happening around me. I soon found the rhythm of the dance when it was time and as the ceremony paced through the long night I became one with the men, we were a whole. We were a strength that protected and guided the initiates, Tom amongst them.

The shadows thrown against the rock walls of the canyon and those that moved under the starlight gave movement to the long night. As did the breeze shuffling the bushes and the stamp of feet disturbing the ground lending depth to the dance, talking to the land.

The Djaranin arrived first, heralding the arrival of Wolgaru and it was the crack of Badjimala's whip that pointed them out to all who were deep in ceremony. It was a rude awakening, one that announced the beginning of the initiation of the young men.

Never have I felt such fear and yet such elation as I tested the power of the serpent killer moving through the night, feeling the weight of it as an extension of myself. It danced with me, along with Badjimala's own whip.

The whips kept the dark dogs travelling with Wolgaru at bay. I had little time to pay attention to what was happening in the Bora Ring. I was too busy keeping the shadow dogs at arms length as they moved swiftly, too quickly for the eye to catch. It was their shadows cast across the ground in the feeble light that warned you.

Occasionally you could catch the reflection of starlight as it danced across their sleek hides, particularly if they slowed in their dance to mark the initiates or Elders in their sight. Mostly though they moved like dark lightening, which flashed and shivered before my eyes. It was only the swift shift of their shadows that allowed you to follow them at all.

The whips danced and sang and the dogs hated them. We gave them no time to mark the men in the Bora ring as we kept the dark dogs moving about us, around and beyond the outer ring. All this time I knew the serpent moved amongst the men within the circle, testing then, tasting their strengths and finding their weaknesses.

I had little time to mark the serpent myself but I knew it was there. Dark and afire with sleek flickers of a light not unlike the starlight that danced off the dogs sleek pelts. Wolgaru had the long dark pointed ears of legend that stretched and whipped about his head like the sonar sight of the bats. His teeth were fangs in his wide snapping jaw, sharp and often coated a brilliant blood, crimson at the head of the long length of him.

The Elders called to him with the bull-roarer and he answered their summons in a dance, attending to the initiates in the sacred rites of passage but I had little time to pay much attention.

As exhilarating as it was I was growing near exhaustion when the thrum of activity around changed and the temper of the dogs I marked moved to stillness. Then suddenly it was a retreat.

It was a moment before I realized that the payment that was the wallaby had been given to the dark serpent As sure as the crack of Badjimala's whip had sounded the beginning, it now sounded the end. I knew all was done as I watched in awe when the Spirit Creatures of the night retreated back into the caverns with a deathly swiftness. I almost collapsed under the flood of relief I felt.

My body hummed with heat as much as the sweat poured from me but as Badjimala came over to hold me to my feet. I welcomed him and offered my own support to his weariness. It was done; we had come through what had been the most trying of nights in my entire life. I couldn't believe that I had not only survived but I was triumphant in what I had been charged to do. Not only were the initiates safe, but they too were now exhausted and it wasn't long before I joined them in our path into the Dreaming. I had shown that I could conquer my fear.

It was deep into the next day when I finally stirred and there was movement about me. Many were up and about but a few still slept on the sandy ground and scree where they had burrowed defeated by their exhaustion. I noted the gashes and wounds on the bodies of the young initiates and decided then and there that I would never become a Kadaitcha as they. I would never step beyond the Lore of the Featherfoot.

Neither Tom nor Taipan was about but when Big Jim came over he invited me down to the creek. Without much ceremony at all we moved off into the forest quietly leaving the initiates and the Elders behind.

"We will wash and head back today young Jeremy. Our job here is done and we best leave the young Kadaitcha to the Elders," he said quietly. We both then washed the earth from our skin in the cool water of the creek not far from the cavern as we prepared to leave.

"Where is Tom?"

"He is with Taipan and is fine. He came through the ceremony well."

"Did he...? Was he cut... in the same way?" I asked, not really wanting to hear the answer having seen the marks of ceremony on the young men.

"The head-cut? Yes. It's a mark of their ceremony and they undertake this themselves guided by the Elders. I have seen it before."

"Why?" I asked incredulous at the ceremony and what would be the attendant pain and discomfit.

"Because they need to spill their blood to the earth. It is an ancient rite of the Kadaitcha and without it they cannot hear the sacred songs, or share the knowledge of such men young Kintji. It is a choice only they can make."

I shook my head astounded at the strength of will that such a thing must take.

"It is a choice Tom has made, one he will make many times. As he spills a man's blood to the earth, so he will spill his own. Death does not come easily and to take a life has a price Kintji."

"It's not a choice I will be asked to make?"

Big Jim grinned at the tone of my voice. "You will not be asked to make such a choice, but one day it may be a choice you will make anyway. It is for you to decide."

"And you?"

"It is not a choice I will make. That is not my way. Come, its time for you and me to leave, the others will follow us later. You have school tomorrow."

"School? Jee-zus that seems a thousand miles away."

The world of school was indeed a thousand miles away in my mind and it was hard to bring it back into perspective for me.

The next day at TAFE, Kelly was curious about my subtle withdrawal, as curious as I was determined to settle my experience back into my life. My friends gave me space though and I appreciated it.

Without Tom around I didn't have the opportunity to get down to the beach. I missed the mindless serenity, you could find in listening to the constant pound of the surf against the sand. I missed losing my thoughts in the swift movement and exhilaration of the waves with the board balanced beneath you. It was a peace that I missed badly and one that I needed more than anything now.

Tom and Taipan arrived back ten days later; both looking stronger for their experiences and that in itself amazed me. I was keen to ask Tom about his trials but it was something that was hard to ask a man so instead I waited. A time would come I figured and it would likely be a time around a fire late at night when we were enjoying a mindless escape together. I could wait.

The one good thing that came of our time in the bush and our ceremony was that we were now free of many of the restrictions, those that had been imposed on us.

While I still was forbidden to use the ililika for my own ends Tom was now released from any such constraints. His trials had taken him beyond these restrictions and while training was a life long commitment for the Kadaitcha he found himself in a place where he could offer guidance.

We would commonly get together and Big Jim would school us further in the use of the whips. Making the whip was an art in itself and one that he teased us with, though I thought with Tom it was a more serious concern. Toms whip, one that Apari had made for him since our dance was even smaller in length than mine and lighter. Big Jim referred to it as a stock whip rather than a snake killer, a whip designed to target well with its handle braced by bone or a wooden splinter as a belly to keep the grip stiff.

I was told that it served a different purpose than mine even though I was unsure of the exact purpose it was to serve. Its use was still the same, to inflict an emotional control in a form and incite fear. Big Jim made it very clear that our whips were tools and he was strict with us about when we would be permitted to employ them.

Tom never voiced my curiosity about when he would use his whip as I had hoped he would, so that I could learn more. He accepted easily the splinter embedded into the handle. Even Big Jim referred to it with some apparent disquiet and I knew there was something about the whole business of Tom's whip about which I knew nothing. It was just another one of the mysteries of the Kadaitcha that I came to accept. If I were meant to know then in time I would be told.

I guess it was this attitude, which fed my respect for a person's privacy and it was an attitude that I learnt was to cause conflict in other ways.

Kelly and I soon were back to enjoying the beach. With many of the restrictions of my training removed I found myself more possessive of her, particularly when Tom joined us and I had need to question this.

Tom picked up on it easily and while he tormented me about it in private, his ribbing didn't extend to when Kelly was with us. I tolerated his attentions towards her, trusting that he wouldn't be taking it further though he often enough challenged me with a look. I felt it had more to do with taunting than intent and in some part it became a game we amused ourselves with. One that Kelly caught onto in time and it was an easy game.

The Business of Men

Jeremy

It wasn't long after the time of our ceremony that Kelly was sketching on my shoulder again as we sat about on the grass at TAFE. She was quieter than usual, though intent on the sketch and I decided that it was the detail that kept her seemingly concentrating.

Over the weeks I had come to like this particular design and it felt as though I was close to choosing what was to become very much part of me. That it was Kelly who had bought me to this made it also in some way part of her as well and I liked that thought.

We had become good friends and I wondered at times like this if it was something we could take further. I felt that she was perhaps the first girl that I had really considered that I might understand.

"What do you think of this design?" I asked, wanting to hear her thoughts.

"It's good. I like it."

As I felt her touch up the lines where they had faded. I waited and then drew a steadying breath. "I think I'll go with this one. I'm going to call into the tat shop today. I was talking to the guy last week and he wants to take pic's, work up the design for me."

Kelly sat back and considered her work. "You're really going to go ahead with it then?"

"Yeah, I always was. That's what I've been saving up for. Didn't you think I would?"

"Well... no... I mean I didn't know. You're not going down to the beach today then?" She asked with a curious tone.

"No. I think Tom is though, I heard him say something about it this morning but I was sorta doing stuff at the time."

"Mmm. I like Tom. He's a good friend."

"Yeah. He has a bit of a rep' with the girls so don't mess with him. I know you like to flirt but he's a lot older... You'll get burnt." I warned on a playful chuckle though I could see an odd curiosity in her glance.

"I can look out for myself. Don't worry over it... we're just friends." Playfully she gave me a small shove and then giggled as my glance slashed back across to catch hers, hearing that something again in her tone that concerned me.

"Just sayin'," I added warily.

I knew my words would carry little weight but I think what I feared most was that if these two got to messing around with each other then that would change things. I didn't want to change things between the three of us.

At the tattoo shop much later that day the artist finally got started onto the design and it was good to see the beginning's coming together. We discussed colour even, which wasn't something I had given a lot of thought to and the tat artist trialled a small patch of ink on my skin near the scars to test if I was going to be able to take the colour. It was looking good I thought.

I didn't see much of Kelly outside of TAFE that week. She seemed as busy as were we all. It was coming up to the end of the semester and the year so we were deep into prep' for the assessments.

I suspected however that she and Tom had linked up and neither of them was going to tell me about it. It was the way Tom wouldn't look me in the eye when I spoke of Kelly, the way he moved at the time, these little things that echoed in his ways.

At first I was angry with them both. It wasn't that I minded about any relationship they may have, but it was more about that they kept it from me. I couldn't confront them though, after all I really didn't know. It was just I hated all this sneaking around business.

Not being sure about it was the most difficult of things. It was only when I found a pair of girl's knickers in Tom's car that I even gave it any serious thought. I couldn't think of any girl, other than Kelly, who had been inside his car and I knew he had no other girls hanging around.

I was at first angry, tempted to confront him over it but was it really my place. Instead, in the end I slipped the scrap of lace and silky stuff into my pocket and contemplated what it meant to the three of us and our continuing friendship, or even if there was to be a friendship anymore.

Determined to confront one of them, I was even thinking on challenging Tom. I had run through the scenario in my head a hundred times but that was all suddenly set aside when the weekend arrived. I found I was unexpectedly off on a drive back up north to the community and I didn't have a lot of say in the events as they overtook me.

In the end I decided that It was only to be a few days really and I figured I could take care of the question with Tom when I got back.

Andrew had suddenly turned up at the door and said that Taipan had already rung TAFE and made arrangements with them. I was told that it was important that I make the trip back to the community with him. It had been arranged for me to be going back only for a few days.

You just didn't argue with Andrew or Taipan, they both had a way that was much too set and serious about the whole business.

When Andrew had rocked up to the house early on the Saturday I realized then that Big Jim had been waiting for his arrival. Tom too seemed to know little about it; even Andrew wasn't very forthcoming about the whole business. If fact he was down right tight lipped and it appeared to me he avoid talking about it around Tom. But as I said, you don't argue with Andrew when he is in one of his singular moods.

"This is serious business Jeremy. All I know is that the Elders want you back in the community for business that concerns them an' I've been sent down to fetch you. There is something going on and I don't know the whole of it myself. Taipan can tell you more when we get there."

The two of us left Sydney fairly early Sunday morning and by the time we drove into the community it was well after sunset. It seemed to have been a lifetime since I had left home and I was surprised at how much the community had changed, and yet it was still so much the same.

The central campfire area was settled into a full swing, as mums and kids milled around. As usual they were making the most of the last of their day before the youngest of kids were sent off to bed early, preparing for school the next day.

A group of teens also had a small campfire going down at the creek, which was something new. It was a larger crowd than I remembered and my inclination was to go straight down and join them.

Andrew shook his head and indicated the path beyond the main campfire that headed straight up to the Karadji's valley, which surprised me some. He said that Taipan was waiting for us to get in and that catching up with everyone would just have to wait.

"Ty wants to see us as soon as he can, they want to settle this business pretty quickly for some reason. Besides you're getting too old for that group." He nodded indicating the gathering down by the creek.

Surprised at his words I glanced back at what I had thought was my old friends, only to realize that there were a lot of new kids amongst them. Andrew was right, while I wouldn't mind meeting some of the girls, I couldn't see many of my older mates and others amongst them.

"Where do the older group hang out now?" I asked curious.

"They have a shanty up the west arm, right at the end of the road. Seems to be where most of them head for now since Alex and I moved into Toms place. I've been up there a few times, it's not much but they pulled it together themselves and its become a bit of a hang-out for many in your old group."

"I might head up that way later."

"Yeah... wait and see what the Elders want first though. Then your time is your own I guess. I have to get you back by next Wednesday though, or it will affect your studies."

The path we took up along the valley was familiar. It was a place that had always held a sense of old Spirits and as we approached along the lower path Andrew took the sidetrack that led up to what was his own place and I guessed he wanted to see his family first.

"I'll just call in to check on Alex. She has her hands full with Yindi and Ellie. Aine was going to keep an eye on her for me. We won't be a minute."

"Yeah sure."

Alex was resting on the lounge when we walked in through the front door and immediately I knew we were both very welcome. Watching the two of them together, Alex and Andrew, was a warm and comforting experience. It reminded me of something Tom had said once about Alex and he at one time being close.

It didn't seem to make much sense to me now, as Alex clearly was devoted to Andrew. It was pretty evident that they were soon to be expecting another kid. Besides, I wasn't much in sympathy with Tom on anything at the moment and if Alex had shaken him off and given him trouble, then he had likely deserved it. Andrew and Alex looked to be in their own little world and it was my guess that Tom likely could have merited what he got.

She greeted me warmly though, something that surprised me a bit but I guess Andrew must have spoken about me a couple of times.

"Jeremy. Its great to see you back, how is the shoulder by the way?"

"Great. No worries now, it hardly ever bothers me these days."

"That's good news. We had heard that it took a time to heal?"

"Yep but it's all good. You look very preggers though?" I asked laughing as I stated the obvious.

"Mmm... something's you just can't account for I'm afraid. These things just happen." She smiled as Andrew drew her to his side obviously content to find her well.

Then he cut in, "The kids asleep?"

"Yep, only just."

"Well since your OK, we might nick up to Ty's and I'll be back in a minute. Anything left in the fridge? I'm starving." He added kissing her lightly.

"You're always hungry. I'll heat up something, don't be long."

It wasn't far to the Karadji's house at the end of the track and as we broke through the forest at the end you could see that everyone seemed to still be up and about.

Taipan was settled in the lounge room with their little boy Kiahan reading to him. He looked up as we came in through the doors on the lower level and then set the book aside with a reassurance to his son as the youngster scrambled off the lounge obviously delighted to see his Uncle Andrew.

His Uncle swung him high, something he clearly expected. We were both soon welcomed and invited to take a seat, one of those gathered around the low burning open fireplace.

Aine was busily bustling around the kitchen pulling together some snacks and warm drinks against the remnant chill of the night air that still lingered before the full flush of summer.

"Trip go well?" Ty asked as he set some toys aside off the lounge, bringing some order to the cushions and making room for Aine and us. She handed me a chunky sandwich while Andrew recounted the easy run we had up the coast and it wasn't long before he had excused himself to get back to Alex.

I wasn't quite sure what was expected of me but I was happy to tuck into the food Aine had given me as I waited patiently to be told what this business was all about.

Ty had settled himself once again when Aine quietly left us wandering off as though to get something. Watching her go he nodded and then he looked across at me with a deliberated expectation.

"We have someone with us that I believe you know. We've been asked to help and I am hoping you will be able to give us a hand as it would otherwise mean I will need to head to Sydney..." Ty broke off as Aine stepped back into the lounge area from the upper landing with someone following behind. Surprised beyond words I froze with my drink still halfway to my mouth as Aine then cut in.

"Jeremy, I believe you know Kirri."

Kirri stood there, quiet and at first my mind just went blank as I returned the cup to the table with deliberation. I straightened to stand completely speechless my thoughts running rampant. Kirri dropped her eyes in a manner strangely demure, totally and utterly quiet even in the way she stood so still.

"Kirri has come to us via an arrangement with the Elders, she has been with us for a few weeks but we were hoping that you might be able to help with settling her in.

She asked how you were and we thought then that you could introduce her to the others more easily than we could. She'll stay here until she is ready to head down to Sydney in a while. Perhaps you can help her settle in down there?"

"Me?" I squeaked surprised and confused.

"Yes. Is there a problem?"

"No… no… no problem. It's just… just that… I mean I don't know how you mean?"

"She needs to learn our ways, there is a lot she will need to understand and while we have been helping her understand our ways, it has become clear that there is a lot…"

"She's staying?"

"Yes. I am hoping she can join you and Tom in Sydney, maybe not straight away but eventually we can bring her down."

"Down? Down to Sydney you mean?" I stumbled still confused. Taipan just grinned and I was sure he understood my confusion finding it entertaining.

"Yes."

Suddenly Kirri stepped forward making her way over to where we stood by the lounges. She turned hesitantly to me while I remained totally stunned by the turn of events.

"Jeremy, I hope you're healed now. Taipan told me how sick you had been. I wondered whether your shoulder healed… after the bite I mean."

Dumbfounded I just stared across at her, not even sure I could or should answer, not sure of anything. It was all just so improbable or impossible to even contemplate. Then I turned back to Ty looking for assurance on how I should answer her.

In the end the silence became stretched and I had to do something. "Yeah… It's good. Nearly healed. I mean it is healed but I'm getting a tat'."

At the corner of my eye I saw Ty sit down again and realised that he just might have something to say about the permanence of this plan of mine. It would be an opinion that I didn't necessarily want to hear.

"I mean… it's all organized." I turned to him reassuringly. Even though I knew it was my decision. It was not something I really wanted to openly discuss with him. Although he must have gathered by other things I had said that this was where my thinking was.

"It's your body son. Your decision," He answered. "I'm sure you've thought about it." He nodded with not a sketch of disagreement evident.

"Yes. I've been working on the design with friends and I think I'm ready." I added confidently as I glanced back at the women.

Kirri was looking confused and Aine surprised, then she must have noted the confusion in Kirri's glance. "A tat is a tattoo, it's an ink design Kirri. It is very popular with the kids of late it seems."

"Oh. Like a drawing on… on your skin."

"Yes a permanent design. You have them for life."

"I have heard of them. They are very painful to do I think."

Still confused and somewhat flummoxed at Kirri's presence I moved to sit down. "I don't understand, I didn't think Kirri... I mean where she comes from...?

"Kirri is here to stay for a while, quite a while." Taipan added in answer to my stumbling question. "The Elders have made arrangements for her to come to us. It is something that has been arranged between the Kadaitcha with agreement from the Elders from the Inlands and our Elders. It is an arrangement that they feel is needed."

"You don't mind?" I asked as I turned to her, gaining my voice with Ty's reassurance. I was remembering the things Kirri had said in what seemed a lifetime ago now, a whole world of experience away.

It now all felt like something that had happened when I was a kid, so much had changed... I had changed. It just seemed so improbable that she was even here.

Aine moved to take a seat on the lounge and invited Kirri to sit also; they both settled as though a pigeon pair. Kirri then began to answer me in the quiet yet confident way that I remembered well. "It is my place now. I will return to the Inlands one day, go back to my country but not until..."

"Kirri needs to learn about our world and to adjust." Taipan once more cut in. "She is here with the blessing of her family and her people and it will take time for her to understand our world. Will you help her?"

I shrugged. "Yeah sure. I guess so."

"Good, then that's settled. We can talk about it later. In the mean time you can both reacquaint yourselves over the next few days and we'll see how it goes. Either Andrew or I can get you back to Sydney on Wednesday, we can discuss later when Kirri might be ready to go down to Sydney."

Aine spoke up quietly. "I think it's too early, the kids need time Ty, and Kirri, well there are things she needs to understand. There is a lot of adjustment for her."

"You might be right. Anyway tonight Jeremy you are welcome to doss down in the spare room if you like. You must be buggered after the drive today."

"Thanks, I got a bit of sleep on the drive but I should go an find Mum, let her know I am here. I would like to catch up with a few of the guys too?"

"Of course, that's fine," Ty agreed. "Kirri hasn't had much of a chance to get out, would you mind if she went with you. She hasn't met any of the crowd her age, I don't think? Though don't go taking her up to where the shaman hang out will you? Maybe the younger group?"

Looking across at Aine, she agreed with a nod while the idea flashed through my mind. What was her age? I seemed to recall that it was older than I, much older than any of us sitting here. The memory flashed still wanting to be denied.

"Yeah sure." My reassurance was impulsive but when I stood as though to act on Ty's suggestion. Kirri too climbed to her feet watching me in that way she had. It was in a way that seemed to see right through me. "We may as well get going I guess. We can go down to the creek where the others were. Meet some of that crowd there."

"Sounds like a plan." Ty stood too, smiling slowly as he swung Kiahan back into his arms. "And this one can go for his bath I think," he added on a confident chuckle. Reassured that all was just as he wanted it.

The trek back towards the main camp with Kirri was at first quiet but it wasn't long before my curiosity got the better of me and I was wondering what the others would make of her. With my own doubts I turned to her to try and find out how she really felt about being here.

"What made you decide to come here, up to … what was it you called it… the Edgelands?" My grin challenged her with humour as I recalled some of our conversations in the cavern.

"My father, he is amongst the Elders and they thought that it was time that we did something to help preserve our balance."

"Your dad?"

"Yes. That is what I said." Confused she glanced across at me. The dark shadow of the night drawing us closer than we perhaps would have normally walked otherwise.

"Yeah … I know. But it just seems so improbable after what you said."

"Why improbable?"

"Well … well I don't know, it just is. I mean, I know you come from underground an' all. I realized that now but why change? I mean… isn't it very different? I didn't think you even liked it up here much."

"I think I like it more now. Taipan and Aine … even Andrew and Alex are so nice, not at all what I thought. I'm sorry about the way I spoke at times. Ty has explained a lot to me about the Edgelanders. I see now that it isn't all like what I thought. Though it still is, only it's… it's different. Taipan has helped me see a lot."

"Have you been here very long?"

"No. Only a short time and I am still adjusting. Aine said I should stay indoors until I acclimatize. Your sun is very strong and it is coming up to its most fierce cycle so I have to be careful out-of-doors still."

"Oh yeah… sunburn. You would be easy to burn with your skin I think?"

"Yes. I have some cream but it will have to be a gradual thing. I have already begun to colour strangely," she added smiling as she held her arm for me to see."

"Not much."

"No? I thought so."

"Your colouring like an English tourist." I added laughing at her confusion.

"I am?"

"Yeah. You look like you might go that golden colour but don't stay out in the sun too long or you will go beetroot red, like the Pommies do."

"The Pommies?"

"The English and Europeans. Lots of them go red really quickly without even knowing it at the time and it is really painful. Sun burn."

"That is what Aine called it. Though she isn't as dark as you or Taipan, or even Andrew. It is so strange that you are all different colours."

"You will probably colour up like Aine in time."

"I hope so. You don't think I will be as dark as you?"

I laughed at that and then shook my head at the very suggestion. "Maybe in like... a thousand years or so."

I found my mum up at the community fire with the other women. After a welcoming bear hug and quick introductions with Kirri she let me get away to join the crowd still down at the river. It seemed that no one had met Kirri and I realized that she must have spent all of her time with Aine and Ty in the valley.

Mum had naturally assumed that Kirri was with me. I could see it in her eyes and I let that slide, as I wasn't sure what the others might have said. There was really no need for explanations I figured even if they were mine to make. I was only going to be here until Wednesday so even my Mum couldn't make much of a fuss in the few days I was here.

When we reached the group down by the river it was great to catch up with some of my younger friends after so many months as I listened to all the community news.

Kirri fitted in easily though she was very quiet and stayed resolutely at my side. It was easy to see everyone thought that she was my girlfriend and that was OK. I found that the others talked more openly when they assumed I already had a girl. It seemed many thought that I was no threat to any of the other relationships going on around us.

The evening tumbled into the late night as we sat around the small fire and laughed at what the others had to say. Some of my old friends asked me about Sydney and how I had found living there. I made light of my experiences and I noticed that even Kirri was attentive to my answers.

Later we were joined by the older guys more my age and listening to their exploits at school in senior I realized that nothing really had changed, nothing but me that is. It gave me a new perspective on things that I didn't realize I had already acquired so easily.

Kirri just mostly listened, fielding any questions and leaving the answers mostly to me, which was amusing in its own way. It was like we were really a couple but to me it was obvious how much she watched everyone. I noticed how she was so careful in studying the kids around her.

Most surprising was when she began to imitate the other girls. I smiled as I saw her practice each mannerism in turn carefully. When I caught her eye with a question in mine she just grinned slowly, knowing somehow what I was thinking of her antics. It was all a bit eerie, as though she knew my thoughts.

Slowly the couples began to peel off from the group while others drifted away or headed for home as the night moved to its fullness.

There was a bit of a racket up at the car park when a few of the older blokes and girls arrived back from where ever it was that they had been in their cars. Most of them headed straight off into the community, giving the younger group hardly any attention at all, aside from the one or two who had walked up to greet them.

The group around the campfire had mostly melted away by around midnight. I was beginning to feel the effects of what had been a big day hit me more surely as I moved to stretch out the kinks in my back.

"You ready to head back?" I asked Kirri quietly.

She smiled and scrambled to her feet. I don't remember her being so compliant before and I wondered if I should challenge her about it; tease her a bit as I joined her.

"See you guys later." I added to the few left around the fire when I joined her and we turned to make our way back towards the track and onto the Karadji's valley.

"You were quiet? What is with the change of attitude?"

Her eyes flashed and then she settled her glance back to the ground. "I have to find my way amongst your people. That is expected of me and it will take time. I'm accustomed to well... to someone my age being more mature and it's hard."

"Mature?"

"Yes mature. We age slowly but our experience is greater than well... many there tonight. It is going to be hard for me to make friends easily. I can see that now."

"Yeah... I guess. I never thought of it. Will you change do you think? Age differently... like physically than you did Inland?"

Kirri shrugged. "It is one of the things we don't know. Mostly those who come to the Edgelands either don't return or return quite quickly. In our histories it is the Edgelanders who come to the Inland more often. Our knowledge of your world however is fairly basic I think now. We thought perhaps that our people, those who never returned to us were killed or ... we weren't sure but maybe I can see how they just decide to stay."

"So what bought you here, now?"

"I have to decide if I want to stay, maybe for some time. I'm a sort of emissary. I've been forbidden to return for some years or it will anger the Elders. They told me that coming here had some risks for them."

I looked up sharply and frowned. "How? Why?"

"Coming up to the Edgelands has many dangers and there were some of the Elders who argued against it. Some were concerned about the Guardians and what they might do."

"The Guardians, who are they?"

Kirri's response surprised me as she looked up frowning. "You know them as the Oruncha Men I have been told, but to the Inlanders they are a guardian spirit people. Our Elders speak of them often, they guard our way to the Inland and we have need to respect them. They protect us. It is from them that we learn a great deal. Not all of the Edgelanders know of the Guardians though, do they?"

"Well... yes and no, they are called by different names too. They are givers of knowledge for us. Teachers, or guardians too I guess. To a lot of other people in other cultures they have become figures of legend. We protect the knowledge of them a great deal ... others wouldn't understand. I'm not supposed to talk about it. We don't talk much to others who can't understand these things. They are strictly men's business I had thought."

As I reluctantly recounted to Kirri what little I had been taught of the Oruncha I wondered myself about these mischievous and knowledgeable Spirit men and the part they play in her world.

They had been instrumental in my initiations. I knew they watched me. But since I wore the Skystone then maybe they couldn't see me as much? Other than that I wondered what did I really know about them?

Kirri listened attentively. She had heard a lot of what I told her before I realized and as her frown gathered I couldn't help but ask. "So the Oruncha are a guardian people you know well?"

"Yes. All throughout the Inlands and in some parts they are the gatekeepers... like Andrew I think?"

"Andrew? Our Andrew… I don't think so? For us the Oruncha are spirit men of the caverns and more part of the Kadaitcha Lore. Andrew has little to do with them I think, he's a Banman."

"But he's is a gatekeeper. I have met him before when he came to the caverns to get you… remember?"

"Yes… well no … not really. I don't remember a lot after that bite but I try not to think about it much either. I mean there is so much more I am learning and the Oruncha…" I shrugged. "They will leave me alone, I'm sorta protected. Andrew is the only Gatekeeper I know of, and his Lore is different to mine. Though Tom too gets into the caverns but he is different, more like me but different. You will meet him I guess when you get to Sydney."

At the mention of Tom, it seemed that I suddenly had Kirri's full attention. So much so that she moved closer in to me as we walked."

"I have heard of Tom, Taipan has talked of his brother to me, that I will get to meet him. Is he a good man?"

"Tom? Well… yeah I guess so." Not wanting to talk about Tom's business I dived into other topics. "In the Inland… are there many communities then?"

Her look was sharp. "Yes, many like your cities I think. Some are large Domilands and others… well others are much smaller, tunnel like or much smaller Domin's and they live in the Outlands of our bigger communities. I prefer living in the Domilands I think. It is much harder to live in the Outland's, they don't have the resources we have."

"A Domiland, what is that?"

"Oh. It's like a umm… a big city I think."

"Underground?"

"Yes. I live in one of the bigger Domilands, it isn't the largest but for this part of the world it is one of the larger ones."

"What is it though… is it a cave or… or… I don't know?" I grinned across at her not sure how to phrase the question. It was just so odd a concept to me.

Kirri looked at me strangely again and then a little confused offered, "A Domiland is… well like a cavern I guess but bigger, much, much bigger. You can't see the vastness of it or like… like you can't see how large it really is all at once." Then she shrugged and smiled. "It's a Domiland."

"Sounds weird."

"It's not weird, it is … well just like your island really."

"You have water around the Domiland?"

Kirri laughed and then shook her head. No a Domiland is not an island but it has islands in it and we have water and... and settlements you would call islands. The Domiland is a place like a huge, huge dome-like place, a bubble. It is a world formed in the earth crust beneath the Edgeland. They are just there... they have always been there like the Edgeland has always been. Only it is so huge you can't see its extremities. Taipan said that your country is a island and that is like where I lived, only..." Looking up suddenly at the sky, lit by a million stars found in the Milky Way, Kirri shook her head again and continued.

"We don't have the sky like you have, no stars or night lights. We don't have night like this at all. It is kind of scary... your night? And... well the sense of nothingness up there, no roof or constraint to space is really odd to me. I don't know if I like it much."

"No night? Then how do you know when to sleep?"

She smiled. "We get tired of course, just like you do."

"Yeah but you can't sleep so well in the light, not in the day like we have."

"Our light isn't as harsh as yours, it is ... sort of muted to your daylight. It is softer, a more gentle light which comes from the top of the Domina. It is easy to sleep ... you just sleep when you're tired. We don't have a day or night at all. The difference in your night and day for me is going to take a lot to get used to. Everyone is around all the time at the same time... isn't that hard?"

Now it was my turn to shake my head in confusion. It did sound confusing to me, really strange.

Ignoring her question I wanted instead for her to answer mine. "Are there many of these Domilands?"

"Yes... I don't know how many, I've never counted them. It's just something you wouldn't do," and then she giggled at what she obviously considered a preposterous thought. "We have different Domilands like... well like you have countries or continents I guess. Some have different communities or dominion's as we call them."

"Really? That is an old word. We have that word but it means... something different I think."

Suddenly Kirri grinned and laughed softly. "There are a lot of words like that. Aine and Alex have been helping me find them. Like... um... like county. We have counties like you have countries. They are different but almost the same. Mostly though our words are not spoken, it has taken me a long time to find the words you would use." Kirri flicked her fingers as I remembered that she had done this before.

That made me laugh but also it made me think. "Maybe we have a lot in common just in some things."

"Well of course we do, we have a common history."

"We do?"

"Yes. I was talking to Taipan about it, but you seem to have lost a lot of your histories since the wars."

"Wars?"

"Yes, thousands of years ago now, in your years there were the wars mostly in your North I think. Ohhh... what was one of those words that Taipan used?"

Amazed I watched as she struggled with her thoughts and wondered about something that happened thousands of years ago, apparently before the other civilizations of the world had even got around to being.

"I know. Gilgamesh, that was it. Or one of the battles in the wars, they are called lots of different names but Taipan said that your histories have mostly been forgotten or lost. Your big countries and societies only believe in written history I am told. Yet there is so much that was not written and the oral stories are no longer told, or believed. It is such a sad thing to lose your histories."

"What happened?" I asked shaking my head with an avid curiosity.

"At the time so many more of the Edgelanders moved down to the Domilands, to survive. Some stayed with the Guardians, your Oruncha people. People found their place, where they felt most comfortable and took on new ways as they have done since the beginning. Much like the Elders have asked me to do now in moving up to the Edgelands. I wonder if it has something to do with that... like reforming links that we once had? They did not say."

"You think?"

Kirri shrugged. "Who knows, not me. I just do as I am told like everyone else." She shrugged smiling as we paced the dark track together, each engrossed in our own thoughts as we made our way through the night towards the Karadji's house. Our minds stitching together the things we had learnt in the last few hours. These were strange and new things to both of us.

As we stepped along the path I thought to myself how this would have to have been the strangest conversation that I had ever had. But I wanted to know more. I wanted to hear what Kirri could tell me of the Inlands and these histories that we shared. It was a knowledge that fascinated me.

Suddenly the whole prospect of helping her settle in took on a new light and I was deep in thought as we made our way back along the path. Which was probably why I had no inkling or warning about what happened next.

Lost

Jeremy

Whatever it was, it came from behind me and I had no idea of it until I felt it. Kirri was in front of me at a low section of the path where it meandered closer to the creek. We had passed the junction where you could turn up along another track to where Andrew lived with his woman.

It was particularly dense and shadowed here so I had set Kirri ahead of me. It was an alternative to holding her hand as we made our way in the deeper shadows of the night, a contact she seemed not to encourage. It was just her way really, a mannerism.

I had already discovered she didn't like much being touched and tended to shy away from any contact, something that I had put down to her natural reservations and mannerisms.

I heard no sound that could have warned me, so when the blunt blow hit me from behind I was unprepared; all I recalled was that Kirri swung about suddenly.

If it hadn't been for the look of fright in her eyes I would have said she had been expecting something, she had been so tense in those moments.

Darkness gripped me, suddenly, pulling me into oblivion and aside from that look, I knew nothing until I began to stir an age later.

It was cold and wet and I was uncomfortable when I next opened my eyes to the dark starlight and smell of the dank earth. With any movement I made my head thundered. Aching with the pain of it so that I settled, stilling my want to move again.

My head was thumping and I squinted with the dull pain I felt. Then again I recognized the sharp prod in my arm that had really been what had disturbed me.

Turning towards the prodding stick carefully I was amazed to see the small grizzled man seated beside me who was watching me intently, waiting, with a stick in his hand as he prodded me irritatingly.

I knew who he was almost immediately. It was a Jongorrie Spirit man, an ugly looking little man of the forest with the most striking eyes. These spirit men never stilled usually. They had a reputation for always being on the move, never ceasing in their movement through the forest.

You usually only caught glimpses of the wizened little thieves as they moved quickly and silently along their tracks. That he was still sitting here beside me where I lay stretched out on the path was an anathema to the knowledge I had of the Jongorrie. His presence confused me and I groaned, wondering if he even was a reality.

"Get-up. Com'on up!" He grated impatiently prodding me again as I opened my eyes to the sight of him. "Up! Up... up ... up. You waste time... time is important."

"What the fuck!" I mumbled under my breath unsure that I wasn't delusional in some way, or perhaps this was just a dream.

"Up. Up... you have a job to do. A job you lazy bugga'."

I groaned, not believing my eyes or my ears as I blinked across at him. He didn't go away, he didn't fade or flash off in a quick movement as they usually did and I stared at him harder as I eased myself up. Sitting about carefully with my hands gently sweeping through my hair looking to feel the damage to my head while I tried to reassure myself I was OK.

I jumped when I touched a tender spot and bought my hand away carefully feeling the stickiness of blood between my fingers. Resting my elbows on my knees I supported my head as the world about me steadied slowly. This must be an illusion I figured, after such a blow it was likely and I glared across at him once again.

"Up! Up." He prodded at me persistently.

"Will you cut that out!" I spat. I was unsure if he was even there with me.

Still not quite believing it despite the evidence of my eyes I waited for him to vanish. When he didn't and when he took to poking me again, I felt like taking that damn stick and shoving it where sunlight never shone.

Instead I straightened up slowly and continued to glare across at him resentfully. He hadn't gone away... he hadn't even moved and I wondered if I was really seeing him there. It seemed as though he was real enough I decided to myself as I continued to watch him amazed.

"Oh I'm here. I need you... need you I do." He spat impatiently as he met my stare with one of his own. "Need you I do, do ya' hear. You get up will ya'. I can't sit around here waiting. Not waiting... too much to do. Up!"

"Why!" I spat back in an answer, still unsure if I was really just talking to myself or not. Reaching around at the back of my head again to feel where the throbbing seemed to come from, I wondered if my injury had anything to do with this grizzled little man. Not really believing what it was that I was seeing, or even if I was awake.

"Cause you gotta go an get 'er. Get her you idiot. Do you think they called on you cause you're pretty... you're not ya' know! Not at all ya'-know even if she thinks ya're."

"What are ya' talkin' about Jongorrie... You are a Jongorrie aren't you?" I wondered aloud as my fingers came away from my head still sticky with blood. It had oozed and coagulated mixed with the mud and dampness of the night.

"Well you might think ya' smart but your not that either. Of course I am what I am! I'm lotza things but to you... well that'll do." He spat impatiently as he then began to climb to his feet in his ungainly way. "I'm here to help ya'. Help ya', ya' hear. Now get up!"

"What for! Why? Was it you that hit me?" I demanded impatient as I carefully glanced around wondering where Kirri had got to and then it started to slowly piece together in my mind.

"She ain't 'ere. She's gone... they got her and you gotta get her back. You hear... get her back!"

"Kirri?"

"Yes Kirri." He repeated as though I was a child he was explaining something to and he was impatient with it. "It's why ya're here. Ya' supposed to keep her safe but you didn't did ya'? Ya' didn't! Now I have ta' do it... an I have other things to do too... otha' things!"

"Geezus it wasn't my fault. Who are they anyway?"

"It's the men of the caverns that have her now... have her they do and I don't know why. We didn't expect that ... didn't expect that at all. It wasn't supposed to be that way."

"The Oruncha Men! Why would they want Kirri?" I demanded as he began to make some sense.

"Cause she is a Inlander ya' stupid man. An Inlander! Maybe they don't like 'er being here... maybe they have a reason and we have to get 'er back. Maybe the wanna initiate 'er themselves... maybe they do. Do ya' hear ... now get up!"

Slowly, still unsteady I climbed to my feet dazed. I was wet too, damp and muddy from the track as I looked about wondering what the Jongorrie had to do with all this. Wondering what he was even doing here and wondering if I should head straight back up to Taipan and sort this out. It wasn't making sense at all.

"No don't ya' go there!" The Jongorrie spat impatiently as though he had read my thoughts. "Tho' you will need your things... yes you will need the Serpent Killer, an... and maybe a knife. A knife would be good."

"What are you talking about little man?"

"You gotta get 'er. Get 'er from the Oruncha Men. Wot do you think you are here for, ya' stupid man. Stupid!"

I glared at him. "Cut that out or I will swat you one."

The Jongorrie just grinned at that and his strange eyes lit with fiery glints in the darkness. "No ya' won't cause you got a job. A job... your job! It's not my job and you… you stuffed it up. One job… that was what ya' had and I had so many. So much talking and getting 'er here and you… you lost 'er!"

"What the fuck're you talking about? Where is she?" I demanded impatient now with his abuse and tone.

"The Oruncha Men have 'er and they are probably deep in the caverns b'now… probably in there they are, and you have to go get 'er."

"Well we need someone… Taipan I think."

"No. No… no, no. Not 'im. Not even Moongunn… we don't want him near Kirri… he will charm her… charm her like he did the other before. They'll not like that you lost 'er… lost 'er! An' he will be angry… angry! And we don't want an angry Karadji to deal with. Not at all! I've had dealings with him before and he took over… took over 'e did and it was not good! Not good for me and it won't be good for you. I will not take you there if ya' go an' get him. I won't! I won't ya' hear."

The Jongorrie began muttering to himself as he edged down the track and I slowly stepped up to follow him. The very thought of involving Taipan was apparently a horror to the little man and it had me thinking.

This was Tom's Jongorrie I suddenly realized, there was just no other explanation for it and I had heard Tom complain enough to recognize the temper of the little man. With that thought I wondered what he had to do with any of this. It just didn't make sense. Tom had complained at length about his Jongorrie, how he was a little pest at times and how much he often annoyed Tom but he had his uses I knew.

"Hold up will you!" I called to him as he meandered down the track in his odd gait. "I'm coming but my head is aching like the buggery."

"Well take a pain pill… a pill will be good. They are good pills I hear, take two or… or even three. If we go to the Karadji's place you can get them… and your Serpent Killer… gotta get that. Hurry. Hurry will ya."

Following the strange little man along the track, trying to pace up with him I was amazed at how fast the little guy could move. He was determined as he muttered to himself and at least I was warming up in the effort with trying to keep up with him. My head throbbed mercilessly however and I decided the first thing I would do, would be to take a pain killer.

It wasn't long before we reached the lower entrance to the house and while the Jongorrie fidgeted he moved stealthily into the night-shadow of the building against the wall that was veiled from easy view.

"You go… you go in. I will… will watch out here just in case anyone comes. Just in case." He whispered, though there was a certain fear in his eyes and I wondered just what he was afraid of.

Maybe he really was afraid of Taipan for reasons I couldn't fathom. I had considered waking Taipan as we moved along the track; despite what the little man had said now though I decided that maybe I shouldn't.

I left him and slipped through the lower doors. Once in my room I stripped off my wet gear and searched around for some jeans, then took the pills I found in the small en-suite off the room.

Ratting through my pack I found the whip and my knife along with a small torch, remembering the strange sticks I had used to light my way in the caverns before. I wasn't going to rely on the Jongorrie. He would be able to see well in the dark I was sure, unlike me.

Coming across the Kadaitcha's belt in my search I decided to quickly fix that around my hips and settled my tools into their holds, winding the Serpent Killer about my shoulder securely as Big Jim had taught me.

The little Jongorrie man had said I would need it and I was going to take him at his word. I just wished for a moment that Tom or Big Jim were here to head out with me. Once again I considered waking Taipan, then decided again not to.

The Jongorrie had to have a reason not to want to take him and I had to respect that if I was going to have any chance of finding Kirri. Hopefully before the dawn or before anyone worked out she wasn't back or even before anyone had missed her at all, or missed us both.

The Jongorrie made his way up the side of the mountain and he really did seem to know where he was going. As I followed him along the overgrown track, I wondered if there was an entrance into the caverns up here. I hadn't ever heard of one but then there were a lot of things I hadn't heard of either.

Keeping up with him was a challenge as he could move swiftly about the tangle of the damp sub-tropic forest. He kept looking back at me impatiently, mumbling something that didn't sound very respectful so I was glad I couldn't make out what it was. I felt like an elephant following a mouse and I think he thought that too, for all that I had been trained to move quietly through the bush.

I was buggered when we finally reached a rock overhang, one that blocked our way as it clung to the steep hillside. It looked to be settled into a precarious hold but it was soundly bedded I discovered. The Jongorrie easily slipped down towards its lower point and ducked under the hard overhang where the earth had fallen away over an eon.

As I scrambled to follow him I noticed foot scrapings and tracks, which had been left behind. It was obviously where someone had struggled and seeing my attention the Jongorrie scrambled back up out of the gloom to check out what was holding me up. I was left with the distinct impression he was not at all pleased to see the evidence of so many footprints before him. Reaching for a tangled branch he pulled it from the bush and then swept the ground around annoyed as he worked concealing the prints, flicking forest floor litter about.

"Careless... careless. Someone should say... they should say I think."

"What?"

Impatiently he looked at me. "The Caverns... the cave entrances are secret things. They know... they're careless. Afraid they are... they must know you will follow. They must, they're hurrying 'cause they know. They're afraid of someone or something. Too afraid to take the time as they should. They know they should!"

Following him as he continued to mumble once he had finished with concealing the tracks, I moved into the tight crawl space. I was amazed when I was able to half slide; half climb down into the space. It opened up into a blow cave, one carved by the winds and sand, and then it went deeper on into the dimness that flowed down into the darkness of the earthen slide.

The Jongorrie kept muttering to himself as he descended ahead of me and I decided they weren't the only ones afraid of something. He too was not happy but he was also impatient as he kept glancing back at me as though to make sure that I was still there.

I flicked on the torch when I was no longer able to see the little man and he grumbled more. Shooting me impatient glances, adding a sprint to his step, he shifted ahead mumbling about me being blind as a bat... but nowhere near as smart. I was able to follow him even though he broke ahead often but he did seem to wait for me and then scoot ahead again.

Many of the passages were tight, while some were cavernous and it was in these caverns that I suspected there were others about. Other strange little people and I decided that they were his people that I saw in the shadows.

Some taller than others, some smaller and misshapen in odd ways but they seem to be gathering, staying well ahead or behind, as though they were avoiding me. I was hard pressed to keep up with the movement around me but that some of the little people carried dull lights helped. I found myself often blinded by pockets of darkness however and this left me stumbling regularly, relying on sound to follow the others.

The Jongorrie complained when I flicked the torch to life so I avoided turning it on as much as possible. It wasn't easy to keep up though.

Within half an hour we had descended into a well trodden passage where a light moss or fungus like growth clung to the ceiling and it was this that gave off a strange blue-green luminance. It seemed to feed from the seepage and it was here that the Jongorrie slowed his race.

"We can rest here... rest for a bit. Just a bit while we wait for the others?"

He had stopped to reassure me. His mood had lightened and he was almost mollifying me which seemed rather strange in the circumstances.

"Who else is coming?" I asked, battling to keep the weariness from my voice as I eased myself down, grateful we had at last stopped. I was carefully watching for the strange slight movements I could see. Aware that there were others in this cavern that shuffled about and had moved around us silently when we had arrived.

It seemed that I was in a bed of Jongorrie and I wasn't sure if I was welcome here so I shifted to where my back was against the wall, trying to ease my strained muscles. I was sore from the climb down that had taken forever and which had taxed every muscle in my legs. My arms had also taken a beating against the walls where I had been unable to see clearly.

I was weary now beyond words but the worry of losing Kirri kept me awake. I worried about where she might have been taken to, or what was happening to her even now. I was worried also about where I was and wondering if I was ever going to get out of here. If the Jongorrie deserted me I doubted seriously that I could ever have made my way out of these caves and it was a sobering thought.

"The Jongorrie are out and about." The strange little man continued as he shifted back in closer. "We are looking for the woman, the one you lost," he added impatiently and I heard the murmur of others about us in the dark recesses. I didn't care much at this point as I was just too exhausted, but the Jongorrie went on.

"We saw them we did, saw that they were going out, up to the Edgelands and they weren't supposed to. It is too early it is ... too early for the Oruncha to be out and about. There was sumthin' up. Sumthin' up there was. I knew it... could feel it in me bones."

"What were you doing here anyways?" I asked distracted for the moment though it was hard holding it together.

"Looking out for the little one, checking up on the women, helping the Kadaitcha... too much to do... way to much. It is wot Tom has me do. Wot I do lots... He's that age ya' know... women... He's one for the women ... he is ... he is."

Closing my eyes for just a minute I took a grip on the Serpent Killer still wound about my shoulder and wondered if I would be expected to use it, reassuring myself that maybe not so much now. Just for a minute I told myself this as I tried to ease the ache still in my head and the tightness of the muscles of my legs. Ease it to a silence and a welcome stillness.

When I woke it was still dark and my eyes adjusted quickly to the strange half-light, but it had been the soft muted chatter that had disturbed me. For the moment I was still as I looked about frowning trying to recollect where I was and what it was that had bought me here.

It wasn't at all cold here. The air was quite warm if somewhat dry and I could see the movement of maybe a dozen little people, the Jongorrie I realized. They had their women here too, women and children settled in small tangled heaps of sleeping kids while others moved about. Some were picking at and eating the small cavern bats, which they held by their wings stretched over a low, smouldering flame. Others were talking in a slow murmur, a babble I couldn't understand.

What struck me the most was that each little person, in their own way was marked by a strange luminescent glow in their hair. It danced when they moved, fired and faded making their locks seem alive and it was the weirdest thing I had ever seen.

When I shifted, Tom's Jongorrie looked up. He seemed busy at something, eating it seemed. Then seeing I was awake he shuffled over and offered me a soft root of some kind. It was an odd colour and he obviously thought I should eat it as I took it from his hands reluctantly.

"There eat, you need y'r strength. I got you this special... I did. I wasna' gone long."

Taking the strange root vegetable I sniffed at it as I watched his hair, it too glowed softly and wondered at it as I bit into the soft baked root. It was a taro of some kind, an odd colour but maybe that was the light. The food was warm and it tasted good none the less, so sitting up more I bit into it again grateful as he also handed me a container of tepid water.

Others looked over but no one stirred or fled. They seemed strangely settled now with me about and as my eyes adjusted I looked across at the Jongorrie with a question I was about to voice.

"Yes... yes they have decided you're 'armless... It took some tellin'... took some talking I can tell ya but it's fine. It's all fine now. They will fix you up in a minute... fix you up they will."

"Kirri?"

"Yes. The 'ave her they do. Down in the caverns, not too far from here she is. Not too far at all. It is where I thought she would be, where she can stay an not be hurt."

"Why? I don't understand why?"

Impatient once more the Jongorrie sat back in frustration. "Not smart... not smart at all. Don't you know anything?"

I shrugged. "She is a friend. But why would the Oruncha take her...?"

"There are them that don't want the Inlanders mixing in the Edgelands at all... not at all. They see a weakness, a problem that isn't there, not there at all. This is a different business... different. So they want to draw her into their ways, the old ways. But it wasn't to have been. Many of the old ways are not needed anymore, it is different and they don't see it... don't see it they don't. They stay to the histories, some do... they don't want you to mix."

"They don't want her on the surface?"

"No. No... not at all. They like to keep things separate... apart. Too much mixing is seen as not good... not good for anyone. They 'ave destroyed whole peoples... whole places when there is mixing. Some 'ave, they 'ave."

I sat back and considered what he said. "She said that she had been told not to speak of the Inland. Don't they know that?"

The Jongorrie quickly shook his head and glanced across at me. "They don't know these things. Don't understand that it's not you. They don't understand that things are different... and it is dangerous for her. Dangerous!"

"Dangerous? But what has it to do with me?"

"Yes. It's not you she is here for. You are not for her... not at all. They want to make her a Iyawo..."

"A what?"

Frustrated he looked across at me. "A woman for the Oricha. You are stupid... stupid! Fancy thinking she was for you!"

"What me and Kirri. There is no me and Kirri! Who are these guys anyway...? The Oricha? Never heard of 'em." I protested.

"They are men of the caverns, special men... men like no other. Like... like Shaman of the caverns. Only they are... they are very Clever Men, men of the Kadaitcha Lore. Men who know the worlds, know these things they know. The Shaman of the Oruncha Men they are."

"So they are the Oruncha?"

"Yes, and no. They are and they aren't... they can be of many things. The Oruncha should be told though... they should be. That is it." He agreed suddenly as though this would settle everything.

Still confused I shook my head, it made little sense this running monologue the Jongorrie often spoke in. "So what do we do?"

"Hmm... we need a plan. A plan to get her back is what we need. Get 'er back before they give her to someone who she's not meant for." With that the Jongorrie shifted quickly and headed over towards the others. He obviously had some intent as I watched him sit down with the small men gathered not far from me. Leaving me to get on with finishing the taro as I watched on silently.

A small woman arrived quietly carrying a bowl and looking up I wondered if I was supposed to drink it. Though when she set it down beside me I followed her carefully with my eyes. She just smiled and bent to wet her hands in the foul looking water. Then taking up the bowl she began to scoop the liquid spilling it into my hair as I made a move to jerk away, frightening her.

Standing still, as still as the rocks in body, her fingers were dancing as though in protest. She then glanced quickly across at Tom's Jongorrie when she realized I didn't understand her. Restlessly he climbed back to his feet and shuffled over impatiently.

"Sit still… sit still will ya'. The woman needs to fix your hair, fix it she does and you should sit still… be respectful."

"What is she doing?"

"She is to prepare your hair, prepare it for the fire water… so you can see, so we all can see. You're a strange one you are… can't feel you… can't feel you. You're like a shadow, not real at all. A strange creature to us, strange … You are not like an Edgelander at all and it is dark in the caverns… dark. Wot did you think?" The strange little man demanded.

With that the Jongorrie shook his head and his hair seemed to flame with the firelight tangled in his greasy locks. Leaving me to frown in wonder as he impatiently signalled her to continue.

So I sat still as she drench my hair in a mix of what looked to be oil and water with some type of herb or gritty clay mixed through it. Once that was done she left me for a while and intrigued I ran my fingers through my hair. There was no luminance like the others had and I didn't understand. Perhaps I needed to wait I thought.

Climbing to my feet I carefully made my way over to the circle of men who the Jongorrie sat with, settling myself amongst them as though I really belonged there. None challenged me, though their glances were impatient.

I was becoming accustomed to this impatience of the Jongorrie though I couldn't understand anything they mumbled. I realized that they often spoke in the strange silent finger language that I had seen before in the caverns with Kirri when I had first met her.

It was a swift and torrid exchange I came to recognize as their fingers flicked and danced and their glances gave way to the knowledge in their eyes. They were discussing me and I would have loved to understand what it was they said to each other.

While I sat amongst them silent, watching patiently, another small woman came over with a gourd in her hands and gently began to pour what seemed to be a soft, glowing ooze that had a gentle yellowish glow. Working it through my hair she streaked it through carefully. It was cool and soothing and the men looked on with approval.

"The fire water will help... help us all it will. Leave it." The Jongorrie warned as I stretched my fingers to touch the water now dripping through my greasy locks. "Don't put it in your mouth, don't drink it will ya. It is not good to drink." Then reaching for a bowl of what I understood was warm tea he offered it to me. "Here drink this, it will help. It is a special drink... a special plant it is. One that will guard you from the fire sickness."

"What is it?" I asked, my eyes pointing out the strange luminescence in the heads of those all about us.

"Fire water... it is good for the darkest caverns, the dark places where the Oruncha are. The oil in your hair will feed the firewater and help it to grow, to light the caverns. It is a good... a good thing."

It only took perhaps half an hour before I realized my hair was as aglow, as were the other heads about me. It was an odd comfort the strange luminance dancing as you moved your head.

You knew immediately where everyone was and it seemed to light the caverns as we set off to move through them. It was a soft light this strange luminescent algae that was now living in my hair. Unlike the much-hated torch that the Jongorrie had at first complained about, but which I still kept tucked into my belt just in case.

The thought of becoming separated from the group was horrific. Though I became more confident as I followed the small heads and the path of the men ahead of me, having left the women and children behind.

They stepped quietly through their own world and once more it was I who felt I moved way too noisily. I was unaccustomed to moving across scree and scraping between fissures of rock that they could fit through easily. We moved as a group deeper into the caverns, every sound amplified and echoing, bouncing off the walls around us.

I noticed at once the growing restlessness amongst the half dozen or so Jongorrie men as they started to flick their fingers signalling between each other. Their steps were eerily quiet and their hand signals flying between them as they slowed their pace.

I could do no other than to follow what they were doing as they approached a dark crawl space raised above the floor of the cavern we were in. The Jongorrie signalled me to move ahead of them so that I could see. Others were laying flat up near the crawl space peering into the darkness ahead. It was a small tight crawl space and they indicated silently when I joined them, that the Oruncha were gathered in the cavern beyond.

I climbed up and had barely enough time to see the men below when the little man behind me nudged me to move. I immediately moved to the side so that the others could crawl up to see as well. Without a word we were shown what our quarry was in this manner and with a silent assent.

Into the darkness below in the wide space you could easily see the movement of what were taller men in the deep cavern below. They too had a luminescence in their hair but it extended across their bodies, their skin was covered in body hair that curled strongly on many of them. They also moved about oddly. Some moved with an apparent difficult gait as I watched, while others seemed more subtle in their movements.

It was obvious that some were of a great age, perhaps Elders amongst them. They wore a ceremonial clay streaked through their body hair in strong lineal designs making them seem much whiter than they really were and they were busy making sure that each of them were fittingly decorated in the cloaking white clay as though for ceremony.

The elders preferred to remain seated quietly as they settled around the central pool attended by others. The pool was a source of much stronger greenish light, one that lit the cavern and I could see they were preparing a food of some sort.

It was then that I caught sight of Kirri, she was curled into a corner sitting on what looked to be some type of matted fibre and the sight of her fired a need for action through me. She looked terrified, hiding her head as she was in the comfort of her arms, curled tightly into a ball with her legs drawn up defensively.

It was as though she didn't want to look upon the men as they moved about her, or perhaps she couldn't move. Perhaps she was semiconscious I wondered as she didn't move at all. Perhaps she slept as I had slept and I looked down at Tom's Jongorrie below me as he nodded strangely as though in answer to my silent curiosity.

Then he spoke up softly. "They have given her something, she likely can't hear you... or maybe... maybe not even see you."

"What will they do?" I whispered back.

The Jongorrie shrugged. "We don't know... it has been a long time... a long, long time since this ceremony has been done. They prepare her for the Oricha."

Sliding carefully down the slight slope of the crawl space I sat before the Jongorrie. "What is this ceremony?" I demanded.

"I told you... I told you I did. You didn't listen!" he accused impatiently.

"Stuff that! Just bloody tell me again!"

Glaring across at me as though I was a halfwit the Jongorrie sighed deeply. "They prepare her... prepare her... and bind her to the Lore. In the old way they want to bind her. Do you hear... do you hear that, stupid man"!

"Dammit! What does that mean though?"

"They will give her only to an Oricha man. They will make it so that no other will come near. It is the Lore. He has been chosen and it is not you!"

I shook my head simply not understanding what he meant. "You mean she is gunna be given to some bloke. Just like that! She has no say?"

"She will decide... she decides but in this way they make the decision easier for her. She will only be his... bound to him... and if ... she decides not to be bound then no one else will go near her... she will belong to the Oruncha then. No-one else..."

"Bloody hell! We gotta get her out of there then... they can't do that. She can't stay here, not here with them. It isn't her world, not her place!"

Turning back to the crawl hole impatiently and with some urgency I stretched to see what they were doing, ignoring those behind me as I heard them scramble about growing excited, strangely enough.

Pulling at the Serpent Killer wound about my shoulders I braced it in my hand and tested the subtleness of the whips weave as my mind searched for a plan, a way to get Kirri out.

I couldn't see much for it but to do as Big Jim had suggested so many times. I needed to scare the shit out of them but it seems such an unlikely thing to me in that moment. I had my knife but I didn't fancy a blood bath and I knew it was not our way. Plus, I wasn't sure I was up to taking on the half a dozen or so men down in the cavern.

Some of them were quite old; most would be quite slow I decided except for maybe two... or three of them, they looked mostly like Elders. I heard the Jongorrie scramble up beside me and settle strangely close as though to share a confidence.

"You do it... it is for you to do. They are mostly blind I know, and now you know... You know... I have heard that they can't feel you nearby and it's true ... true it is 'cause we can't. We can't feel you at all. That could scare them you know... not feeling you nearby, like we can't feel you near but only seeing you and not knowing... not knowing what you are."

"Really?" I was surprised that I had forgotten that, and now I could see how it was the very thing I could use against them. As I turned it over in my head, assessing the mangled old men below me I grew more confident.

The Skystone was still on my finger and I doubted if the Jongorrie would know of it but then... I looked across at him. He knew something, he saw me but could not sense me as other than a part of his natural world. Maybe, just maybe though he had heard something from Tom or Taipan? Maybe to these strange little cavern people I was just a shadow in their world.

I didn't have time for this though. It was a sudden thing when I clearly saw what was needed and there was no time for grappling with it in my thoughts.

Gripping the Serpent Killer I scrambled up further into the tight crawl space and then on a thought I pushed my way through it, dropping and sliding suddenly. Slipping down the rubble onto the cave floor, landing with a stumble as I fell awkwardly to my knees near to the group gathered in the cave below.

Fighting for balance I stepped up quickly and braced myself into a crouch for a fight. My stance was deliberately aggressive and I faced whomever I thought was the quickest and the more powerful of the men amongst them.

It was a second before I remembered to flick the whip before me and it was two or so flicks before I got it to snap loudly in the confines of the cavern. The men were already fighting to their feet in surprise when the whip finally cracked heavily and they had scrambled back warily at my first attempts.

They said nothing, a few grumbles and a defensive stance amongst some but mostly they moved back with their fingers flying in that silent talk, realizing I was there now, challenging them.

Again I flicked the Serpent Killer aiming it towards the strongest of these strange Oruncha Men and hearing a satisfying crack of anger I then tossed my glance towards Kirri.

"Kirri!" I yelled into the deafening silence as my glance flashed between the others.

The sound of my voice echoed loudly through the cavern and it was followed by the disturbed murmur of the men. "Get up!" I yelled again.

Kirri lifted her head and seemed to sway with the movement. Realizing that she appeared to be drugged and out to it, I began to move my way in a high dance step towards her. Flicking the whip and winding it quickly back behind me into another angry cracking coil with each step.

I had to move fast, move before my impetuousness died within the grip of a fear that I had a need to control. Shifting towards her more quickly, I realized that she too had the strange luminescent goo through her hair. Only her hair was also streaked with red clay as well ... tangled in heavier coils and not as oily and loose as mine.

It was a second before I reached her but it wasn't until I laid my hands upon her that the murmur of the men really stepped up. One of them moved as though to stop me but I thwarted him with a loud bellow, flicking the whip angrily in his direction. It made him freeze and crouch warily as though he didn't know what I was.

"Stop! Stop right there!" I roared as I flicked the serpent killer menacingly and wished in that moment that the bloody Jongorrie would get their arses down here, but it seemed this was going to be left to me.

"Shit!" I mumbled as I carelessly pulled Kirri up with my free hand, gripping her arm tightly as she shifted with a lazy, confused compliance. My eyes searched the cave about me for something... anything that would provide an exit.

I knew Kirri would never make it up to the crawl space and I realized I should have figured this part out first. It was then however when I saw the Jongorrie emerge from a smallish crevasse in the wall, one of the many dark lines of shadow and I felt a sense of relief.

If we were gunna get out of here it had to be now... speed and confusion were what I needed about me. As the small group of Jongorrie moved warily towards me I wrenched at Kirri, almost throwing her towards the few of them now gathered in the dimness.

Again I flicked the whip into a dance about me with all the momentum I could draw from my shoulders and arms. The Oruncha Men moved as though in stealth, a slow and wary step as the Jongorrie approached Kirri, where she now lay sprawled on the floor of the cavern between us.

It was a wicked and rapid dance I stepped, all the more threatening when I grabbed at my knife and held it at any of the Oruncha who even looked as though they would move towards us. I bellowed with the crack of the whiptail snapping savagely then I saw out of the corner of my eye, Kirri and the Jongorrie scramble off towards the deep crack in the wall.

I kept it up, aiming at those who moved in any way towards the retreating figures. I was almost enjoying the dance of my feet beating against the ground while I watched those about me move back and stumble in the dimness while they made louder their protest.

The crack of the whip echoed and bit about the walls and the strain of maintaining the dance of the serpent killer stretched through my body.

Suddenly I stopped, taking a moment. I was breathless as I stretched for a renewed strength. I wove the whip about menacingly still growling with each reach for air. When I knew the last of the Jongorrie had slipped through the deep crack in the rock I swung suddenly to retreat.

Without much pause I shot off after them bellowing in the hope that the confusion of movement and sound would thwart them. Not wanting to hang back unless one or more of the Oruncha Men challenged me.

I didn't look back, I didn't need to as I cannoned into Kirri inside the narrow cavern while two of the little men tried to drag her along. She was groggy, sloppy footed and weeping in a quiet painful way as I grabbed at her. Pulling her up against me I began to half run, half drag her along.

The Jongorrie ahead of us scattered as some ducked down different paths, taking different tunnels and I realized that they had a plan of their own. Kirri was clutching at me; she was struggling to keep up and fighting to keep a sure footing. I tried to stay tightly behind Tom's Jongorrie but it was difficult with so much scrambling going on around us.

It was as though the Jongorrie knew what he was doing and I realized if the Oruncha were following us they would be unsure of which path to take. It was a good plan and for the first time I recognized the wisdom of having so many with us.

Kirri faltered but I kept dragging her along, trying to quietly reassure and encourage her as she stumbled and the Jongorrie grew impatient.

"Carry her! Can't ya' carry her!" he demanded savagely. "Big enough you are, or can't ya?"

"Geezus, I'm not super man. Just shut up an' move before they get here."

It was a wild scramble that seemed to last forever and as I dragged Kirri along. Fighting with her lack of sensibility I wondered how long it would be before we reached far enough along the deepness of the caverns to be safe.

Kirri was able to crawl, able to scramble when I faltered but she gripped at me looking for support. The small sounds of terror in her breathing and voice kept me moving. Dragging her, I half carried her when her steps faltered, as giddy as she seemed to be at times.

It seemed like an hour before the Jongorrie slowed. Then at last he finally stopped, leaning up against the rock while we all reached for breath. I couldn't have gone much further and it was a relief to settle Kirri up against the cavern wall for a moment, though she slipped down exhausted to sit against the earth with her weight resting as though it was simply too much to hold herself up.

After a minute reaching for breath I dropped down beside her. We all strained to listen to any sounds or movement in the caverns and paths around us. All was quiet, or as reassuringly still as it should have been.

"How are you feeling?" I whispered gently pulling her to face towards me with my fingers so that I could more easily see for myself while I checked her eyes, her breathing. Looking for anything that could be found about her in this dimness.

"Jeremy... Oh Jeremy. Thank you... I didn't know... I was so scared." Her words were a frightened whisper in the dimness. She looked so strange, struggling to speak lucidly. I could see her fighting with her senses trying desperately to understand what was happening about her.

The Jongorrie moved up beside me after a short time and fingered her hair carefully. It was a rich red ochre colour that seemed tacky from what could be seen. The luminance from our hair, which lit the caverns softly about our faces, was much duller in hers than ours. The light of her hair strangely muted by other things. Stuff that had been mixed in with the goo they had used in her hair.

"It is blood they have mixed in her hair," he whispered and then added questioning her. "Is it yours? Did you eat?" The Jongorrie demanded this with more compassion than I had ever seen him show before.

Kirri nodded. "Just fish, it was just fish in a sort of watery stuff. I was so thirsty..."

"Tsk... no... no no no," he protested quietly, shaking his head.

"What! What was it?" I demanded.

"It is done. Done it is... there is nothing we can do."

"What do you mean nothing! Have they poisoned her?"

"No... no, no not like that. They wouldn't do that... it is why she is so bad... so slow. Does your bingie hurt... does it hurt?" Rubbing his tummy he waited for the question to reach her understanding.

Again Kirri nodded as she pressed hand carefully against her stomach.

"Sick... sick it is she needs. Put your fingers down yer throat woman." Then looking at me suddenly, impatient once more he demanded suddenly. "Down her throat. Make her sick! Do it!"

"What!"

"Do it... do it for her. Get it up and it wont be as bad... not as bad."

Horrified Kirri looked at me and then suddenly she stretched forward quickly stuffing her own fingers deep into her throat making her retched with the action of it. She kept retching until she was able to bring up some of what ever it was she had eaten and then she sat back swallowing, hopelessly despondent.

"I can't," she said as she wept softly. "There is no more. Will it kill me?"

"No. Not kill you but it will bind you. Bind you it will and it will make you sick for a time... sick as a dog."

"How... I don't understand?" she whispered as confused as I.

"It will bind you to him. Then you must decide because he too is of their world, the Oruncha. He will be as they are one day because they are men of the caverns like him. In that day... you... you haveta' decide if you want to stay too. The choice will be yours woman... yours it will be. In time the bind might weaken but until then... he too must choose and there is plenty of time... plenty of time woman. But you can make no other choice but him in the Edgelands... no other choice. It is done. It is the old way... the old way."

The Jongorrie didn't look at all perturbed by the events but to me it seems an impossible choice. One I still didn't understand as I thought of Kirri living amongst the Oruncha, deep in the caverns with one of them.

I was about to demand more when the look the Jongorrie gave me silenced me. His look was so hard, so savage and it was directed at me. But in that glance there seemed to be a satisfaction.

I decided then that the Jongorrie had other allegiances than our own and he was going to be difficult. The uncertainty of it kept me quiet, at least until I could learn more for myself. I didn't trust the strange misshapen little man and I let him know it with a hard look. There was some secret here he was keeping and I could feel it in my own bones.

"Come on... come on. We have to keep going. They are all about ... all about and we need to get out of their caverns. The Karadji will be angry by now... very angry when he finds out. I don't want to be there... not there... that is your fault!" He accused suddenly as he swung about and stepped off, his hair still aglow strangely with his movements within the dimness of the cavern space.

Looking across at Kirri I started to gather her up. She seemed to be at last recovering a bit but she was still very weak. Being much too weak to walk without my support as we stumbled along behind the Jongorrie, for the most, silent, as I tried to help her along.

It was a long and torturous trek and when we finally broke out into the daylight an age later I realized from the height of the sun that it was another day and we both flinched with the brilliance of the light. How long had it been I wondered... was this the next day or had it been twice that. I simply wasn't sure anymore how much time had passed deep in the caverns.

The Jongorrie just looked across at us as he waited for us both to gain our way into the sunlight after the slippery climb up the inner bank. Waiting for us to scramble out from beneath the tight crawl space into the light of the day.

"You take care of it! You explain to the Karadji I've got stuff to do... important stuff to do..." he mumbled stubbornly as he suddenly turned away and in a flinch he was gone.

I couldn't believe it. I just straightened and stood there astounded as

Kirri collapsed at my feet. I couldn't believe he had just off and left us the minute we emerged into daylight. However it was the quiet little hick of a sob that Kirri made which shook me from my stillness.

"Hey... hey hey. Kirri come on. It's not that bad. We're out." I whispered trying to reassure her as I bent down and she folded into my arms, nestling into my grimy shoulder exhausted. "Come on we should get cleaned up. They can't reach us here... it is over. Over!"

Shaking her head she struggled to gather herself together. "What will Taipan say... the others. We have to tell them."

"Yeah... I know. Taipan will know... he knows about this stuff. I will tell him all about it, don't worry. Look, lets just get back to Aine. She can help you I'm sure."

Rolling one of Kirri's long locks between my fingers I realized that what ever it was, the luminance in our hair that had begun to fade only slightly in the dimness of the caverns, was not evident out here. Instead our hair just felt greasy. It had dried in some part but it no longer glowed in that strange soft way.

It was just too much to take in. Too much like it was an impossible nightmare and I hoped to-god that Taipan would have an idea of what had happened to us over the long darkness deep in the underworld. I hoped that he and Aine could help Kirri, and even perhaps help me to understand what it all meant for both of us.

This was all just so improbable, so impossible to comprehend fully. Would the Oruncha ever seek her out again and what was it that they had really wanted? What was it that had really happened down there in the caverns? I didn't even understand what it was we had just escaped from.

I didn't think I even knew the half of it and I hoped that Taipan at least would have some idea. As I helped Kirri scramble down through the sub-tropic forest and back along the path towards the Karadji's home I ran the whole dark experience through my mind again.

Picking at it, recalling the fears and the things that had happened to us both I tried to find a reason, seeking a rhyme even to our experiences. I didn't understand it much at all and it became imperative that we reach Taipan. I had every faith that he would understand, hoping that he could tell me just what it all meant.

The Truth of The Oruncha

Jeremy

It was quiet as I sat across from Taipan in the bright space that was the dining area. I had slept soundly, fully exhausted and had not seen Kirri since Aine had taken her into her care when we had stumbled into the lower lounge area near on twenty-four hours ago.

The look on the faces of the others had told us how bad we had both appeared to be. Aine had let out a cry at the sight of Kirri as she had just collapsed in my hold. It had been Taipan who had gathered her up while I had found this very same chair I was sitting in now to crumple into.

I felt better, having slept like a log after demolishing the brunch Taipan had made while Andrew and he watched on. He too had been with Taipan when I had emerged from the small guest room earlier.

The concern raised in our absence had been kept amongst the three of them. They hadn't raised questions beyond enquiring in the following morning amongst some of the other kids. Though the look in Taipan's eyes had a savage edge when we had first stumbled into the house.

Andrew had known the questions to ask I realized, he knew of the dark caverns and the places of the Oruncha. Even Taipan had listened quietly as he had explained their world and their interest in Kirri to us both.

"Ty has spoken about what is going on. I think you need to understand this business, particularly if you are to keep Kirri safe, young Jeremy. We need you to do that when she gets to Sydney, at least for a time."

"Me! I don't know… don't understand it. How can I do that…? I mean I can't even keep her out of trouble. I failed miserably! How's she going anyways… is she OK?"

Taipan settled in the chair across from me, setting his drink on the table in front of him easily. "She's fine now, Aine has been with her most of the night and they're both resting now. Which is why I would like to get Kirri to Sydney as soon as we can. With our baby due soon, Aine tires easily and I can't ask her to do this again, not now. I'm sorry. And Alex is due to deliver in the coming months too so it is something we really don't need to deal with around here at the moment."

"Why Sydney though, I mean can't she go back home for a while. Surely they wouldn't mind with all that's happened?"

Taipan's look slashed across to Andrew and then back to me. "She must stay because she needs to make a decision. Sydney is the best place for that. It's far away enough from here for her to think objectively and yet we can still protect her. Kirri has come to our world to learn to understand our ways. Her husbands family has made a claim on her, it's all been arranged Jeremy."

"Her husband! Jeesus… she's just a kid!"

"Not so." Andrew interjected. "Look it is a complicated business but she is much older than any of us, much older than most anyone I know. Well in the terms of our years that is. Physically she looks young but her experience goes well beyond ours. You need to remember that."

"Older…? Like what she said you mean?" Then I thought on it. "She said something about aging slowly in the Inland. I mean… I never really believed her I guess."

Shaking my head I looked between them seeking for answers.

"Yes." Taipan agreed. "In physical terms she's a teenager, but in Inland time she is much older and ready for marriage, ready for that stage of her life and their lives… Their lives are very regulated in the Inland, very much a social order they have. It's part of living so long a time for them and it is a very different world to ours."

"Part of why she is here is to help the worlds come together." He went on, "We need to better understand each other. Her Elders believe it's time for worlds to merge in part, a quiet thing. They… well they believe that we, the Edgelanders as they know us, are destroying our world and theirs. They want to help stop that… to bring us some of their knowledge and in doing so preserve their own world. They believe that in time we'll go too far and it… it will bring us to the very edge of our survival."

Seeing that I was struggling with this Andrew jumped in. "Since your time down there, since you and Kirri met, there has been a lot happening. The Inlanders had given up on us, feeling that we were slipping away into… well a more animal state, into chaos. I think you realize that they feel we are primitive enough not to overly impact their existence aside from the damage we do to their world. But Kirri has helped them to see that there is a hope… since she met you."

"They feel that our intelligence is misguided and that there is hope, or that they can help. I can't say I agree but to help us now is important to them. They want to help us preserve our lands, as well as their own. I don't know what you said or did, but it gave her people hope and now they want to help. Where as before they had meant to leave us to our fate. But they don't know how to go about it. This is a beginning Jeremy."

"But what has all this to do with me. I mean if she is getting married to some guy…"

Again that look between them silenced me as Taipan jumped in. "That's not for certain. That can change… well we thought so but I don't know now.

We are still waiting to see...?"

"See what?"

Taipan drew a breath. "Kirri is ill. It is an illness that has been given to her and we have to find out if we can manage it. We will know once she gets through the first of the toxins."

"That soup... the fish food they gave her was toxic?"

"Yes. It's a toxin; or rather had a toxin in it and it depends on how she can deal with that. Her immune system is a little different to ours. The Kadaitcha are looking for a cure, or something that can manage it."

"But why... why would the Oruncha do that?"

Ty drew another deep breath, though his look was steady and deep. "Because it binds her... it will bind her to her husband. It's the old way and we thought that it was unnecessary but in the old Lore such a thing would bind her to... to the Shaman chosen for her. The Oruncha follow a Lore that has amongst them a higher order, that of the Oricha or higher order Shaman of the Caverns, men of both worlds and more experienced than most in spiritual things."

"Oricha? The Jongorrie spoke of them. But how can a soup bind her to someone, it can't do that can it?"

"You have to understand that the toxin is a survival technique, one used in the caverns and the shaman chosen for her is of the caverns as well. It is a ritual or ceremony given to the men of the caverns from the Dreamtime Jeremy. It's part of an old ceremony of the Oruncha. The Oricha are like ... like a caste or an enclave group and are drawn from the Oruncha Men. Or even the Kadaitcha, a man drawn from the Featherfoot as long as they are of spiritual experience."

"We know them by many names but that is neither here nor there." Ty continued in a quiet sure voice. "Her husband would also once have had this toxin in his body in the old ways and it was seen as a sacred thing that preserved life. A thing they shared and one, which was sacred to the Shaman and would not be shared with others; None other than those who follow the Oricha or the Kadaitcha Lore. It is unique to the caverns where these Lore's are nurtured. This knowledge is not shared amongst anyone who is not from the caverns usually. Though Apari has told us of these things as we needed to know them now, so that we can help Kirri."

"But why are you telling me this, I'm not from the caverns."

"I know, but you are of the caverns. The stuff of the serpent runs through your blood since your bite. You can know these things. The Kadaitcha have trained you and continue to do so. You can be of a help to them; but that is not much in all this business. This is about Kirri and there are other things you need to know."

"Will she be OK?"

Taipan nodded and smiled. "I think so. What it is, this thing she now has is a type of ciguatera or fish poisoning. It comes from bioluminescent plankton or fire algae. It is the glow that can be in the water at times. It isn't as weird as it sounds. People around the world get ciguatera from eating infected fish particularly in the tropic regions. To the Oruncha men though it is a survival technique in the caverns and as I said, it is sacred to them as is the use of fire water in their world."

"But how can they... how can that stuff bind her to some guy?"

Taipan's smile confused me further but the manner of it gave me hope also. "The Oruncha and the Kadaitcha have a lot in common, they are the same but of different worlds. The Oruncha see Kirri as more of their world than ours. There are some things that we Edgelanders are good at and medicine is one of them. We know these things and we can manage this illness."

After a moment he went on to explain. "As Kirri will live in our world, at least for a time, the Kadaitcha feel we need to manage this thing with her. The binding business is the Lore of the caverns, not the Edgelands. We can manage this, though not with the normal range of meds. We will use a more ancient medicine. It is a tea that Kirri will become accustomed to in managing her sickness. This is what the Kadaitcha are doing now, sorting just what mix of tea or medicine to give her."

"They are here, the Kadaitcha?"

"Yes. Andrew bought them in this morning after we spoke to Kirri and worked out just what had happened."

"Is that why you want Kirri to come down to Sydney, because Tom can help? He is stronger at this than I am ... an ... an he is a full Kadaitcha initiate isn't he?"

The look Taipan gave me was the strangest of looks and Andrew sat back suddenly and grinned, crossing his arms across his chest, waiting.

"No... and yes. Kirri must choose if she wants Tom to be her husband. And Tom, he must choose the same but it is not something we want Tom to know yet. I have been in his position and it is not time yet for him to know that his Grandfather has arranged a woman for him. That time will come soon enough when he is more open to it."

My jaw dropped and the silence in the room was palpable. I was astounded as I realized that it was Tom who Kirri was to be given too. He too was a shaman from the caverns and I had not seen it fully. It was he who had been chosen for Kirri. Tom...! Shit!

"But why? I mean why Tom! I was thinking some creepy guy from the Oruncha or... or even the Kadaitcha but Tom!"

His elder brother just nodded before he continued. "Apari, his grandfather has arranged this thing for him as he feels it's the best way. Tom is... well, Tom is Tom. He needs a strong hand in his life, a strong woman and Kirri is this. He is strong headed and God knows constantly he is in strife. Even now as we speak he is deep into something that is causing dissension in everyone's life, mainly from choices he has made. He can't control himself sometimes I think."

Taipan shook his head and the laughter in his eyes took the sting from his words as he continued. "That boy...! That man is a handful and yet he is who many pin a future on. He has a way... and he has been chosen for whatever reason. Kirri can guide him in the choices he will face in his life. Kirri will be the tempering influence over him. But because he is who and what he is, she will need her wits about her. However this is... all that business is for the future. For now we need to lead him to accept what the Kadaitcha hope for him and he has to make the choices in regards to his future. The Kadaitcha know these things, they can see into what is life. Kirri too can sense these things, she has this gift that will help Tom."

"A gift? What?"

"She can sense the future and that is something which Tom needs to guide him. Tom's senses lay mainly with the past and the past can have too greater influence on him."

Astounded I looked across at the two older men, these two men in my life who had guided me and were helping me become a man.

Andrew cut in suddenly, unexpectedly as I grappled with the things I was being told. "Tom has known a few women in his life Jeremy and each was chosen for a reason. Even Alex." At my surprise, Andrew shrugged and nodded in agreement with my thoughts, my shock. "Yes, my Alex. And I will not give her back to Tom, which is why I have helped in this. Why I will fight to see it succeed. Kirri has been chosen now, over Alex as they both have a similar gift; that of the sight of women and Kirri is a much better choice. She also understands many things in Tom's life that Alex will never understand. She is a much better choice for him. And Alex is a much better choice for me." He finished softly with a certainty in his tone that you couldn't dismiss.

"This... this is just bloody amazing! Does Tom know all this?"

Taipan shook his head. "No. It's not time yet, but he will know these things when Apari decides it is time. For the moment we just have to manage Kirri's health and then Tom will be told when he's ready. He isn't expecting a woman but Apari has made this decision for him and it isn't the time right now, just yet."

"Tomorrow Andrew will run you back down to Sydney as planned and Kirri will stay here for a little longer, until she's recovered. As I said, Tom is knee deep in something else and Apari tells me it needs to be resolved and that you are needed down there to help him. There is a ceremony afoot which you're needed to be a part of. Big Jim can't manage this one on his own. It is an important ceremony for Tom."

"Big Jim knows what has happened."

"Yes. I spoke to him last night and he bought us up to date on Tom's antics. The Kadaitcha are planning something in Sydney and are on the hunt with all that has happened. You are both to be part of this. I believe the Djaranin, the death dogs are restless and also on the hunt again. Something is seriously afoot down there, although Apari has asked that we not intrude. It's Kadaitcha business and it is a dangerous business."

I shook my head astounded, remembering the dark dogs all too readily. I wondered what had happened or what had been going on while I had been dealing with Kirri in the caverns.

"Have you heard Toms in hospital?" Andrew suddenly cut in.

Surprised, I shook my head.

"Yep. Seems he got himself beaten up in town over the weekend. You met his Jongorrie, from what Kirri has said. I take it that it was Jep you were with? Apari said he was with you both at times and I hear that he has been mighty vocal about the demands that have been placed on him."

"What was his name ... the one you just used?" I cut in curious having missed the reference.

"Jep. Least that's what we call him. Apari has sent him down to Sydney to be with Tom. He has been a very busy little man by all accounts, between you and Tom he has been on the wind a lot. He won't be happy about being called away from Tom so much. But I suppose with Kirri in trouble he had no choice. Apari probably stepped in about that."

"He is a rude little shit that Jongorrie!" I said softly.

"That he may be. But without him, Tom's life would be near impossible though I don't think Tom appreciates him that much yet. It's a good thing Kirri has come to know the Jongorrie. She will know when he is about now that she too is bound to the caverns in all this."

I shook my head still astounded. "I can't believe all this has gone on. Tom...? He's never gunna get it all."

"He will." Taipan reassured me. "Just don't tell him yet of Kirri. I mean not that it is hoped that she will be his wife. It is the business of the

Kadaitcha and his Grandfather. You don't want to be upsetting the fire there. You can guide Tom but you can't lead him. It is for Kirri to win her place in his life and she understands that. Once she has decided then it will be for her to take care of what is... well, women's business. As women do in their own way."

I nodded astounded at what I had been told. As I thought of Tom, of Kelly and of Kirri, I wondered somewhat confused at what was going to come of all this. I questioned myself also if I should tell Taipan of Kelly even, but then decided that perhaps it should be left to the fates. I still wasn't so happy about the whole Kelly and Tom situation anyway.

I caught up with my mum and other friends later that afternoon saying little about my experiences of the last few days. I felt that there was a certain disconnect in all this and I realized that I had grown beyond the Community. I knew then that I had already really left home in my mind and it had taken coming back to the community to discover it.

Yet I knew that it was I who had changed, others were mostly the same. While it was good to see everyone they were very much a part of community life. The seemingly trivial realities of friendships, fights and the many things that made up life in the place where I had grown up, seemed nonsensical and unimportant to me now. It left me wondering exactly where my place was to be found.

Returning to Taipan's later that evening I was deep in thought about what my future would be and just where it might take me. When I approached the tall bush house I saw Kirri sitting very still on a small grass patch, seemingly also deep in reflection. She sat carefully watching the darkness of the night skies with an odd expression on her face.

She looked strangely lonely, a part of the stillness of the night. Her skin almost luminescent against the dark shadows running along the ground she sat on. A sole figure in this world I thought and this was probably how she felt. Her light coloured hair hung restless down her back, sweeping around her now. I wasn't accustomed to seeing it loose as she had always contained it in some way but now it cloaked her, hiding her from the darkness of the night it seemed.

Wandering over to where she sat I joined her quietly on the grass, greeting her as easily as she had watched my approach, even though I was conscious of breaking into her silent reverie.

"Taipan said you were ill... how are you going now?" My softly spoken words flipped about us, enveloping us strangely.

"Much better, though I feel sore all over but I've stopped being sick since Aine gave me a tea, which seems to have settled my stomach."

"Was it very bad?"

Kirri made a squint of her face, reflecting her opinion and then shook her head. "Not as bad as that soup stuff I had, that was really awful but I was so thirsty. I wish I hadn't drunk it now."

Looking up into the brilliance of the heavens above Kirri sighed, as though weary and lost in her thoughts.

"What is it?"

"The sky," she said softly. "I just can't get used to it, it is like it is falling in on me somehow or maybe I am falling into it. It is the vastness of it."

I grinned on the thought, remembering a lot of what she had told me of her world and the place she called the Domina's. "Yeah ... I guess it must seem strange to you being underground and all. It is pretty awesome though don't you think."

"Awesome? That is a strange way to think of it. It is just so huge ... so empty. Like there is nothing overhead, nothing is... is contained. Doesn't that scare you?"

"No, not at all. Why would it?"

Again she shook her head. "It scares me. I get a sense of falling into it and that is really strange for me."

"There must be a lot that is strange, stuff you have to get used to?"

"Yes. There is, but Aine is helping in that way."

For a moment I wondered if I should say what was skating around my thoughts and then I suddenly made a decision. If she was coming down to Sydney, then it would help to know how she felt.

"Taipan told me about your marriage, about your husband and all. You could have told me."

Kirri looked at me strangely. "About my husband Ariaka? The one they have chosen for me. Aine told me they were sending for you because you were close to him and you would be able to help me in this."

"Yeah that's him."

"You are both companions I realize, but..." she shook her head as though confused. "This business is not something between you and I, is it? So I couldn't say really. It is still to be decided and I wasn't sure."

"Well no... I guess not but ... well if you are coming to Sydney then maybe it is. I mean Ariaka... Tom, he is a good mate and I wouldn't want to see him hurt or angry."

Pausing a moment she said softly. "His Grandfather said he was a good mate for me. I didn't know that it was like this for you also, do you mind?"

I was arrested by the question in her eyes and then it dawned on me what she was asking. "Geezus no! I mean it isn't like we ... he and I aren't like mates like that. No... we're friends! Friends like mates... we just ... I mean friends!"

"But you said mates? Is it not like this for you and he."

"Yes... but not that way. I mean no! Mates ... that is friends here, that is what I meant." I protested seriously.

"Oh. I thought you meant..."

"No! Geezus no." Chuckling, still shocked I shook my head denying the question lingering in her eyes. "Mates is just friends here, it doesn't mean mating or anything like that. Just friends! Good friends. Not like girls and him... not that way..."

"Oh. I see now." Her smile was somewhat amused and strangely relieved. "Our people are different, they have different ways and I have learnt this much. I can see your way is different from where I come from."

"Is it that different?" I asked curious.

"Yes. We live together in different ways even. Women live together and there are also communities for men, but we have those who live with their partners. Our families are more diverse. I don't think I really understand your way yet but I want to learn."

"Isn't that like us, now?"

"It is different, in many small ways. I wonder what my husband will be like. If he will understand."

"He will I think, If you explain to him what you need or... or think.

"What is he like then? Can you tell me something about him?"

"He's a good m... friend!" I grinned errantly. "I mean he likes women, gets on well with them really. Too well sometimes I think." I shrugged, "What can I say? He is a good bloke... he's fair."

Kirri just smiled again and looked back up at the stars almost reverently and it was some moments before she continued. "This is not like the Domilands at all. It is so different here. We can't see the stars at all, we have none but we don't have the night either. This is the time when so many things hunt here on the Edgelands I think. They must wait for the darkness or maybe they wouldn't catch much food otherwise. The dark is a dangerous time I can see that now. Once I thought it was the safest time but it isn't, is it?"

"I think it has more to do with the heat of the day with the animals, not the dark. It is hard to run fast and work hard in the midday heat across most of Australia. Yeah ... I guess you could say night was a more dangerous time though."

"I'm accustomed to the heat, but it is a different heat here. It is moist all the time where I live, but we get the winds with the current shifts. Aine told me of your storms. They are far worse than ours. I haven't yet seen one of your storms, not like the ones which Aine spoke about."

"You get storms in the Inland?"

"Yes, electrical storms but they are mostly high in the Domina and they are more like electrical sheets. They are wonderful to see. Though they never arc to the ground like Aine said lightening does here. I think I would like to see that. Is that where your love of fire comes from? It would start fires I am sure."

"Yeah the lightning starts fires all the time. You'll have to wait for summer, the summer storms are great and they aren't too far off. We get them around Christmas."

"Christmas? What is that?"

"Oh… kinda when we give each other presents, the end of the year. We celebrate Jesus's birth I think, sorta like a birthday party."

"Really? Who was he?"

"Geez… umm… some prophet or son of God or something. They have one in each religion I think… like a prophet or something."

"Why?"

I laughed, not really sure how to answer. "I don't know. It's a churches thing. It's OK… it can be a lot of fun too."

"Oh… You have some strange customs I think. In our beliefs we are all people alike and we celebrate our world and what governs us."

"You don't have Christmas then?"

"No. We celebrate our harvest and that is our fun time. It goes on until we have our harvest complete after the growing season. Some harvest fruits, others harvest from the water and so on. We all have different times for our harvest feasts and preparing the food for the time until the next harvest. I love that time, and you can work in different harvests if you want. Everyone is involved in the season in some way, it is part of being in our communities."

"What about your family? What do they think of you coming up to the Edgelands… do they like it?"

Her look was odd, as though she didn't understand the question. "It was my choice. My … family thought it was a good idea and it's not forever, I can go back. It isn't like I will never see my people again but it will change some things."

"Like what?"

Kirri smiled suddenly, the humour sparking her eyes. "I'll probably go back all dark like you and that will be very odd. But it is worth it for what I will be able to tell my people about the Edgelands. Taipan and Aine has told me that the burn on my skin will go away in time, she called it a tan; I can tell that I already am going dark."

Inspecting her arms quietly she then added. "And you said you can't even notice it. But I can."

"No. I can't notice much." I chuckled, seeing the paleness of her arm in the starlight.

For a time we sat still, reflecting on the differences in our world, at least that was what I was doing.

"So how long will you stay do you think?"

With a small shrug she astounded me. "Until Ariaka no longer wants me. Or maybe I will find another husband but I have this disease now... this ciguatera. It is infectious I think, so maybe I will not find anyone else."

"Infectious? Did Taipan say that?"

"Yes; He didn't seem to think it was too bad a thing; but to me... to us from the Inland disease often means death and our Mage needs to be called. He did say that it was transferrable to my husband or any mate I might have. We don't have a lot of diseases, maybe because our Domilands are so small compared to yours and we are more isolated from each other. Maybe too my husband will not like that I have this thing, I think? I will have to tell him."

"Mage? Is that like a doctor or something?"

"Yes. Like Taipan, only he seems very knowledgeable. The things he knows are very valuable. You are very lucky to have such a mage. The first few days I was here Taipan organized inoculation's for me, which was a bit frightening when he explained what they were. I thought that they might make me sick but ... well it didn't. There are still some that I will need when I am feeling better... or so he says."

Uncomfortable, and unable to think of anything to say to reassure her I frowned at the simple statement of Kirri's about Tom's opinion on her health. I couldn't see how it would really matter to him, not if Taipan didn't think it was serious.

"I don't think this illness is that bad, not if Taipan says it isn't," I reassured her. "I haven't heard of it before, I don't know what to tell you."

"Taipan said I might get sick again if I eat shellfish or some seafood's. Or even drink your alcohol, but there isn't a cure and even if there was, the Edgelanders would know I think. They have a tea to drink, it tastes horrible but if I add sugarbag it isn't too bad really. I will get used to it."

"That sounds pretty bad. I never even knew this disease... this thing existed ... haven't ever heard of it before."

Kirri just looked up at the skies, a little desolate I thought and I wondered what it was that she was thinking.

"Taipan did say that lots of people have it, didn't he? They just don't know a lot about it." I added as though in consolation and then I thought better of saying anything more. It didn't seem to make much difference to her somehow.

After a time she looked across at me. "You know it is transferrable across to any child I might have, it is a toxin. That is the hardest thing. I don't think I want to have babies anymore."

I shook my head, part in denial, part in sympathy and I could see that this was what Kirri seemed most upset about.

"Look don't let it worry you. Seriously… if lots of people have it then maybe it's not so bad."

But I don't think she really heard me.

Path to the Present

Jeremy

When I got back into Sydney the next afternoon Big Jim was waiting for me. He had heard from the Jongorrie of our exploits and was pleased that I had handled it all so well it seemed. He was less happy about Tom for some reason and I figured it had a lot to do with his antics over the weekend.

Tom looked the worst for wear and I was glad to be flying under Big Jim's radar, leaving Tom right up there to take a lot of the flack. It gave me time to think about what I was gunna do about Kelly and Tom, which was something that was playing on my mind.

I liked Kelly a lot but since finding out about Tom and her, and even now with the knowledge of Kirri just around the corner, I found myself out of sorts and annoyed with my mate. He seemed to be moving towards another of those monumental messes, which years ago he could get himself right into the thick of without even trying.

Andrew didn't stay long after we'd arrived. He was on a round trip, which was a hell of a drive. He was keen to get back to Alex and the kids so we saw him off soon after and I knew he was planning on a sleep break somewhere along the way tonight.

Big Jim also seemed to know about the Inlander, Kirri, and he mentioned her only once while Tom wasn't about. Reminding me that it was not my place to tell him of his wife but that Apari would do so in good time, as was his privilege. You didn't cross men like Apari so I left it at that and decided that Tom could sort this out himself, but Kelly... that I felt I should do something about.

Tom was still recovering from the beating he had taken over the weekend and it was hard not to annoy him about it, particularly in my current frame of mind. He was something of a mess but each day he was looking better, though he refused to be drawn on what had actually happened. In the end I put it down to girls and too much to drink. I couldn't think of anything else that would make him so reluctant to talk about what had happened.

He and Big Jim spent a lot of time over the next few days on the whips and occasionally I joined them but I was glad to get some time on my own to catch up with my studies. The academic year was coming to an end in a few short months and while I couldn't see a path ahead for me, at least I could ensure I made passing grades and that meant knuckling down and getting stuck into the work I'd missed. The teachers were great and had notes that I could use, which mean it wasn't too long before I was up to speed with the rest of the class.

When Big Jim and Tom headed out that week for a few days in the bush, I was glad to see Tom get out of the house. He too felt the same I was sure as he seemed to have withdrawn into himself as only he could do at times.

Dealing with Tom when he was in a quiet place was difficult, as you never knew what he was thinking or what in his life was influencing him. At times like this I had learnt to just back-off and leave him to work through his thoughts and concerns in his own time and way.

Over the months he had taken on that certain look that many of the Kadaitcha could adopt. It was a look that travelled right through you as though it addressed your very shadow. It was a look that in time could send shivers across your skin, although mostly he and I shared a good knock-about relationship.

I knew he could raise that look, like an inscrutable knowledge he possessed. At any time it would be enough to pull me up from annoying him and I would leave him be, happily.

I caught up with Kelly on Thursday a few days after the guys had headed out and she was strangely quiet. I was still of two minds on what to do about her knickers that I had found. That scrap of silken fabric that had been in Tom's ute.

I had tucked them away in my bag and was seriously thinking of confronting her over it. That I figured would give me an open to discover just what the relationship between her an' Tom was.

I even considered returning the scrap of silky stuff just to see what she would say about it. This idea I had played over in my mind a dozen times and while that thought built in my head I struggled with what I felt about her as a friend.

I guess I just didn't want to know if their relationship was really what it seemed to be. What did I want in regards to my friendship with Kelly anyways, and did it even matter any more?

Part of me wanted to punish her with my knowledge of Kirri but that was a path to serious conflict, not only with her but also with the Kadaitcha and with Taipan. That was somewhere I didn't even want to go.

As much as I wanted to punish her there was part of me that wanted to warn her. A part that tore at my loyalties as a friend and it was a confusing place I was in, particularly in regards to her.

I knew that few amongst Tom's family would accept Kelly while the girl from the Inland who had been chosen for him, was even at this moment becoming very much part of the family.

The outlook for Kelly was not good, even without the complication of this other guy she was hanging out with. I struggled with telling her this, or leaving it to work itself out.

The opportunity to talk was welcome when it came up after lunch when we both had a spare class and I decided to join her. She was doing some reading, while she sat in the shade away from anyone else enjoying the quiet time between sessions.

"Hey you, mind if I sit here?"

Kelly looked up and closed her research text on the table with a little pout as she rested her elbows in an attitude that seemed fed-up. "Nup. This stuff is boring... how are you finding it?"

Her book was on our health and safety unit, one of the assignments I had at last completed and I smiled my consensus. No words were needed as I settled across from her at the table.

"I've been meaning to catch up... see how it's all going?" I added discounting her question and getting ready to test some questions of my own. She looked a little worn around the edges as though things were not going her way much either and I wondered what was happening in her life.

Shrugging, she clearly was bored and irritated. "I think I am over it all... I'm seriously thinking of dropping out."

"Why? It is only a few weeks till the end of the study and the assessments aren't so rough. Seems a shame after doing all that work getting almost to the end of it."

"It's a bit pointless. There is so much else in life you know."

This was a new development and I wondered what had happened to bring it about. We hadn't seen a great deal of each other in the last week an-a-bit and with Tom being largely absent, I considered the question of whether this would have had anything to do with her mood.

"Like what? What else is going on?"

"Well..." Kelly shrugged, "Life! Have you ever wondered if it is all worth it? I mean all this?" Sitting back irritated she continued restlessly having dismissed her reading so easily. "It seems so disjointed somehow, almost an extension of never ending study."

"It's OK. Sure... it is schoolish but it is different."

"You think so? I don't know... I just want to get out there and do ... something, anything with my life."

"Like what?" I asked after a moment.

The pause was poignant and I wondered for a minute if she was even going to answer me or just fob me off. It gave me a sense of being played somehow.

"Some of the girls I know... friends in town, are talking about going interstate and well ... I am thinking about it."

"Yeah? Where?"

"Melbourne, Western Australia even. There is work over there you know and it would be easy I think."

Surprised I sat back and considered it. "Have you been offered a job or something then?"

She shrugged. "Yeah, sort of. It's ... like contract work really. The pay is good too and... and I'm thinking about it. They want to go soon, maybe in the next few weeks. I can go with a group of the girls"

"That sounds very different to what you always talked about doing. What is it? What about your boyfriend, whats-his-name?"

Her look was not pleased. "It's the entertainment industry, sort of dance an ... that sort of thing so it's a bit different... but I like it. I don't know about Pete though. I think I might break up with him soon, it's not going real well, sometimes I think he's a bit of an arsehole."

Restlessly she shuffled about before she continued, her mood strange. "We had a fight, a real bad one."

I tried not to smile in my sense of satisfaction, struggling with the thought of her knickers, even now in my bag as my thoughts stretched to Tom. I nodded as though understanding. "That happens when you cheat on a guy Kell'." I said quietly, still feeling that sense of wanting to punish her for trashing our friendship so easily.

Her look was sharp. "What do you mean?" she demanded on the very edge of resentment.

"Well you cheated on him didn't you?"

"You have no idea what you're talking about. What is it to you anyway ... what I do!"

I shrugged. "Look I found your ... things ... in Toms ute."

"What things?"

"Your knickers ... they had to be yours..."

"That's none of your business!"

Again I shrugged. "Seemed like my business at least I thought so. I thought we were all friends. You could'a said something you know if that is the way it was. It's this creeping behind my back that has pissed me off ... both of you."

"I don't have to explain anything to you, even if they are mine. It's between Tom and I and it has nothing to do with you!"

"Look. I'm not blaming you or anything, I'm just saying the way it is."

"Did Tom say anything?" she demanded suddenly, her tone odd.

For a moment I hesitated, then shook my head.

"Well he better not! He's got me into enough trouble. Where is he anyway I haven't heard from him for ages, over a week?"

Again I shrugged. "He's away for a few days. Anyway don't ask me, ask your boyfriend ... Tom. Not the other one."

"He's not my boyfriend. We're just friends!" Kelly protested resentfully, "Both of them! I think boyfriends are just trouble ... why would you want one? They think they own you! I don't want to talk about it." She spat resentfully, bringing the whole discussion to an abrupt end.

For a moment we just sat there, while I contemplated what to say. After a time, instead of saying anything I just searched about in my backpack. Finding the scrap of silky stuff and lace I placed it on the table scrunched into a ball between us. A part of me was even reluctant to see that scrap of lace and I part company, along with my imagination.

Kelly looked up suddenly. Quietly gathered the scrap up she tucked it into her own bag almost negligently.

"OK. I could have told you," she said softly. "But it wasn't like we were serious or anything. It was never like that. I didn't want to hurt you."

I shrugged, realizing with her words just how much it had affected me and I hadn't realized it fully until she'd acknowledged it. "Don't worry over it. I'm not. It's just the way it is." I added as dispassionately as I could. "So tell me about this job? You said it was with a group of girls?"

Strangely she smiled and dropped her glance for a moment, almost as though it was a secret, which was odd. "It's sort of a dance group we are putting together, that would be the best way to describe it. They're talking about travelling over to Kalgoorlie. They have been invited to perform there at one of the clubs."

"A dance group?"

"Yes ... like burlesque really. There is a place called Langtree's. It's all above board and the money is good. Good enough to travel all that way and stay over the Christmas season even. There is even a chance of more work over there."

"I didn't know you did burlesque? Isn't that like stripping or something?" The idea was intriguing and I suddenly realized looking at her that she could be really good at something like that. If she knew how to dance that is.

"It's not stripping, it's dance. One of the girls has worked at it before and it's something we have been playing at. She's teaching me a routine. It's a lot of fun... and it's harder than it looks."

I grinned. I couldn't help it. "You'll have to show me sometime. I think you would be good at something like that."

"I've been doing dance class even, just informal but I like it. It helps with steps and stuff. You could tell me what you think about the routines, some of them, if I show you them … if you like?"

"Yeah sure. Anytime. I'd like that." My grin about said it all as I thought about how much fun it could be to see Kelly in action.

"Well how about later on this arvo? I've been practicing in the garage at home. It's where I hang out and my Aunt goes out Thursday's with her boyfriend. So we won't disturb them, they won't even know."

"I can't today, I'm going down to the tat shop. They are starting on my shoulder."

I had to admit I was more concerned with my first big visit to the tattoo shop, a visit planned for that afternoon. They were finally going to start on the design that we had been working on forever.

Kelly grimaced eloquently and then added with a thread of mischief in her eyes as she suddenly smiled. "I could come with you? Hold your hand even."

I laughed at the thought, but then considered it. It would be nice to have someone there with me, break this sense of solitary I was feeling. Someone to distract me even, and Kelly could do that easily.

"OK. Maybe I can come over on Friday... and you can show me your routine..." That idea had more appeal the more that I thought about it.

Shaking her head she broke into my suggestion. "I'm going into town Friday, I told Pete not to pick me up. I was going to catch the train early and do some shopping, take my time."

"Well how about I run you into town. I can take Tom's ute he's not home. Probably won't be back till the weekend at the earliest and he won't mind … won't even notice really. It's an early finish Friday so we can take our time an you can do the shopping you want along the way."

"I didn't know you had your licence?"

"I don't, not yet." Grinning I shook my head. "But I can drive, I am near ready to go for it anyway. Just a timing thing... I should be OK."

With our arrangements settled I made a point of cleaning out the ute as best I could when I got home from a long session at the tattoo parlour. The place was still quiet and I figured at least if Tom found out about my expedition he might go easier if I made the effort to clean the ute up.

It had taken a while at the tattoo shop to etch the fine, moderately sized design in ink into my skin and it was going to take more than a few visits to complete, but I was glad that it was underway. There was something satisfying in this. It was sorta' like I was fighting back against the Serpent and the Oruncha, making a stand on my own.

I felt I was taking a grip on their strange world, one that I seemed to be a part of now. The tattoo for me was like a badge of achievement in my own strengths, even if others didn't see it beneath my shirt or didn't even know what it really meant for me.

I was claiming my place and my understanding of the spirit places and it settled well with me as I had watched the ink stain my skin, ignoring the bite of the needle. It was a much lesser pain than the actual bite of the serpent had been, but it went on for an age and I struggled at first to separate myself from the process.

I'd decided to wrap the slender tail of the serpent about the side of my chest, laying the design down under my arm and curling from my shoulder. It wound around my back with the front claw sitting on my shoulder announcing the presence of the tat. I rather liked that whole design. It effectively blanked out the fang scars where I'd been bitten.

With the others away it was easier to organize myself and deal with the discomfit of it. There was an eerie peace about the cottage that was undisturbed by anyone or anything. It also allowed me to get into my study. The new ink on my skin made sleeping difficult but I was really pleased with how it was looking. They had said that the discomfit would only last a week... perhaps three at the absolute most.

The fishing was good from the end of the wharf for when I needed a mindless break. That offered me a quiet solace and entertainment so I had little to really complain about over the time the others were away. There are times when you just need those moments to yourself to help you settle the things in life about you.

Driving into TAFE Friday was a breeze. Driving practice and getting my licence was something that had been going on for a good few months and it wasn't the first time I'd taken to the wheel of Tom's ute. He had often let me drive on our runs from the beach to home and I was more than familiar with the stick-shift along with the routine of driving. I felt I could pass it off easily and with any luck no one would be any the wiser.

We left TAFE about midday Kelly and I. She had bought a small duffle bag with her that I figured was her weekend kit. This we left in the cabin of the ute when we pulled into the shops along the way. I was surprised at how much I enjoyed the shopping with Kelly though.

That she didn't go to regular dress shops and the like, had a lot to do with how easy she was to take out shopping. She turned out to be great to shop with even though it wasn't something I enjoyed usually and she was entertaining to watch.

Preferring the op-shops, she obviously had a plan on where we were going and what she was looking for. It was all something of an experiment really. Often the prices were as cheap as chips and the variety was great in some of the out-of-the-way centres that we cruised through.

There was even stuff for me to look through, tools and books. Her tastes seemed to be eclectic, even bordering on garish but it was a lot of fun, which surprised me.

Kelly was also certainly in a good mood, the odd diffidence from the day before seemed to have vanished. So I just put it all down to the strange brand of fun girls seem to get out of shopping.

By the time we got into Kings Cross district I was shopped out and looking forward to putting my feet up for a time somewhere. Kelly suggested we go straight on to her place, where she stayed on the weekend. It was only a short distance along the backstreets below The Cross central district where I could find free public parking in the street. Here we could easily get to Kelly's digs, drop the gear off and head out for something to eat, to just about anywhere I figured.

The place where she hung out of the weekends was a tenement of a sort and it was a hive of activity when we arrived. Kelly headed straight up the tight front internal stairs, greeting some of the girls on the way, those who were milling about in the rooms downstairs. They seemed a lively lot and no one questioned my accompanying her, laden down with shopping bags as I was. One woman she introduced me too as a friend, she was a little older than Kelly but seemed quietly entertained by my accompanying her.

They all appeared to be about their own business and I thought them a friendly group. It was easy to see why Kelly enjoyed their company. Anyone would do so I quietly thought to myself as I followed her upstairs with complete ease.

Once upstairs in her room at the end of the hall I dumped the shopping bags on the large bed, which was neat and orderly like the room on a whole. Kelly surprised me by closing the door behind me and went straight to emptying her shopping loot all over the bed while I watched the childish delight on her face. Leaving her to rummage through the collection of clothes while I lounged up against the window overlooking the small backyard area.

It wasn't a bad room, a bit crowded it seemed though the heavy curtains were off putting. Drawn back as they were now it at least softened the effect somewhat. She prattled on mindlessly in the meantime about the clothes she was rummaging through and how they could be improved or changed, which really didn't interest me much at all. It was however an endless curiosity with her.

Kelly was in seventh heaven and without thought she stripped off her top and began to try on some of the gear she had collected, almost as though I wasn't present.

It was amusing and certainly entertaining as I lounged back against the windowsill and tried to contain myself with my arms crossed steadily about my chest watching her quietly. She posed and pirouetted with different outfits draped in front of her before the large pitted mirror bedded into the centre panel of the heavy old-fashioned cupboard. I was enjoying myself happily just watching her get so much delight over so simple a purchase as some of the things were.

When someone knocked suddenly on the door however, Kelly froze with a startled yet curious fear in her eyes. When they called out and it was obviously one of the girls she relaxed immediately as she reached for the door to let them in. The odd fear I had seen for just that moment in her eyes had melted away in immediate relief.

"It's just me sweetie..." A tall and confident middle aged woman said as Kelly swung the door open. "One of the girls said you had popped up here and I wanted to catch up..." Seeing me lounging against the windowsill she suddenly stalled. "... well and who do we have here?"

"Ohh... Sandra this is Jeremy. He is a friend and we've been shopping. You should see some of the things... you'll have to help me. I think there is a nice one that we can do something with. Let me show you."

Dancing with enthusiasm Kelly stepped over to the pile on the bed. "This one... we can add some bling I am sure. It would be lovely don't you think." Holding it up as the silky stuff slinked out beneath her hands I watched as Sandra picked at it, feeling the fabric.

"Yes. I think so... something ohhh... feathers with some beading on the bodice maybe along here... But we weren't expecting you until tomorrow. Pete said you might be in though, he was very sorry about ... what happened. I'm sure he didn't mean it. He was very concerned and asked after you but I told him to give you time. I know you need to think about... well some things?"

Glancing across at me Sandra smiled, almost as though to reassure me for some reason.

"Did he say when he would be in?" Kelly asked with some reservation.

"No... no he didn't. He was here yesterday but he didn't stay long. I wanted to talk to you...?" Again she glanced across at me oddly.

Kelly smiled. It was obvious she like the woman as she added. "Oh Jeremy is fine, I told him about the idea and he's fine with it. Thinks giving Melbourne a go is a great idea."

"So he's a friend… as you said. Of course he is!" she finished as though coming to a decision. Turning to me she continued. "You look out for our young girl here I take it. Friends?"

It wasn't so much a question as a statement but I nodded just once in agreement none the less.

"Well that's good to know. I'm not so sure about your Pete," she added turning back to Kelly. "It's… well difficult sometimes. He can be… difficult the silly man."

"I haven't told him yet about going to Melbourne…" Kelly reassured her and this had me wondering just what this exchange was all about really.

"Well don't dear. He wouldn't like it much at all I think. You would be such an asset for the group, so young and pretty. An what does your young man think of you moving onto other adventures then?"

I shrugged noncommittally when she turned back to me, with a careless surrender. Again leaving me to wonder just what the plan was between them. It wasn't my decision what Kelly did but it seemed that her friend Sandra was encouraging her in whatever it was.

"Well that is good then." Sandra announced as though it was relevant. "I'll just leave you both to it… whatever it is you are doing. We can look at those things later. There just might be a place for some and well… you know us girls!" Chuckling she had moved over towards the door as she spoke with humour and irreverence, closing it softly behind her with a significant look.

It was in that moment I wondered if she was actually cross-gender, it was something in the way she moved, the manner in which she flung her hand about dismissively and then I shook myself mentally. It was Kings Cross after all and the manner of the people who seemed to gather in this area… I was likely being over imaginative I decided.

"I think she likes you." Kelly challenged playfully moving over towards me. The laughter in her eyes was intoxicating and that she still was wearing just a little strappy bra over her low-hipped jeans was distracting beyond believable. I could feel my body tighten as she moved up daringly close and within reach of my breath.

"You think so." I chuckled nervous as she shifted closer still.

My hands easily found her waist. Leaving me unsure if I was trying to keep her at a distance or draw her to me as they settled there and she leaned into my warmth.

"Hmm…" she whispered on a light note. Her fingers dallying at my throat, light and playful. "We've never really done this have we? I mean we sort of played a bit… but?"

I winced slightly as she put her hand to my side and curious she frowned.

"Ohh… your tattoo. I forgot! Let me see?"

Tugging at my shirt without reservation she hauled it up obviously curious. Helping her I grabbed at the shirt fabric and pulled it over my head, tossing it carelessly to the side and turned the design to her, waiting for her scrutiny. It was very much like the one she had worked on with me over the months and the tattoo artist had made a few improvements that I rather liked. Kelly stepped back shifting me about under her hands so she could better see the design.

"It looks good! Like really good! I love it."

Her fingers skitted lightly over my body exploring the design carefully and with some gentleness at the same time she was giving me goose bumps that raced around my skin. "Oh I like this… is it sore?" Running her finger about my ribs I felt her trace the tale of the dragon as it tried to wrap about my lower ribs.

"No. Not really, just a little uncomfortable sometimes. It's not finished yet, still a bit to go."

Quite suddenly she leant in reaching up and lightly kissed the scars on my shoulder where the serpent had bitten me. "I never really believed you about these. One day you'll have to tell me how you really got the scars?"

Her voice was soft, seductive and I was completely distracted from her question. I took her back in between my hands, shuffling her easily as I half stepped us, half tugged her restlessly towards the cushioning of the bed beside us; it was a single, easy step away.

Kelly chuckled, seeing my thoughts in my eyes. She was a lightweight and as we tumbled playfully onto the covers she squirmed towards me, moving amongst the strewn clothing.

I felt hesitant and unsure though, my actions a question in themselves. I was driven, seeking escape from her questions and my need to avoid the answer to them. Anything… anything to escape questions I told myself.

"I don't want to talk about that now." I laughed low as I shifted my weight in towards her, pulling her closer to me.

Kelly chuckled as I moved in quickly, my weight moving easily over her as my lips found hers so simply in the end. She was warm, soft and inviting and my fingers found the naked skin under my touch irresistible.

I felt the warm desire for her body shift through mine. I wanted to feel her touch. The inviting warmth of her body shifted into mine so easily, inviting other things. My thoughts were scattered and yet focussed purely on the warm pleasure that was swamping me.

Wrapping her arms about my shoulders she seemed to encourage me as my body spiralled into the heat I felt. It seemed like an age since I had held a girl closely or touched her so intimately. My hand moved up over her breast hungry for the feel of the delightfully firm and yet delicate skin.

For just a second, as I drew an intoxicated breath my thoughts flicked to Badjimala. It was as though I felt his presence but then I tossed the thought.

What I was feeling beneath me captured and held me filling my mind. Kelly's warmth was a delight, the sweet smell of her a lure. My lips found her breasts when I swept and pulled the fabric there aside impatiently. Searching about her back for the clip, those elusive little flick hooks that I struggled to manage while I pulled at the scrap of fabric between us. I was drowning slowly in the scent of her.

Laughing Kelly twisted, grabbing handfuls of my hair. Pushing against me I flipped easily onto my back, my weight buried into the covers of the bed. Kelly moved over me, straddling my body low on my hips. Her fingers dived for the button of my jeans impatiently. I couldn't have stopped her. I didn't even want too while my hands and eyes gloried in the sight and touch of her.

Breathless I was, my mind in a spiral of anticipation as she bent to me and I felt the moisture of her lips descend in a heated path down my chest. Reaching my belly, she pulled at the fabric around my hips having loosened my jeans.

Helping her was a compulsion as I lifted my hips and felt my jeans drag over my skin roughly. Kelly's touch was warm, moist and completely thrilling as her fingers danced over my body cupping me, wrapping about the hardening strength of me, now throbbing with a impatient heat. Then I felt the wet heat of her mouth in sweet delightful relief as the fire burnt a path up through me at her touch.

My groan was helpless as I arced my hips towards the sensations sweeping me. I tightened my belly into the warm flood of her touch, inviting her when I knew I should have moved away. Unable to do so I let the sensation swamp me, the pleasure was so sweet.

I didn't want to move... I was losing control of my body. My thoughts were scattered all about the pleasure I felt. The building heat was intense as it shafted through me again in a scorching path.

"Kelly! Geezus girl..." Was all I was able to whisper belatedly before the traveling heat in my body wildly seared along my groin way out of any control.

Kelly didn't shift, didn't move away and I had lost control over what happened. My body and belly tightened and exploded into its own quick shift, spiralling towards an ecstasy that I had missed so much. This wonderful intimacy I understood well and it was all mine.

I wondered at the uncontrollable power of it as I groaned a small agonized apology hoping she had heard me, hoping desperately that she wasn't about to get angry, disgusted or bedevilled over what was happening.

Her hair still spilt out about the skin of my hips and belly, her lips moist and warm. Her hands holding me, tormenting my body in a soaring pleasure while I was gripped in the helpless surrender found at the heights and release of my passion. I gave into the deep groan of surrender that ripped along my ribs and deep into my gut.

Then she stilled after a time as I eventually did. The fire that had raced through me slowly uncoiled. Her touch was suddenly gentle and I was helpless under the impish laughter in her eyes.

Totally hopeless I felt as helpless as a baby for those next few moments. Never had I been so lost, so inconsiderate, so completely out of any type of control. I eased back against the bed drawing deep draughts of air while I struggled for some semblance of mastery over my own body.

The dusk of the early evening had swept into the room while I hadn't noticed and at some point the traffic I could hear had built in its subtle roar. The world had shifted just a little and I, in this moment felt helplessly abandoned as I reached for her.

Kelly shifted her weight stretching out beside me as I reached up and gentled my hand against her flushed face while she grinned down at me mercilessly.

"Geezus! Kelly I'm sorry... I didn't mean to..."

Shaking her head she chuckled without any mercy. "That wasn't your fault, I wanted that. You didn't have a lot of say in it much."

"Shit, you're a little witch!" I laughed at myself softly... ruthlessly admitting my lack of control over my own body. Laying back, my hand heavily on my brow I considered the truth of her taunt giving myself over to her small giggle, while I still felt hopelessly out of control.

A quiet giggle filled the fast darkening room taunting me again as she shifted her weight once more, sitting herself up in a cross-legged fashion all the while scrutinising me dispassionately. There was a certain triumph in her eyes that laughed at me as I watched her, my breath steadying.

It was then that I felt my hair stand up on end, my senses freeze when a dark shadow of movement flicked heavily across the last of the light spilling in from the window, where the curtains were drawn back.

In a quick shift, struggling to see what the movement was I sat up onto the edge of the bed while Kelly too, swung to the window leaving me to pull at my jeans absently.

It shifted again that dark shadow; its presence flitting across the light spilling into the room announcing a movement and this time I knew that I hadn't imagined it. It has passed in front of the window between the darkness and the growing shadows for a second time.

This time I had surely caught sight of it; just a glimpse in its heavy movement in the shadows and then it was gone. It had moved swiftly into the deepening shade of a deepening night.

"What the hell...!" I exclaimed softly, unbelieving of the hint of another fleeting presence. "What was that?"

Kelly looked across as confused as I struggled to my feet and fastened my jeans. "Did you see that?" I demanded quietly.

"What?" Climbing hesitantly off the bed to join me, she and I both stepped over towards the window.

"There wouldn't be someone out there, ya think?" I asked unsure.

"No... No of course not."

"Then what was that...?" My senses were screaming in alarm, a strange and acute awareness overtaking me. It was as though something had stepped across my own shadow.

Kelly shrugged it off. "Probably just a cat or something. Stop it... your giving me the creeps," she warned hesitantly.

It was then that we heard the soft pad of feet against the tin overhead causing us to freeze suddenly. Alarmed Kelly moved quickly and grabbed for her top, tugging it over her head, her eyes to the ceiling in question. Having lost her bra somewhere in the clothes still strewn about the bed she didn't bother with that at all.

"It's probably a possum." I said, reassuring her though I knew that the shadow had been of too big in size to be simply a possum. "It was just a shadow really, it crossed the window. It might be a trick of the light even."

"Yes... you're probably right," she agreed as she finished adjusting her clothes. But still my senses were screaming at me and I was at a loss to understand why. Kelly too was growing nervous and every part of me wanted to protect her, to settle her down from where my own nerves were reaching.

Moving over to the window I looked out again, studying the shift of shadow across the darkening scene, looking for anything that would reassure me. There was an odd sound overhead, a shuffle of feet or perhaps a shift in the air and then it was gone.

Its presence lingered though, a perceivable threat or even a promise but maybe I was being fanciful. There was something about the threat however that I recognized, something I understood on the edge of my senses and I found that alarming.

"How about we go and find somewhere to eat, my shout." I suggested quietly. Thinking that we would be better off away from here if there was someone on a clandestine mission of their own, sneaking about outside.

"Suits me," she agreed readily as she grabbed at her jacket. "There is a place nearby where it has a great menu so we don't have to go far if you like?" Then she prattled on with a reluctant reassurance. "Maybe its just nothing, I mean..." she shook her head shrugging. "What could it be?"

"Come on then. I'm starving actually, I could do with a feed."

With my hand on her back I motioned her ahead through the doorway. Tucking her under my arm I felt strangely protective of her as we both headed off down the long hall and on out through the front door. There seemed to be fewer people about now, though you could hear chatter coming from the ground floor towards what I thought might be the kitchen at the back.

I was glad to get out of the place and the more distance we put between the place and ourselves had me settling down. I felt that we were stepping steadily away from the edge of something I didn't understand and that which I was unsure about altogether.

Yet somehow it all felt strangely familiar.

Shadows of the Night

Jeremy

I had always enjoyed any visit to Kings Cross, it was a place with a life and excitement of its own, though it was still very much too early for the life of the night to start up.

The dusk had moved through the city and into the night quickly as it did on the edge of summer. By the time we reached the little restaurant-café it was near enough on dark for the traffic and the streetlights to take on the garish aspect of the night. A good time to settle indoors I thought as the night began to settle into the streets, turning the narrow alleys to deep shadows best avoided.

Settling at a table towards the back of the café we could watch the passing parade of people hurry off towards home, while others emerged to begin a nights entertainment. Kelly and I decided easily on something to fill our bellies.

"You never said what you like about The Cross, or what it is that brings you here every weekend. If it's not this Pete guy then what is it?" I asked easily, looking for simple chat to fill in the first shadows of the evening.

Looking across at me she smiled confidently. It was that inscrutable smile she had whenever she spoke of her weekends. "It's the company I think. I like being around the girls … from the house. They're nice and … well we're like a club of people almost. It's fun and we get out to parties and the like."

"It really isn't so much Pete then?"

Kelly shook her head. "I think that's what I like about the idea of going down to Melbourne. I can get rid of him."

It was an odd thing for her to say, almost a challenge somehow and I frowned. "Why not tell him just to hit the track, ditch the guy."

Shrugging she frowned. "He pays rent on the room so I feel … I don't know? It's as though I'm obligated to him."

"What about Melbourne? Do you have somewhere to stay?"

"Yeah. Sandra has a boarding place down there. Much like here I think but I can rent a room when I start working. Mostly to keep my stuff she was saying. I would be independent and I sorta like that idea. Though at first we would be going to Western Australia, to Kalgoorlie for a month or two and I will have a place there too she said."

"Sounds like your set on it Kelly."

Nodding she agreed. "Yes. I think I am. I'll come back to Sydney again, like she does. She travels between Sydney and Melbourne a lot, organizing troupes of entertainers and well... she is more into the entertainment side and we get on well. I would travel too with the troupe I think. We would do different gigs and things. Sandra organizes all that."

"And here I was thinking we could have a great thing going here?" I commented laughing, not half kidding either.

"We can still be friends can't we?"

I nodded. That was the way it was going to be I realized as I tucked into the meal the waiter put in front of us, perhaps a little disappointed at the turn of events.

I wondered too what Tom would think of her plans, though I didn't want to think of him now and I guess I was feeling a bit guilty, or maybe a little obligated. I wasn't sure but either way it wasn't happening if Kelly was headed south to Melbourne.

"Are you gunna tell this other guy ... Pete?"

Kelly shrugged. "I guess so, maybe this weekend. He's not going to like it much, but then he..." Instead of finishing the sentence Kelly looked up at me, as though just realizing it was me she was talking too and then smiling she shrugged and popped another forkful into her mouth.

It was in that moment that my phone went off. It was Tom.

"Hey." I greeted him frowning.

"Hey yourself. Where's the ute?"

"Umm... I've got it. I just needed to get into town for a bit..."

"Bloody Hell Jeremy! You haven't got your licence yet! Are you out of your mind! Get the bloody thing back before Big Jim goes ballistic!"

"Umm... where is he?" I asked reluctantly.

"He's outside." Tom cracked quietly down the phone link. "Probably ringing Ty now... or the police... geezus I don't know. He is not happy with you. He figured you had taken the thing out when we got back and he has done nothing but growl about it for the last fifteen minutes! You are in deep shit!"

"Dam... can't you put him off, make some excuse or something?" I half whispered.

"You're in deep shit with me! You idiot! Get the thing home! No! Hang on don't... Wait there I will have to come and get you..."

"I can get it back." I protested defensively.

Yeah sure... Big Jim will kill me ... and you! No ... just wait there. Where are you?"

"The Cross."

"Where's the ute parked?"

"Umm… It's in a back street, not far from Kelly's place."

"Kelly's?"

"Yeah. Kelly's with me, I ran her home this arvo, we had bags and stuff."

"OK… look I'll meet you outside of Kelly's, you should know where that is I take it? We'll come in by train. I can walk up from the station to there. Bit of a walk but it's better than changing trains and buggerizing around and Big Jim might be calmer by then. He wanted to go to they city himself."

"Does he have to come in though?" I asked reluctantly.

"Yeah… he's meeting some mates in the city, they have some business going on tonight. I was going to run him in you idiot!"

"Oh."

"Look I'll see you in an hour or so. With any luck I will be able to calm him down before he gets his hands on you."

"OK then, look I'm sorry Tom… I didn't think you would need the ute…"

"Yeah save it! We can talk about this later."

"OK… sorry mate, really."

"Yeah you will be."

Tucking my phone back into my pocket after Tom had hung up I glanced across at Kelly who was finishing off the last of her meal.

"Good news?" She quipped, knowing that it wasn't"

"I'm in the shit."

"Tsk… sorry. Maybe you shouldn't have taken the ute. We could've caught the train."

"No. It's OK. Tom's not too wild he just wanted the ute is all. We'll work it out."

Kelly shrugged. "I feel responsible."

"Nah… it's not your fault. Come on… lets finish up and walk this off. I gotta meet him near your place in an hour or so, maybe more, so I can walk you back if you like. We have plenty of time."

The night was quiet down this end of town as we turned our backs on the lights of the Cross having dawdled over our meal easily. People were coming and going all bent on a good night, eager for the lights and the excitement and entertainment of the Cross.

The main artery travelled between the city centre, skirting Hyde Park and the Domain then ran up into Kings Cross.

There the streets were wide and busy, humming with the growing traffic. Kelly's place was off this artery a bit, stepping higher between this area and Surry Hills to the south. It was an area where the people lived in the quaint and narrow two story terraces of last century, which rubbed shoulders with each other and yesteryear while the bustle of the big city encroached.

A number of these places had been built by convicts, or by tradesmen who were the early Currency Kids, Australian children and grandchildren of these same convicts and emigrants. Many were also kids of the local Aboriginal people who had once lived around the harbour and on the fringes of the city. Those considered Aboriginal, were a displaced people, a mixture of blood and cultures who had lived and fought together in pockets throughout the city and who still had a presence in the city very much so today.

The squattocracy from the outlying pioneering stations and homesteads a century before had once also had their summer-homes here. Buildings that stood broader and taller than the others, they had settled into the city with a certain pretentious regality. The same regality their owners had tried to establish and thankfully had failed in doing so during the often violent land-grab of the colonial era.

Big Jim knew many of those descended from the Aboriginal Eora people, those who had survived the disease and mayhem colonization had bought to an ancient race. He had told us many of the old stories, some entertaining, some tragic, while we had sat out under the stars at night around the fire.

I walked these streets with Kelly for quite a while, talking softly of things we saw and thought about. All the time I could feel the pull and the presence of the old people and it was disturbing in its own way.

Deeper into the shadows of the back streets it was more prevalent. Here the shadows moved dancing under the lights of the night and shifting in strange ways that had my senses on edge.

From behind the curtains of many of the tenements, people went about their business. Some had left their front doors open, people stepping through them easily while others were shuttered against intrusions. There was a secret world going on behind the curtained windows. The world of life and city living and at times you could glimpse the movement or hear the sound, which gave its presence away.

Still in some way on edge from our experiences this afternoon, those memories of Kelly that I was unable to so easily dismiss, I watched the shadows with a keen eye.

It wasn't until we came closer to her digs some time later, after we had strolled around for an hour and more, that I became aware of a heightened sense of threat. A sense that crept along my nerves and flicked something deep within me as we came closer to her place.

I was expecting to see Tom perhaps, or that he would soon be arriving but despite that, shifting closer to Kelly I attempted to carelessly drape my arm across her shoulders. I tried to keep her close but she laughed and dodged my intent.

"Not here," she complained softly as we turned into the narrow street and Kelly stepped ahead impatient with me. "Tom should be here soon I think, it's been ages."

I frowned and followed her silently, but that didn't release me from the sense of something wrong, which was hanging about and growing stronger the closer we came to the tenement.

It was the shift of a shadow in the corner of my eye, the tread sound of weight in a dry garden... perhaps the hints of movement in the city of the night. Unable to see into the dark corners, beyond hidden gardens and shadowy verandah's had me on edge.

As we approached the building I noticed movement across the street and almost immediately realized that it was Tom stepping out from the shadows where he had obviously been waiting for us.

He crossed the road quickly while we both watched and waited expectantly.

"Hey you two. So where's the ute?"

"Its back a few blocks, parking wasn't easy to find. Have you been waiting long?"

"Nah. Only maybe five minutes." His glance suddenly shot to Kelly as he frowned and then returned to me. "What did you two have planned?" He asked quietly.

"Well... nuthin', Kelly is headed back and I guess... I was going home."

"Big Jim wants to meet us down the Domain way."

Now it was my turn to frown, on the edge of a feeling that there was something more to this. Tom's look was too steady, too expectant and I wasn't at all sure about what to say.

While I dithered though, there was a racket building slowly, just within hearing and as we all glanced off towards the noise, it was Kelly who stepped up first.

"That's Sandra...?" she said softly mostly to herself.

Moving more quickly in her step she began to walk off ... and then move faster towards the noise while both Tom and I hesitantly followed.

It was a building racket, an argument of a sort coming from the tenement building and as we got closer we realised that it involved more than one, maybe two or three people. They were all yelling at someone and the din was obviously violent.

Kelly swung quickly in through the gate and trying the closed door through which the din was growing more harsh, she all but burst in through it swinging it back on its hinges, leaving us to follow her lead.

It wasn't hard to find the room the noise was coming from. Sandra was screaming in a harsh and protesting bellow as we first heard the angry tones of a male voice arguing with her.

By the time we both reached the door, the one off the front hall, Kelly was in the thick of it and screeching at the guy who I recognized as Pete. I had only seen him from a distance but now what I saw of him I didn't much like.

He was dark haired and almost scrawny but he thought more of himself obviously, than anyone else despite his savage anger. He was not a man you could feel easy with and his cruelty in dealing with the woman crumpled at his feet had my temper up instantly. In fact there was little that I thought would commend him as a friendly type, he was too slick, too sleazy looking and that Kelly flew into the fray immediately had me wanting to intervene as quickly.

"Let go of her! You bastard... let go...!" Kelly demanded as she launched herself at the guy with her fists flaying around.

Pete was standing over Sandra, his own fist curled viciously into her hair, forcing her to her knees as he spat his contempt over something she had done. A contemptuous drivel that Kelly was interrupting apparently without thought while I took another moment to try and gauge just what this was all about.

It was a disturbing sight as he then lashed wildly out at Kelly, hauling Sandra along with the movement while she arced in painful protest in the savage treatment.

"You bloody bitch!" he ground as Kelly fell under his wild blow. "So you think you can just leave!" He demanded of her harshly.

Tom, not hesitating, moved in an instant passing me. His aim focussed on Pete as he swung back his bunched fist, putting all his weight behind the move. Pete, seeing his punch coming lurched back, dragging Sandra with him by the hair.

The punch went wide but Tom didn't wait, he swung quickly grabbing the finer built man by the shirt and lifting him, slamming him up against the wall. He then buried another punch heavily into his gut.

Pete had let go his hold of the woman's hair as he took the full force of the blow leaving Sandra to scramble, howling bitterly towards where Kelly was now cowering up against the other wall.

Tom had then just let him crumple to the floor but he wasn't done with him I could see. When the other man struggled and ripped at his jacket desperately, he succeeded in pulling out a blade. The flash of which caught the harsh light of the room.

He pointed it at Tom as he struggled to gain his feet and protect his paining gut in a retreating step.

We all stood frozen for a second as the mans challenge danced between Tom and I, shocked by the threat of the knife Pete was wielding wildly between us.

I don't know what had happened to the others, but their screams and protest had faded down the hall as though they had scattered. In an instant it was deathly quiet as our eyes held onto the blade.

It wasn't a big thing, but it was sharp and new and it reflected the glare, the light in the room glinting with threat. It was a threat that had frozen all of us but Tom... he just crouched facing the blade held by the other man squarely on, as he chuffed softly. A threat buried deeply in the sound he made as though to test the man balanced before him.

Stunned I watched as Kelly screamed a warning again, it broke the tension about us shattering the moment as the high sound echoed through the house.

Pete staggered for just a second, his glance wild and in that second I knew he wasn't going to use the blade. He simply didn't have it in him to take on someone as powerfully built as Tom in a fight of wits or strength. Tom looked bloody fearless. He was a force to be reckoned with all on his own, even without a blade and he seemed to have no fear in him.

In a quick movement Pete faltered and then suddenly dived for the door as Kelly screamed once again. I guess she thought that he was going to knife me for some reason. I was closest between them but I knew Pete didn't have that in him either... he was a cornered rat bent on escape. His glance didn't even graze mine as he ducked past me diving out the door and Tom and I both shot out after him almost immediately.

My mad and angry scramble down the hall was suddenly arrested though, as Tom grabbed at my arm pulling me up and I realised it wasn't Pete he was chasing but me.

"Let him go," he ground determined... "We aren't done with him yet."

It was the look in Tom's eyes that pulled me up ... something in his voice. "Leave him!" he said again quickly seeing the surprise in my glance. "Let the Djaranin round him up we have a place to be at."

"What!" I demanded. "He's a shit! You saw what he did to the girls ... he doesn't give a shit about anyone but himself." Then suddenly what he had said to me sank in through my anger. "The Djaranin?" I questioned in disbelieving whisper.

He just nodded, a strange look in his eyes one that again arrested me.

"Can't you feel them about?" He whispered in a voice from the depths of knowledge, one laced with expectation.

"The Djaranin?" My question was breathless… still unbelieving.

Tom just nodded again. "They're on the hunt. I could feel them before but I wasn't sure. Now I am. That is what this is all about. Jeremy … mate you just don't know the half of it." He said softly with some frustration as though seeing the full view of something that I couldn't see. Then he stepped towards the door, moving quickly beyond me.

"But he'll get away." I protested still on the edge of disbelief. "He'll come back for Kelly!" Not even sure I had truly heard what Tom had said.

Turning back to look at me quickly, his glance returned torn from looking after Pete's swift moving shadow. The other man was racing down the street, the pound of his feet carrying into the night as it faded. Tom in that moment had the strangest of expressions. It was as though he had just recollected that I was even there.

"No he won't." he said softly. His eyes then quickly travelled beyond me to the sound of the women entering the dark hall. "Look stay with Kelly, see her safe I have to go."

"But… but what about the ute?"

"It's not going anywhere. You better go and collect your whip if you want to be around for this… it's in the ute I think, leastways it was when we left. I'll meet you down near Lady Macquarie's Chair when you're done. An' lose that distemper of yours… rein your anger in a bit. It won't help you, or Kelly for that matter."

"The Botanical Gardens?" I asked confused… totally flummoxed now by Tom's sense of purpose. It was only then that I noticed he had his own serpent killer wound under his shirt, tucked in about his shoulders and chest as he reached for it, slowly drawing it from its warm cocoon. He wound it tightly in his grip concealing it in part between us as his eyes flicked to the now silent, uncertain women approaching from behind me.

"Yes. We'll be there in the gardens… don't be long." Tom flung as he took off.

In the next moment he was gone, off down the street and I knew the thrill of the hunt suddenly surge through my body pulling at me. I wanted to go with him, leave the women but Kelly had now reached me. I felt the light touch of her fingers on my back

"Are you OK? What's happening … is Tom going after him!" she asked uncertain, not sure what had gone on or why even I was still there.

"Me? Yeah sure I'm OK." I answered absently. I wanted to follow Tom.

It took a minute... just a minute for me to collect myself. What was it Tom had said? Look after the women?

My glance took them in and I felt a sense of resentment. The women...! I've been given the women to look out for... this was men's business and I had the women to sort out.

Dammit this wasn't what I wanted. I should be running now with Tom and the Djaranin... after whatever this was about. But I didn't have my whip; it wasn't even in the ute I realized. I had failed to return it, failed to keep it within reach as I had been told.

Keep it nearby you at all times Badjimala had said and the warning rang through my mind uselessly.

The women...! They were fine and I reassured myself of this as my eyes dived between them. However Sandra had other ideas.

"OK... that's it! We're leaving now... right now. And if your coming with me Kelly then you better get your arse into gear."

Surprised I looked over at Sandra. Gone was the soft feminine voice and the playful ways she had used earlier. Now there was a force with a masculine tone to the very tip of her fingers as she pushed ahead of Kelly.

"I mean it girl." She... he threatened as she swung up onto the narrow stairs leading onto the second floor. "I'm leaving tonight!"

Said with intent she glanced back down at Kelly, who was equally surprised. We both stood staring up at her.

"Well what has got into you!" Sandra challenged and then continued up the stairs purposefully heading for what I imagined was her room. "Don't you know a performer when you see one. It's the performance!" She flourished her fingers waving her hand high above her dishevelled head in a crescendo of motion. "And I'm gunna be performing in Melbourne come the new week my girl... So get your arse into gear if you're coming 'cause we are quitting Sydney for a time!"

With the flourish done she pranced with determination on up the stairs, bent on quitting Sydney. Both Kelly and I knew it without any room for doubt that this was an invitation given only once.

"But..."

The look Kelly gave me was anguished, confused and looking for guidance. I couldn't leave her like this even though I wanted to.

Every fibre of my being screamed to be racing out of here but Tom had given me a task and I had to see to it. My indecision and uncertainty tore through me. Then I realized that I didn't want Tom or Big Jim to find out that I had left my serpent killer behind as well. They would be sure to find that out quickly if I were to follow Tom. I understood that with a horrible moment of realization.

"What should I do?" Kelly whispered confused, suddenly seeming very much the young woman she was.

"Will he be back?" I asked with an edge of accusation, anger still sweeping through me at the thought of the weasel that Tom was likely tracking through the streets even now.

"Tom?"

"No Pete for Christ sake! The bloke you're going to ditch remember." I said with some impatience.

"Pete? Well... yes. He always comes back. Even after..."

"Well if he is coming back ... do you want to be here?" I demanded impatiently, angry with myself more than her.

Kelly looked across at me surprised at the question. "No!"

"Then maybe you should just go home. Don't see him anymore. Ditch the bastard."

She shook her head indecisively. "But he'll come and look for me. He will!" she said afraid. "I'm going... I'm going with Sandra... tonight."

"Is that really what you want to do?" I wanted to push the point... I wanted her to say that she preferred me, or even preferred Tom, but she didn't. Her mind was filled with thoughts other than us, thoughts I didn't understand.

It took just a moment really for her to answer me.

"Yes."

"OK." I said seeing the decision reflected in her face. It was then that my own thoughts kicked into gear, touched with disappointment. A flush of resentment resurfaced also with her decision but I tried to ignore it.

Look after the women he had said. "What about your Aunt?"

Kelly, for a moment again looked confused. "It... it doesn't matter. She doesn't like me much anyway and she knows I want to leave. But ... but I need to get some things." Hopefully she looked to me for help and I felt resentment rear its ugly head again.

"Oh no ... no I ..."

"But Tom said to look after me and I need to get away Jeremy. Truly I do ... don't you see. If I stay here I will never get away from Pete. He'll find me, come after me... it's what he does!"

"You want me to run you back to Cronulla, to get your stuff. Sandra said she is going tonight..."

"And she is!" Sandra's voice echoed as she clambered to descend the narrow stairs. "There is a Melbourne train out in the morning and I aim to be on it. Are you coming my girl? You had better make up your mind quick."

"Yes. Jeremy is just going to run me home to get some stuff... I'm coming too... honestly I am."

That was how I found myself sitting outside of the interstate station at Central, hours later. I didn't want to be there, I wanted to be with Tom, even Badjimala, despite the suspicion that he would still be angry with me.

It was just coming on light when I had pulled up. The night had crept into the piccaninny dawn when I had finally organized Kelly and dropped her off to catch the train to meet the others.

They wouldn't have long to wait and there were four of them now. Sandra had found others to travel with them it seemed and they had been waiting at the train terminus for Kelly to arrive.

They had a surprisingly small amount of luggage between them but it was enough to make managing it cumbersome. Kelly had been sparing in what she had packed. Leaving a great deal at her Aunts but she seemed to care little about it.

It was her old life she said and it had nothing to do with the new adventure she was on. The things she had thrown into the old travelling bag had surprised me. Things hauled from a chest in her room at her Aunts ... things I dare say the Aunty knew little about. A lot of it seemed to be performance gear, cute wispy bits of lingerie and silk or fluff stuff but it was all the stuff she needed or wanted it seemed.

Sparing with the more practical gear she had stuffed that into her carryall as though it was of little importance. She had changed too in the time we had spent at the house. It was as though I was no longer there, almost as though I was of little account in her life and I guessed that this was the way it was to be.

What had become of our friendship I didn't understand but it was almost a relief to see her meet her friends and see them on their way. They would be in Melbourne by the nightfall and I wondered if I would ever see her again.

For a moment I just sat there in the ute and watched them make their way into the shelter of the station. I found myself alone and it was an odd feeling. I eventually turned the nose of the ute back in towards the city on what had been a strange night and headed back in towards the Domain.

It was at least time now to join the men if I could even find them. I was almost too tired to drive, certainly too tired to care much as I wound my way around the city, avoiding the main streets where I could. That was how I found myself up behind the National Art Gallery where I tucked the ute up into a space that seemed designed more for the services and headed out on foot down towards Lady Macquarie's Chair. This was at the very tip of the Domain area, which wrapped itself around the Botanical Gardens.

Macquarie's Chair was the old colonial landmark jutting out into the harbour of Sydney providing a small place of refuge for the city. It was all quiet as the sun broke over the settled city, flushing light into the dawn of a new day.

Dawn in Time

Jeremy

The full breaking of the dawn was eerie in the city as it began to flood over the horizon. I knew I had missed whatever it was that had kept Ariaka and Badjimala in the city but I also knew that the men should still be around. It wasn't long since the Spirit hours had passed but with the quick shift of dawn this time would be coming to a close.

Why they had chosen Lady Macquarie's Chair to meet I wasn't sure but then it probably had something to do with the ancient Bora ground nearby I figured. It was an old ceremonial site of the Cadigal people, the old mob that had lived along the foreshores south of Sydney Harbour, one of the of families of the Eora people.

That the Bora ring had been buried within the Botanical Gardens for a century or more now had little to do with the places where the Spirits touched our world. The Bora Rings after all merely demarked where the men were protected. They were places of spiritual power like churches I guess but much more ancient. They didn't actually protect the men it was the Dreaming and the Lore, which did that.

Cutting across the Domain grounds I headed down towards the path running along the eastern edge of the peninsula, across from the old dockyards. Here it met the sheltered nature walk that ran along the foreshore.

I had been this way before. Badjimalla and Taipan had bought me here and Tom also had known of this place, though not its history. That had been for the men to tell us about, gifting us the stories of our old people, now that we were not only many tribes but also a people within a nation. We were learning be become a nation unto ourselves but it was a struggle and we still needed to find our way.

I knew that this had once been a sacred site of ceremony, though once the reserve of the local mobs. The foreshores of Sydney Harbour also held its secrets; the secrets of the Spirits and the Serpents. Little had changed for these ancient Lore givers, even though the city had grown up around them.

The first Governors of Sydney Town had acknowledged these sacred things and the gardens helped preserve them for the people. Even today they were the preserve of the Spirits. These things that we touched in the Spirit hours, a Lore we preserved in our ancient time honoured way.

That I had missed the ceremony that had been a part of this night was what irritated me the most. There would be other times, other ceremonies but perhaps this was to have been my first big ceremony where I could have stood as a warrior, a man amongst men. I had missed it and it would be something that I would not soon forget.

As I reached the headland, I had passed only a few other morning runners. The first of the cities athletes and they bothered me not at all. To them I was just another runner out for morning exercise and I tried to look the part though I was hardly dressed for it. No one would take notice though. I would be just another teenager running along the pathway for some reason that was my own.

It was quieter once I went around the headland that was known as Lady Macquarie's Chair. There for a moment I paused to catch my breath, stretching my lungs carelessly.

It was then that I saw them, a small group of men down by the rocks at the head of the small cove that wrapped around the Gardens.

The first rays of sun had flooded across the harbour; it was the last moments of the Spirit hours.

Reaching for breath I watched gathering my breath. Tom was finishing up at the waters edge, wiping off his body with his hands. I knew from his movements that he had been washing away the marks of ceremony, though few if any other observers would realise this.

He was wearing only his jeans I could see and that they were dry told me that he had been dressed for ceremony and the jeans hadn't been a part of that. Even from where I was I could see his expression. He was well pleased with himself and I wondered what the ceremony had been all about as I began my stride down towards the group of men.

The Gardens would have provided an ideal place, sheltered from curious eyes it would have been a ceremony hidden by the trees and gardens, concealed within the land folds of the gardens and cove. The gardens were peaceful like that and it was hard to believe you were in the heart of the city.

Even from the Sydney Opera House and along the harbour-side you would be hidden. For a moment I thought about how the first Governor must have got something right when he allowed the corroboree and other celebrations to continue here in this quiet space. Even though his house was just up on the hill. Even he would not disturb the ceremonies. It seemed to me then that perhaps it all had been of a design in that way.

The men who were gathered around the rocks were perhaps a dozen making it a larger group than I had first expected and already they were beginning to disperse. I could see several who had begun to wander off and others were sorting gear as I approached.

Big Jim was not about but Atari was, he was seated quietly among the older men up on the rocks. He was also watching the movement of his grandson in a way that had me wondering just what it was I had missed. That the old sorcerer was here was the biggest surprise of all. Would he have marked my absence I wondered?

When Atari looked up noticing my approach he caught my glance. He then simply nodded in acknowledgement, returning his attention to those seated about him almost immediately. He didn't require my presence and in that moment I knew all was well. He would have turned his back on me if it was other than this and relieved I began to make my way down towards Tom.

"Hey ... Jeremy."

"Tom," my acknowledgment hinted at my disappointment in missing this ceremony.

"You should have been here earlier mate."

Tom's grin was wide, but it was also serious as he continued. "It was something you should have been a part of I think. But not to worry, Badjimalla managed it and there were a few others who were able to control the Djaranin."

"Geezus!" I shook my head feeling the disappointment like a physical blow as Tom stood by having reached me then he signalled that we should take a seat.

"I came through good." He said softly, the thread of serious business still evident in his brow. "It wasn't easy though. It is one thing to learn how to do something, another to actually take a life."

Surprised I looked across at him, I could see the pain he was in but couldn't make sense of his words. Had I heard him right I wondered?

"Take a life? What the hell happened? You didn't... kill someone?" I said, finishing on a disbelieving whisper.

The face he made answered me... his expression was in no way conflicted but yet concerned in a small way as though he was unsure or perhaps saddened by what had come about. It wasn't at all like the man I understood him to be.

"What the hell happened?" I asked again.

For a moment I didn't think he was going to answer me and then he did, his voice as quiet as the morning. It was barely a whisper as the sun began to roll across the grass of the foreshore.

"It's not the first time ... that I have taken a life. But this time it was something different. I had decided that it was needed and that it was what I would do. It was my decision. I wasn't angry or... or unsure even. It was simply something that was to be done. He couldn't be allowed to live… the pain he had bought the young kids. The pain he would continue to bring, to him it was nothing…" He shook his head as though drawing on the growing strength of the dawn before he continued on.

"I didn't know though … The Wolgaru serpent … I didn't know about that but the Kadaitcha did. They knew and now so do I. It is done. I am what I am I guess."

"The Serpent … was here?"

Tom just nodded then added. "This is her place, she is here. I didn't know that either but she is here. She lives beneath the city and it is here that she comes to dance. She has family here … in the gardens and I have watched her dance Jeremy. I'll show you one day … her dance."

Looking around I wondered at his words, noting the soft and serious tone and then I noticed that we were alone. The others had left, fading off into the new day as though they had never been.

I could also see Big Jim pacing along the walkway leading from the Botanical Gardens, coming towards us. His stride was determined and with purpose, that he was going to join us was plain.

"Can you talk about it?" I asked quickly. "I feel I really should have been here but I … I wasn't."

Tom looked over at me and then he too noticed Big Jim's approach. "Yes … with you. We can talk about it later when I'm more settled maybe. Where have you been anyway? I thought you might be here sooner than this."

"I was putting Kelly on the train, she and a couple of friends have headed down to Melbourne I think, or maybe Kalgoorlie. They have work there. Did you know about that?"

"Yeah. It was on the cards."

"What about this Pete bloke?"

Tom's look was sharp, surprised even. "He won't bother her. It is done with … that part of it."

It was then that I realized that it was Pete who he had been talking about. Pete … he was the man he had dealt with tonight and surprised I stumbled over my next words.

"It was him you hunted down wasn't it? … But how? Why?"

"The Death Dogs caught him, that wasn't my part. The Djaranin play their own part in this. There is nothing they don't know when all is said and done. It's as though the Serpent and the Dark Dogs are one really. They are the judges in the evil in man. I made no judgements on that."

"God! What did he do? I mean … Kelly was afraid of him an… and so was

Sandra. She's a he you know?" I added inanely, it was so much to take in.

Tom just grinned. "Yeah ... I think there is a lot you don't know. Maybe it is time you knew. Come on. We better go find the car before too much longer. It seems the men are finished in the gardens and they have opened the gates by the look of it, it must all be cleared up." Standing suddenly Tom prepared to greet Big Jim.

Big Jim also turned to greet me after he had released Tom's firm grip in a handshake. "This was a good business. Tonight has been a good night. And where were you while all this was going on young Jeremy?" He demanded suddenly.

"Tom said ... I was to look after the women so I was. I got the women away; they've left ... down south for good I think. I only just got here."

"Yes I know. It was a hard job to keep the Dark Dogs at bay without your hand in it. There were others to help fortunately," He added softly with some satisfaction.

"I don't understand." I asked suddenly, interrupting the two of them as they were quietly congratulating themselves. I was at a loss to understand what had happened and it was starting to peeve me some.

"What is it that you don't understand?" Big Jim asked patiently.

"Well what has happened? Tom said ..."

"Lets talk about it then. You need to understand young Jeremy." Big Jim continued cutting me off suddenly as he turned us away from the gardens and back towards the public walkway of the nature strip on the foreshore. "You don't understand what has happened here ... is that it?"

"Well yes. Why...? And the Serpent ... what ...?" I shook my head.

Big Jim nodded and then looked across at me searching my thoughts for threads of understanding. "Young Jeremy ..." His tone was serious and patient as he continued softly. "You have to see things through the eyes of others if you are ever going to understand the whole of anything. And that son ... is a talent you need to learn. Now listen up to what Tom can say and you will see what I mean. It's OK ... you're young. It will all be clear to you in time."

Through Other Eyes

Book 2
Rated MA

Read Tom's story.

Discover the story through other eyes.

A tale about the birth of the Kadaitcha Men and the mysteries of the caverns.

www.ingramcontent.com/pod-product-compliance
Lightning Source LLC
Chambersburg PA
CBHW051510170626
46811CB00002B/739